BUT CAN THE PHOENIX SING?

"Follow me," she commanded, and immediately we were darting between what seemed to be an endless succession of small uninhabited huts. We had at all costs to remain hidden. We skirted an area of rubble-strewn waste ground, overgrown with tall weeds, and then crept down a couple of heavily bombed streets where the remains of roofless houses stood jagged in the moonlight. At the far corner of the second street we heard noises in the distance and pressed ourselves into what was left of a doorway. My heart was back in my throat, for I knew very well that the only people who could be out making such a noise at that time of night would be either police or soldiers. Sure enough, we heard laughter, shouts in German, banging of doors. They must have been a couple of hundred yards or so away, but the sound of an engine springing into life was horribly distinct. It revved louder and louder; it was surely approaching us.

CHRISTA LAIRD

BUT CAN THE PHOENIX ⌖ SING? ⌖

BEECH TREE

NEW YORK

The lines from "To Those Born Later" and "Motto" by Bertolt Brecht
are reprinted from *Bertolt Brecht Poems 1913–1956*, edited by John
Willett and Ralph Manheim, translated by Edith Roseveare, 1976,
by permission of the publisher, Routledge, New York.

The Library of Congress has cataloged the Greenwillow Books
edition of *But Can the Phoenix Sing?* as follows:
Laird, Christa.
But can the phoenix sing? / by Christa Laird.
p. cm.
"First published in Great Britain in 1993"—T.p. verso.
Summary: Seventeen-year-old Richard discovers the incredible details
of his stern and remote stepfather's hidden past when he is left
a manuscript to read while his stepfather is away in Australia.
ISBN 0-688-13612-5
1. World War, 1939–1945—Underground movements, Jewish—Poland—
Juvenile fiction. [1. World War, 1939–1945—Underground
movements, Jewish—Poland—Fiction. 2. Jews—England—Fiction.
3. Interpersonal relations—Fiction. 4. Stepfathers—Fiction.] I. Title.
PZ7.L1577Bu 1995 [Fic]—dc20 94-28422 CIP AC

First Beech Tree Edition, 1998
ISBN 0-688-15860-9
10 9 8 7 6 5 4 3 2 1

FOR
MY
MOTHER

IN LOVING MEMORY

In the dark times
Will there also be singing?
Yes, there will also be singing
About the dark times.

BERTOLT BRECHT,
"MOTTO"

PART 1

RESISTANCE—

IN THE FORESTS

And yet we know:
Hatred, even of meanness
Contorts the features
Anger, even against injustice
Makes the voice hoarse.

BERTOLT BRECHT,
"TO THOSE BORN LATER"

JULY 9, 1971

Dear Katie,

I hate him, I really hate him. I thought it might be better once you left and he didn't have us to moan about, but if anything, it's getting worse. I've just had a really good evening at The Tavern and got back about midnight. Mum and Misha went to a party themselves, and I thought they might even still be out. No way. They must have had a row or something because Mum was already in bed, but Misha was still up, just sitting there in the dark in the living room. He told me off for making too much noise out in the street with the others and then made a hell of a fuss when he smelled the alcohol on my breath. Well, what of it? There was no need to go on like he did. He's so old-fashioned and strict and puritanical. All the things my dad isn't. Dad wouldn't mind me going to the pub and having a drink or two, I'm sure. Just look at the booze he brings with him when he turns up. Mind you, I've not noticed Misha refusing any of that when it's offered. But that's another thing: the way those two get on—like bloody brothers sometimes. It's almost as if Misha worms his way in to stop me having a good time with Dad. I don't think Mum likes it either; she always looks a bit left out when Misha and Dad get talking to each other. I don't blame her; it must be strange to see your husband getting on like a house on fire with your ex. As if they're ganging up on you.

Well, it's late now, and I'm glad I've got some of that off my chest. It all seems worse since you left, somehow. But at least he's off to Australia soon, and I'll have six weeks' peace and quiet with Mum. And with that bit of trouble at school about to erupt any day, he can't be gone too soon.

Let me hear from you again soon, Katie. I miss you.

Rich

JULY 12

Dearest Katie,

At last a nice letter from you this morning. Yes, I know you write much longer letters than I do, but that doesn't mean you only have to write half as often! I had a card from Dad in Montevideo by the same post. He certainly has an exciting life. He doesn't seem afraid of anything: war, famine, earthquake, revolution—you name it, he's there. This time it's terrorists, or freedom fighters, as he calls this lot. Mum says he's addicted to danger and that this makes him impossible to live with. I'd say he's pretty bloody brave. After all, someone's got to report on what's going on in godforsaken places like Uruguay. I just hope I have his guts when I'm older. I think guts are what I most admire in people.

Anyway, in his card he didn't mention my schoolwork or the week's truanting in Wales, which I know Mum wrote to him about. I expect he'll yell at me for a bit when he comes home, but he won't go on and on about it like You-Know-Who. All Misha ever seems to care about is how much work I'm doing, what time I come in at night, and what I'm doing when I go out. I don't know why he's so bothered about my stupid school results. I'm glad he isn't my teacher, that's all I can say.

Anyway, Simon sends his love. I reckon he and Jackie are about to split up. She's turning into a real little swot, as you would say, and never wants to go out. No developments over the business at school yet.

Misha's off to Australia tomorrow—thank God.

Take care. Miss you. All my love,

Rich

JULY 13

Dear Katie,

Thanks for the funny card. This morning Misha left for Adelaide. I was really glad to see him go, as you can imagine, but I must admit he was actually quite nice before he left. He even gave me some money to take Mum out and told me to take care of us both. She drove him up to the airport before she went to work, but they got off to a pretty late start, because Misha kept coming back in for things he'd forgotten. Very unlike him—he's usually so damn organized.

I'm so jealous—I wish I was going to Australia. Michael Pennington's got family out there and says it's fabulous especially if you like sport and an outdoor life.

I hope it goes all right for him despite everything. I can't work up the energy to hate him so much when he's hurtling through the air away from me at about five hundred miles an hour. In the meantime, though, there is a large and ominous-looking envelope propped up on my table in front of me as I write. When I first saw it, I had a horrible suspicion that it was going to be a moral tract on what I must and mustn't do while he's away. But I must admit it's way too thick for that. When I told Mum what I had suspected, she put on her all too familiar you-make-me-so-sad expression and said the least I could do was to keep an open mind. She went all mysterious when I asked her about it and said it was for me to read and find out. She said she knew the gist of what was in it but had

not read it. Apparently Misha intended it first and foremost for me.
Confessions of a middle-aged teacher? A lamentably belated
explanation of the facts of life . . .? Joking aside, it makes me feel
intrigued and uneasy at the same time. It's late now and I'd like to
leave it till tomorrow, but I think I'm too curious to do that.

  Good night, I'll keep you informed. Here goes!

  Rich

—

The following narrative contains the text of Misha Edelman's "letter" to his stepson, Richard Buchanan. Like
Richard's own few letters to his girlfriend, Katie, who recently moved away with her parents to another town, it is
reproduced here in unedited form.

—

Dear Richard,

Over the years people have often asked what happened to me after
I escaped from the ghetto. Several of them have even encouraged me
to put my experiences on record, but I've always resisted. With you
it's been different. You've never seemed to want to know the story
of my past, but you have sometimes asked me direct questions as they
seemed relevant to you at the time. Such as how I came to understand
Italian or, very recently, had I ever camped out or slept rough? (That,
of course, was just before you went off on that escapade to Wales
with Simon, about which the less said the better.) I'm aware that when
you've asked me such questions, I've often been evasive or curt, but
recently things between us have deteriorated to such a point that I feel
I can no longer afford to be either. Our relationship has suffered for
a number of reasons, not all of them my fault, but I readily acknowledge
that I must take some of the responsibility. That may surprise you.
Anyway, I now believe that the time has come to talk, or rather write,
to you about the experiences which went into making me the person
I am. I would like you to think of the result not as any sort of apology
but rather as an extended confidence, offered in the hope that if nothing

else, it may provide context to the things you find hardest to bear in a substitute and second-best father. I should add that both your parents, particularly Jack, have encouraged me in this.

But before I begin, and at the risk of boring you, I need to try and explain—for myself, as much as for you—why I've never attempted this task before. It may seem strange to you that I've allowed nearly thirty years to go by without talking about—or putting into writing and, therefore, into some sort of shape—the events which led me ultimately to become part of your family. Despite people's requests that I should do so, I had powerful reasons for refusing; they remain the reasons why I am bound to be, even now, an unreliable narrator of my own story.

Firstly, my experiences were not mine alone and were shared with people who were important to me, some of whom I loved very much and scarcely any of whom survived. To tell the story inadequately, incompetently, would have been to misrepresent them, to let them down all over again. That was a risk I couldn't take.

Secondly, there was a language problem. Despite my accent, which I know often annoys you, my English has, for many years now, been very good indeed, excellent even. I don't have many achievements to boast about, but my English is one of the very few things I am proud of. My reticence wasn't due to that sort of language barrier; it was just that to write in English about Poland and the people of my adolescence would have seemed like a sort of desertion. Silly, perhaps, when I think of the strange jumble of Polish, Russian, Ukrainian, and Yiddish that was spoken in the forests, but there it is.

My third reason, which even now I can barely admit to, was a reluctance to delve into the past for fear, perhaps, of the sinister things I might still discover.

How the reasons crowd in on one another now. For there's still one more, and it's the most powerful of all. Cowardice. I was afraid to tell the story, Richard, quite simply afraid of the pain. I wonder if you will understand that.

The longer and fuller a story, the more difficult it is to find its beginning. I know that another source can give you a picture of my life in the ghetto and an account of my escape through the sewers to the non-Jewish part of Nazi-occupied Warsaw, but it would feel all wrong simply to continue where that left off, without a brief reminder of what I was leaving behind on that terrifying evening in August 1942, some three weeks after my fourteenth birthday.

Already that is badly put. For it was not I who was doing the leaving, but rather I who had been left behind. My father had died of typhus not long after the Nazis sealed off the ghetto in 1940 with their ten-foot-high wall, their barbed wire, and their armed sentries. My mother, already ill from consumption and without the means of supporting us, asked the famous Janusz Korczak to take my two younger sisters and myself into his orphanage. "Mister Doctor," as he was always called by his children, readily agreed; he already had nearly two hundred other charges, but he'd briefly looked after my father in one of his prewar orphanages and saw us as sort of honorary grandchildren. I visited my mother almost daily and helped to support her with the proceeds of smuggled goods and with offerings from Mister Doctor, until her death in June 1942. One of Korczak's triumphs was to procure her a half-proper burial place all to herself in a corner of the Jewish cemetery; in those days dead bodies were usually just heaped onto carts and taken away in the mornings with the refuse. I remember the funeral very clearly; much more clearly than my poor father's for some reason. Our family was never religious, and neither was Korczak, but nevertheless I said kaddish, the Jewish prayer for the departed, and my sister Rachel planted two geraniums, which she'd carefully nurtured from Korczak's cuttings for Mother's birthday, a couple of weeks before. It was typical of Korczak that amid the unbelievable squalor of the ghetto, he managed to keep a couple of window boxes going, partly to help with our botany lessons but partly, I am sure, as a symbol of hope in a landscape desolate with death and despair. I think that's probably the image he would have most liked to be remembered by: two colorful window boxes overlooking the gray murk of Sienna Street.

Anyway, not long after that I left the orphanage—"Our Home," as it was called—not at all because I was turned out but because I had become involved with one of the new resistance groups. I was working for them—distributing leaflets, helping in a soup kitchen for children, and such things—when the deportations began. That was on July 22, 1942, Korczak's birthday, strangely enough. And, just over two weeks later, on the morning of August 6, to be precise, Korczak himself and all the children in Our Home were deported to the death camp at Treblinka. I was helping to sort leaflets that day, in the house where the illegal printing machine was hidden and which overlooked the route to the assembly point, or *Umschlagplatz*. Here thousands of people a day were herded into the cattle trucks and sent off to their claustrophobic deaths, if not by trampling and suffocation in the trucks on the way, then in the more efficiently sealed gas chambers at their destination. So I was well placed to see the Doctor and our children file past, all two hundred of them; nearly at the end of the procession I caught a glimpse of my ten-year-old sister Rachel, now painfully thin, staggering under the weight of a toddler. Of course, you know about my other sister, Eli, whom the Doctor had arranged for me to smuggle out of the ghetto to non-Jewish foster parents when she was eighteen months old, and whom I've since spent so very many years trying in vain to trace. But I wonder if you knew before about Rachel— dark-haired, bright-eyed, and certainly more Jewish-looking than anyone else in the family. Together Rachel and I had watched both our parents die, and, until I left the orphanage, we'd scarcely ever been apart. She'd been a tough, cheerful, rather bossy, but reassuring little companion, and that day I just stood by and watched her, quite literally, walk out of my life forever.

Within minutes I'd made the decision to agree to what the resistance group had been trying to persuade me to do for several weeks: escape to some of their people on "the other side" through the sewers, now considered to be the only safe route. With my horror of enclosed spaces the prospect had filled me with sheer physical panic, but you'll understand that I no longer had any choice.

And so, finally, to that all-too-clear moonlit night when, saturated by the sewage I'd half waded, half swum through, I emerged from hell. Make no mistake, it's no coincidence that hell in both mythology and religious imagination is usually belowground! When I slopped into the embrace of the stranger who whispered the prearranged password, "Orphans' Home," I felt, as well as relief, acute embarrassment at my stinking condition! It's curious how, when you're very young, embarrassment manages to spoil the most sublime and memorable of moments. The stranger drew back from me quickly with a laugh and said, "Don't worry, we'll get you cleaned up in a minute. We're going to a safe house not far away for tonight." I couldn't see what she looked like in the deep shadow, except that her hair seemed to be half pulled back in a sort of ponytail, with the other half escaping around her face.

"Follow me," she commanded, and immediately we were darting between what seemed to be an endless succession of small uninhabited huts. However good my counterfeit papers were, my foul-smelling condition would have been an instant giveaway, and in any case it was long after curfew. We had at all costs to remain hidden. We skirted an area of rubble-strewn waste ground, overgrown with tall weeds—my nature-starved eyes actually gave them a second glance— and then crept down a couple of heavily bombed streets where the remains of roofless houses stood jagged in the moonlight. At the far corner of the second street we heard noises in the distance and pressed ourselves into what was left of a doorway. My heart was back in my throat, where it had been most of that interminable evening, for I knew very well that the only people who could be out making such a noise at that time of night would be either police or soldiers. Sure enough, we heard laughter, shouts in German, banging of doors. They must have been a couple of hundred yards or so away, but the sound of an engine springing into life was horribly distinct. It revved louder and louder; it was surely approaching us.

My companion put out a hand and touched my shoulder. Flattened into the shadow of the wall, she turned an eerily pale face toward me and whispered, "Don't worry. That's a popular bar. They'll be making for the main road back into town in a moment. They're bound to turn left at the crossroads."

I was grateful for the reassurance but could feel the tension in her as her hand pressed harder against my shoulder. I was beginning to wonder whether "freedom" was going to be any different from captivity in the ghetto. By this time I was also aware of the heavy physical drag of exhaustion.

The noise of the engine faded as the car indeed turned away, and my companion removed her hand. Immediately we seemed to be passing the edge of another piece of wasteland, at the far side of which we stopped in front of a tall end-of-terrace house. She tapped a light staccato tune on a shutter. Noiselessly the door beside it opened a chink, and the next thing I knew I was in a narrow, dimly lit hallway and the door was closed behind me. An old woman, she seemed to be at least eighty, was peering into my face.

"Bless you, my child," she said, "you need a wash. Come with me." You can't imagine what a comfort those few wonderfully obvious, practical words were to me!

I followed her into a kitchen where a freestanding bathtub was covered by a wooden board. She removed the board effortlessly, frail and little though she was in her ankle-length black dress. She turned on the tap and then went across to the range, where a huge kettle was steaming, lifted it across with both arms, and poured the contents into the tub. I was too dazed to offer to help her.

"They said you'd be coming through the sewers, so I've had the kettle on for the last hour or two. Now take your clothes off." She must have noticed some hesitation because she went on, severely, "Don't bother about me. I've had four grandsons, and I've bathed every·one of them."

I did as I was told. In any case exhaustion had by this time got the better of embarrassment, and I thankfully peeled off those disgusting clothes—though not before I'd carefully removed the packet containing my papers and the photograph of my parents. It's strange, but I don't think I ever had a photograph of Rachel. A small thing, I suppose, but I regret it bitterly, if only because whenever I think of her, it's that very last image which flashes before my eyes. And there are so many other, more cheerful ones.

I remember every detail of that bath: the large square tablet of carbolic soap—the sort people only scrub floors with in these affluent days—and the wooden-backed nailbrush with its flattened overused bristles. Dr. Korczak had been a stickler for cleanliness, and we often had to have our nails inspected, but never before had I scrubbed mine so carefully. Despite her fierce words, the old lady did actually leave me alone but returned a little later with a towel, which she held in front of the range for a few moments to warm, and a change of clothes. After I had dressed—the baggy trousers and shirt, though spotlessly clean and pressed, were worn and patched, and I wondered if they'd belonged to one of the four grandsons—she came in again and took me into the little front room, where my guide looked up from what she was reading.

"My goodness, what a transformation! I'm sure that feels better!" She wore a long skirt in some dark material, a white blouse, and dark cardigan. In the soft light of the one gas lamp I could see that her hair was reddish brown, more red than brown, in fact, and much of it, as I'd already noticed, had escaped from the green ribbon at the nape of her neck.

"Come on, Granny, I'll help you now he's cleaned up."

I wondered if she were indeed the granddaughter, but later I was to learn that this marvelous old lady was known as Granny to a large number of resistance workers. Her wartime life merits a book of its own, but suffice it to explain here that she had good personal reasons for wanting to fight the Nazis in all the ways still open to a woman of seventy. (I had misjudged her age by ten years, but no doubt you'll understand, you who write off anyone over thirty as "ancient"!) In 1940 two of those grandsons, aged fifteen and sixteen, had been walking along a country lane minding their own business when they'd been picked up by an SS patrol and sent off to forced labor somewhere in Austria, by then part of the German Reich. The boys weren't even allowed to go home to say good-bye, and it was weeks before the family learned that they were still alive. Two months later they received the news that another son, their eldest, a conscripted soldier of nineteen, had been killed at the front in Russia. Granny's daughter, their mother, had become almost crazed with grief. So that is how, although Granny didn't have a drop of Jewish blood in her, she came to be a most courageous and trustworthy friend to many an escaping Jew.

Before long Eva (as my guide eventually introduced herself) and I were balancing on our knees great plates of thick vegetable stew, heavy with chunks of potato and full of flavor. It was wonderful, but it was asking too much of my poor starved stomach at the end of that day, on top of the exhaustion, the terror, and the ferocious nausea that had almost paralyzed me in the sewer. I felt it again now, surging up from deep in my gut, and I managed to rush out of the room and back into the kitchen just in time to bring up all the stew into the sink. At that moment I was almost broken; the image of my mother propped up against her gray pillows flashed before me, her face full of fear and love just as it had been every single day of the last two years of her life. Then I saw again the scene of the children being driven to their death, Rachel among them. I think it was only then that I finally realized how utterly alone I was in the world. Tears involuntarily ran down my cheeks. I retched and retched until it seemed that the last ounce of moisture had been forced out of me. I stayed there, hunched over the sink, too mortified to rejoin the others.

But eventually the old lady came for me. She put a hand on my shoulder, and the firmness of her tone was again a huge relief.

"Come on, it's time for you to sleep. But first drink this." She handed me a glass of something that tasted like peppermint and helped to remove the foul taste from my mouth. She led me upstairs by the hand as if I were a little child again, and showed me into a room with a high bed, its head- and footboards made out of very dark carved wood. I don't suppose I noticed that at the time, but I did next morning.

"There, you can take your things off and sleep under the covers. You'll not be disturbed until morning." And my body's desperate need for sleep put an immediate and merciful end to the humiliation.

JULY 14, 12:30 A.M.

I said I'd keep you informed, but I think that's going to be harder than I realized. He's written me an account of his early life, and it isn't the sort of stuff that one can summarize too easily. It's certainly not what I'd bargained for—though come to think of it, I'm not at all sure what I was expecting. Why on earth didn't he tell me some of this before? I still don't really understand, despite the reasons he gives.

One thing I think I do understand, though, is why he was so surprisingly nice when I threw up after your party. I thought he'd be furious, but he was actually pretty sympathetic. Come to think of it, he even made me some tea to take away the taste. I can see why now—because of a similar experience he once had. Though actually it wasn't at all similar—he hadn't drunk too much. Rather shaming really!

To be honest, Katie, this document makes me uneasy. I'm not even sure I want to read it all. It was simpler the way it was—just disliking him in a straightforward sort of way. I think I'm afraid I might have to feel sorry for him, and that'd be very complicated. But if he thinks it'll win me over, he's likely to be sadly mistaken.

What a bastard I am. But as you've said before, you love me for it! Sleep tight.

I probably slept better that night than I had for years, quite literally. It was a deep, dreamless sleep such as I never knew in the ghetto, and I woke refreshed. I remembered almost immediately what had happened the night before, but now it was with mild embarrassment rather than searing shame. I lay there savoring the exquisite comfort of real linen—in the orphanage we'd had to make do with rough blankets and lumpy mattresses stuffed with newspaper because the Nazis had confiscated all the decent bedding—when there was a light knock at the door. It opened before I said anything, and Eva's face appeared around it. I'd never been particularly observant about such things before, but I did notice that her reddish hair was now all neatly brushed back and caught by the green ribbon.

"Good morning. Feeling better?" She put a mug of coffee on the table beside the bed and announced cheerfully, "Enjoy this. You won't be waited on again where we're going, young man!"

When she'd gone, I snuggled down again under the feather-filled cover. I had a ridiculous sense of being secure, invulnerable, as if that little bedroom with its sloping ceiling, its heavy dark furniture, its crucifix on the wall, and, above all, its soft white linen provided a sort of oasis in a wasteland of fear and menace. True, I had actually escaped the thousand mortal dangers of the ghetto, but Eva's cheerful greeting made me face the question, Where *were* we going now?

We had bread and lovely homemade plum jam for breakfast. "My little plum tree is one thing the Nazis haven't taken away yet, and she seems to yield more every year—as if in defiance!" The amazing old lady chuckled as she watched us tucking in.

Then Eva told me. "We're going to take the train for Lublin. It's likely to take several hours, maybe more, you can never tell these days. Then we'll make our way to a farm on the outskirts, from where I hope we'll get a ride to within a few hours' walk of our partisan group in the Parczew forest. You don't need to know any names until later. On the train don't on any account get into conversation with anyone; people ask too many questions, and it's dangerous to start telling them anything. Just smile sweetly if anyone tries to talk to you, but don't fall into the trap of replying. If the worse comes to the worst, you're my little brother and we're going to visit a dying aunt, our mother's sister, in a village outside Lublin. You can't remember the name; you've not been there since before the war when you were quite small, and your sister—that's me, remember—has all the details. That way we won't have any trouble with our stories' not tallying.''

I nodded dumbly as I took all this in, not at all sure whether I liked the idea of being Eva's ''little brother,'' or anyone else's, come to that. I was too used to being the responsible ''elder brother.'' But of course, I had no choice. As we left, Granny pressed a bundle into my arms; it was my sewer-soaked clothes, which, as Eva told me, she had boiled after I'd gone to bed and left hanging over the range to dry overnight. ''Make sure you change if you get wet in the rain,'' she said in the most matter-of-fact and grandmotherly way, as if I'd just been going out to play in the garden. But at the very last moment, just before we opened the door, she whispered urgently, ''God bless you both,'' and made the sign of the cross over us.

It has often been said that Christian Poles did nothing to help Jews during the war. Don't believe it. There were indeed those who turned their backs on the hounded, hungry people who came to them in desperation; there were others who did their little bit to help where they realistically could, often not without some risk to themselves; and there were those who were ready to risk their lives and to share their last meal with a fugitive. I don't believe that in these matters the Polish people in the last war were different from any others caught in a similar stranglehold. And what is more, the rescued have no right to assume that they would automatically become rescuers if roles were reversed. We simply don't know, any of us, how we would react until put to the test. And the not-knowing troubles me. You see, I don't believe, as many people do, that courage is a characteristic, like optimism or generosity; I think of it more as a mood, like laughter or sadness, a child of the moment, which might come to any of us in certain circumstances—and desert us in others.

It was strange to walk openly to the station in full daylight, as if we had nothing to hide. I would have liked to go via our preghetto home in the Old Town, in the shadow of St. John's Cathedral, but it wasn't on our way, and I dared not suggest it. It made me angry to see how people in the Aryan part of the city were going about their daily business, on foot and trams and bicycles, as if oblivious of the teeming walled torture chamber in their midst. Unreasonable anger, of course; after all, if I'd passed Granny in the street, I'd have had no way of knowing the extent of the risks she was taking to defy the Nazis and help Jews. In fact, I even remember wondering if I might pass, unknowingly, my sister Eli's Aryan foster parents. But illogically, I was angry all the same. I don't know what I expected of these people, but I just hated them for being on the right side of the wall. They were poor and shabby and hungry, of course, severely rationed as they were by the occupying forces. I saw beggars and food queues there, too. But I didn't see corpses half covered by old newspaper waiting to be carted away with the refuse; I didn't see stick-legged children rummaging in dustbins for any old scrap they could lay hands on; I saw no one beaten to death by guards in full public view. No, these people may have been downtrodden and deprived, but there was not the same dull-eyed despair on their faces. And the smell of death, that was missing, too. The peculiar smell of the ghetto, made up of dirt, disease, and the sweat of fear.

If I had imagined for one moment that the journey to Lublin might be a relaxing interlude, I was sadly mistaken! For one thing, the train was incredibly crowded; it seemed to me that half the population of non-Jewish Warsaw had taken it into their heads to travel to Lublin that day. To begin with, it looked as if we'd have to take turns in the one seat we could find, until, shortly after the train had started moving, a huge peasant woman lifted her cage of chickens from the place next to her and, nodding at me, patted the tiny bit of empty space. I was quite grateful until I actually sat down and caught the full power of her body odor. Eva was sitting opposite me and must have seen me recoil, for the look she gave me was of undisguised amusement; her green eyes positively danced with merriment. And without any doubt at all, it was at that improbable moment that I fell in love with her.

It's an apt expression, "falling in love." It accurately describes the physical sensation of something dropping or falling inside, which I experienced as I sat crammed into that stuffy, crowded, smelly railway carriage. Perhaps you'll think it sounds ridiculous? After all, Eva was a lovely, intrepid young adult of nineteen (as I had guessed and which was later confirmed), and I was a tatty ghetto urchin of just fourteen, whom she'd been ordered to collect and deliver in the guise of an older sister. Don't forget, though, circumstances had made me grow up very quickly indeed. My childhood even then was already buried in the distant past. I remember Dr. Korczak once shaking his head sadly and saying of us all, "My poor children. Children without a childhood!" And perhaps my feelings for Eva were all bound up with relief and gratitude and apprehension in the face of my unknown future.

But anyway, love is always more than its analysis, and what is important for me to record is that Eva, my mysterious, capable, and laughing rescuer, was my first love.

I grinned back and tried to concentrate on being as small and inconspicuous as possible, perhaps as much for the sake of following Eva's instructions as of saving my own skin. But we had both bargained without the interference of a child. She belonged to a young woman huddled in the corner who was much preoccupied with a restless baby. The older child took in everything around her with the sharp-eyed questioning gaze of a five-year-old. For the first half hour or so she fixed her attention on an elderly couple opposite her who seemed quite happy to tell her where they were going, why *he* had a scar on his face, why *she* was carrying a stick. Unfortunately they got out at the first stop, and the large peasant woman with the chickens didn't prove such a cooperative audience, not really surprising as the first question directed at her was "Why are you so fat?" The child's mother, blushing, scolded her loudly, but the damage was done, and an uncomfortable silence hung in the carriage. Eva pretended to be reading a newspaper, but I saw it quivering and was afraid that I, too, might at any moment lose control and start to giggle openly. I longed to catch her eye again.

Not long after, though, Eva lowered her paper sharply, her laughter gone. The little girl had started on me. "What's your name?" she began, innocuously enough. For a dreadful moment I thought, Oh, my God, what *is* my name? I smiled and looked away, trying to show that I wasn't interested in dialogue. I should have known that that would only increase her interest. She took a step forward and patted my knee. "You, what's your name?" Her mother obviously decided she could bother me, a mere teenage boy, with impunity, as she made no attempt to divert the child's attention. I'd never thought that danger could lurk in such innocent clothing. The second time she asked, I looked at Eva out of the corner of my eye and saw her give a tiny nod.

"Janusz Damski," I said, glad of the practice Eva had given me on the way to the station.

"Where are you going?"

"To see my aunt."

"Why?"

"Um—because—she's not very well."

"Where do you live?"

Eva was getting restless. She folded away her paper and made to join in.

"We live near Warsaw. Where do *you* live? And what's *your* name?" The child answered readily and immediately began to lose her interest in us. Of course. That's what I should have done—turned the questions around. I really should have known, with my experience of all the children in Our Home. It was a salutary lesson to me of how anxiety and tension can make you forget things you know perfectly well, can stop you from thinking quickly, can, in fact, give the game away.

The wretched train seemed to stop at every station and barn along the Warsaw–Lublin line, and there were also several unscheduled stops in the middle of nowhere. They were the most worrying. Why had the train stopped? Was the line blocked? Was there a search for Jews? Had they somehow found out about *us*? I began to recognize one of Eva's characteristic gestures when anxious: She would grasp her ponytail in the right hand and run it through her fingers, losing more from the ribbon every time she did so.

And it wasn't long before real danger did loom again, this time in a much more traditional form—that of the German guard who came to check our tickets and identity papers. It was the first time I had had to produce my new "Aryan" documents, and I felt sure that everyone in the carriage would hear the thumping of my heart. The guard was a young man, probably not much older than Eva. He barely glanced at me to check my face against the photo, but he glanced twice and then again at Eva, before asking her where she was going. This is it, I thought. He suspects. There was another moment of tense silence in the carriage. Even the little girl sensed the atmosphere and was quiet, looking up at him with wide, suspicious eyes. Then, with a shrug, he handed her back her paper. "Too bad. A long way from where I'm billeted." And Eva managed to give him a lighthearted friendly smile as if she, too, were disappointed.

We eventually arrived in Lublin after a fraught journey which lasted all day, at least twice as long as it should have done. Dusk was falling, it had started to drizzle steadily, and our reception on the crowded platform was the most unnerving thing of all. Several guards in SS uniform were circulating among the people, shining flashlights directly into faces. I heard "*Jude? Jude?*" and realized that we were in the middle of a search for Jews. Eva took my arm tightly in hers and guided me quickly to the barrier, skillfully avoiding the roving flashlights. "Don't hide your face," she whispered, almost without moving her lips. I noticed that a few people were being marched away to a building at the end of the platform.

"That train took forever," she complained loudly to the Polish official at the ticket barrier. "Was there any particular reason?" I admired her daring, but wouldn't it have been better just to surrender our tickets and make a quick getaway?

"Yes, there's been a big breakout from Majdan Tatarski. A lot of local trains have been delayed by the search parties."

To my horror she then said, "Well, let's hope they found them."

"Not yet. They will. But they'll be more dead than alive when they're caught. They should have stayed in Majdan Tatarski, don't know when they're well off, the scum. Got gardens and everything there, they say."

An impatient queue was forming behind us, so Eva bade the man a friendly good evening, and we were, at last, through the barrier.

As we hurried away from the station, I whispered, "Why did you say that, about hoping they'd be caught?" I felt angry because what she'd said had felt to me like a sort of betrayal. She seemed to understand.

"I'm sorry if I upset you. I hate doing it every time, but it's a way of coaxing information out of them. At least we know now, you see, that whoever escaped hasn't been found, and I don't know but that may be of use or interest when we get back to the others. You're going to have to learn, Jan, that we work in some very devious ways. It's not pleasant, but we don't have the luxury of choice." I heard the defensive note in her voice and was sorry that I'd criticized. There was so much I had to learn.

We took a bus to the outskirts of the town and then, because curfew was approaching, walked quickly to a farm about a mile into the country, where we could count on overnight shelter. By this time it was raining hard, and I thought, already nostalgically, of Granny and her admonition to change my clothes if I got wet!

I didn't like that second "safe house" at all. For one thing, I didn't really feel safe there, and for another, I didn't at all like the way the man of the household looked at Eva. *Leered* would be a better word. I was given a bed of hay in an outhouse, which I shared with a cow on the other side of a thin partition; they brought it in at night for fear of theft, for a cow was a very valuable possession in those days. My uneasiness didn't prevent me from having a surprisingly good night's sleep in the sweet-smelling, if rather itchy, hay; not even the thought of Granny's linen kept me awake. In the morning the wife, a diminutive lady with red, calloused hands, gave us fresh milk and bread and honey for breakfast, so I couldn't complain at our treatment, but I still didn't like them. The husband, Tomasz, took us quite some way on his cart to just past a village called Ostrow, where he dropped us on the edge of the forest.

"Give us a kiss as rent, then." His eyes followed Eva as she got down from the cart. Politely she offered her cheek. "Not like that, silly girl." He dropped the horse's reins, leaned down, and, taking her face in both his hands, planted a smacking kiss on her lips.

"That'll do till the next time!" For a few moments I watched, full of disgust, as the cart bumped away into the distance. Then I turned to Eva; she was wiping her mouth with the back of her hand and shivering, and tears glistened in her eyes. I wished I could think of something comforting to say.

She managed to laugh. "Silly, aren't I?"

"Not at all. I thought he was horrible," I said, with a vehemence that surprised us both.

She looked at me with interest. "Discernment! That could stand you in good stead. But come on now, little brother, we must get off this track and into the woods!"

As we walked out of the morning sunlight into the deep immediate gloom of the forest, I asked why we had to rely on the help of people such as this Tomasz.

"Zofia, his wife, had a sister who was married to a Communist. They perished with the first of the Jews from Lublin—back in April. No, I don't think they would ever betray us, and they've helped us quite a lot with shelter and food. But he can't keep his hands off young women. He tried to come into my room last night, but fortunately I'd anticipated that and I'd dragged a heavy chest of drawers against the door!"

We walked on in silence. Eventually I said, "As if you didn't have enough to be scared of." And it's true; our women fighters always needed that extra bit of strength—and cunning—to protect themselves from the appetites of men. The best of them, and Eva was one of the very best, were very special indeed.

I was to spend just over a year in the forests, and many of the memories from that time merge into one another and are blurred and generalized in a way that the events of those first few days of freedom will never be. The most dangerous, the most frightening episodes stand out, of course, as do certain personalities, but I know I have forgotten a lot. That troubles me. In fact, I suspect that my uneven power of recall is another of the reasons why I've always been so reluctant to talk or write about the past. A selective memory can, after all, give a very false impression of an event, a situation, a character, and I feel this burden of responsibility to tell it like it was. I don't know if you can understand this, but I also bitterly regret the forgetting because it feels as if I am once more losing control of my life: If I can't remember it, then it might as well have happened to someone else or not at all. That's absurd, of course, as it suggests that experience has no worth in itself but is validated only by memory. That can't be true. And yet, and yet—what is forgotten *is* effectively lost. Along with so much else.

But now these reflections threaten to become self-indulgent. What I certainly do remember is my first impression of those forests. It was, overridingly, of a deep, brooding silence. Consider the effect of mile upon mile of dense—impenetrably dense at times—silent forest, apparently empty of everything except trees and undergrowth, on a boy accustomed to noisy, swarming ghetto streets. Before the deportations began in July 1942, over half a million people were crammed into an area enclosed by a wall of no more than ten miles' circumference. Perhaps that won't mean much to you. If I tell you that the average density of population has been calculated at thirteen people to a room, that might mean more.

I was certainly no stranger to fear by this time. Life in the ghetto had been stalked by an omnipresent dread of death in one form or another, either one's own or, worse, that of someone close to you. And of course, there had been tearing panic in the sewer; there has never been anything quite like that, before or since. But the fear I felt that first day in the forest—and I'm not sure that it ever totally left me—was of a different order altogether. It was more a sort of prickly unease and was perhaps the first time I had been afraid without knowing what I was frightened of.

We seemed to walk for hours through thick, tangled undergrowth along a barely discernible path under birch and fir trees which, like some breed of giant guards, menaced without shouting or moving. Once we startled some crows, which rose flapping and clamoring into the air, and I thought my heart would stop. Otherwise the only sign of life was the abundant blackflies which followed our progress with infuriating insistence. I walked close behind Eva as if my existence depended on her—as it probably did in fact! Occasionally she'd look over her shoulder to make sure I was all right and to say something encouraging, but always in a whisper, which heightened the eerie sense of being watched by unseen eyes or heard by hidden ears.

Eventually she suggested that we stop for a rest and something to eat. Zofia had given us bread and goat's cheese and apples, which Eva carried in a shoulder bag. We sat in a clearing with our backs against a tree trunk; sunlight slanted across the surface of the forest floor, making the ferns and damp grasses glow golden above their buff and brown beds of decaying leaves and old pinecones. As we sat and ate and watched, I became aware of more and more signs of life around us: A black and yellow butterfly flickered over a clump of tiny white flowers embedded in spongy moss, and across the clearing a black and white bird hopped around on long, brittle legs. There were insects, too, not just the flies and gnats I would come to know only too well, but also ungainly sticklike things with diaphanous wings which hummed and rattled as they flew. Even before the ghetto days I had been to the country only a couple of times, to my father's sister and her family who had a farm near Kielce, and so this was for me quite literally a glimpse into an unknown world.

A strange green creature with angular, crooked legs alighted on my cheese, and I jumped back. Eva laughed.

"Don't worry. It's only a grasshopper; they're quite harmless! All a bit different from Warsaw, isn't it?" I smiled, though I was close to tears. It was just that I felt so tired again, as if I had come to the end of my resilience; the smallest thing, even a harmless grasshopper, threatened to break me.

"Don't worry, little brother! You'll get used to all of this. It's very strange at first, I know. The silence especially." I would have liked to ask her to drop the "little brother" pretense, which seemed to be becoming a habit, but didn't quite know how to.

"Now the mosquitoes in the evening are the things you do have to watch. Some people are lucky and don't seem to get bitten at all, but they just can't get enough of me." I understood how the creatures felt!

"The doctor, Henryk, can give you a solution to deter them if the worse comes to the worst, but he keeps it for the most susceptible as it's in limited supply, like everything else. You mustn't scratch the bites, whatever you do. Seriously. It can lead to infections, which are very hard to get rid of, living the way we do out here."

At this point I was actually more interested in her mention of a doctor than in the mosquitoes. I plucked up the courage to ask. "Where exactly are we going, and who will be there?"

"I can't tell you where. I just recognize it when I see it. And no surnames, Jan, that's a rule. [It still came as an unpleasant little shock when she used my adopted Aryan name.] In case any of us are captured and tortured." There was a pause while the horrible reality of our situation loomed before us. "What I can tell you is that our band is commanded by a man called Ilya, an escaped prisoner of war from the Red Army, and his deputy is a Dr. Henryk. Henryk is from Warsaw, and he's a cousin of big Joseph, who knew you in the ghetto and arranged for you to join us. We're made up of Jews who've managed to escape from the ghettos or the deportation trains—that's people like my brother and me—or, very occasionally, from the camps. Then there is another escaped prisoner of war from the Red Army—there were more, but they've gone away to the forests in the east beyond the river Bug—and a few Poles who are Communists and left-wingers. We're about fifteen in all, at the moment."

"And what do you do?"

"Anything and everything to save Jews and hurt the enemy. That's usually the Nazis, of course, but it also includes some of our own countrymen, Poles whose anti-Semitism puts them in league with the Germans."

"And you fight alongside soldiers from the Red Army?" I was confused. In the ghetto we were starved of news of the outside world and of the war, as well as of everything else. We children had been especially sheltered in the orphanage, where Dr. Korczak had tried to shield us as much as possible from the grim realities outside. I may not even have been aware of the end of the Nazi-Soviet Pact. And I knew that Russia was traditionally a bitter and hated enemy of Poland.

"Certainly. Communists and the left are our natural allies these days, and since the Germans invaded the Soviet Union last year, that means Soviet as well as Polish Communists. The London-controlled Polish underground doesn't seem to want anything to do with Jews or with the partisan struggle. They've deserted us." She paused and added sadly, "Until 1940 I thought of myself and my family as Polish, not Jewish. We're not in any way religious, and we've been here for generations. It was Hitler who taught me that I'm a Jew, Hitler with the help of all too many of my Polish compatriots."

"Why? Why? Why?" I asked the question with anguish, and by no means for the last time. In fact, I'm still asking it, and I suppose one of the reasons I'm writing this for you, Richard, is so that you will ask it, too. I don't ask it only as a Jew but as a member of any hated and persecuted group of people, whoever they are. Like Eva's, my Jewishness had never seemed a particularly important part of either myself or of my family life—until the occupying forces made it *the* most significant thing about us. We weren't religious, and my parents, though not well off and belonging to the class of small-business people, had always set a lot of store by education, making sure that we spoke Polish as well as Yiddish—which we did, much better than they did, in fact. Sitting in that remote forest clearing with a little time to reflect, I contemplated the hatred that had been let loose in the world and shuddered at its elemental power and scale.

"Why? Who knows, Jan, who knows?" There was a sadness in her voice that made me turn and look at her. A ray of sunlight had set light to her auburn hair, and I wanted desperately to prolong that little interlude.

"It's so silent everywhere. So empty!"

"Don't believe it, little brother. There are a lot of people hiding in these forests. Refugees from the villages, partisan groups like ourselves, and a good many isolated Russians as well. And they're not *all* friendly." Little did I know what a prophetic understatement that was to prove.

Eva explained to me that although the camp was, as the crow flies, only about three and a half miles from where we'd been dropped off, we had to take a much longer route around to avoid the marshland which lay between. I wondered how she could be so sure of the way, especially when, shortly past the clearing, the mossy path dwindled away to almost nothing; but she assured me that there were signs to follow and began to point out odd-shaped trees, certain broken branches, and other landmarks. Sometimes we took off our shoes and walked along the beds of streams to avoid leaving continuous tracks.

Eventually, just as I was beginning to wonder whether we'd reach our destination before it got dark, and to recall all the fairy stories I'd ever heard about evil spirits that lay in wait in dense forests for defenseless children, I became aware of unmistakable signs of human activity. An obviously man-made clearing, where several piles of logs lay scattered, led off into the gloom. Suddenly a young man of about nineteen or twenty appeared without warning before us. I stopped in my tracks, very startled, and my heart was back in my throat. I fixed my eyes warily on his rifle, while he just stood there.

"Password?"

"Don't be silly, Franek!"

"You're late, Eva. Nearly twenty-four hours late. We were getting worried." I noticed how he devoured her features, as if checking that each one was exactly how it had been. He seemed angry and relieved and loving all at once, and forgetting my fear, I knew instead my first pang of jealousy.

"The train from Warsaw was badly delayed. It's the work of those bandits in the Parczew forests, if you ask me!"

His face relaxed, and they grinned at each other.

"No, apparently there's been a breakout from Majdan Tatarski, and there was a big search on. We had to stay over with Tomasz and Zofia."

The young man's face darkened again. He swore and spit expressively on the ground.

"Did he try anything on this time?"

"What do *you* think?"

"Bastard."

We had started to walk across the clearing. I noticed that the young man had a pronounced limp.

"Franek, don't you think it'd be polite to say hello to our new comrade? His name from now on is Janusz, Janusz Damski."

"Of course. I'm sorry!" The young man looked at me for the first time, and with interest. He gave me a friendly smile and held out his hand. I noticed that his coloring was similar to Eva's, but his freckles gave him a boyish, almost mischievous look.

"Welcome, Jan. It's an honor to have one of Dr. Korczak's orphans with us. You see, we've been told a little about you." He clapped me on my back, and I felt, instinctively, that even if he were Eva's lover, I wouldn't be able to help liking him.

"We want to hear all about everything: the deportations from Warsaw, any escapees you know about, exactly what arms the Dror and any other resistance groups have got by now—"

"Franek, leave him alone. He's exhausted. And I've been very controlled and not asked him anything because I knew it would all have to be repeated for Ilya and Henryk. I think you should get back to your post now. We'll see you later."

I thought it strange, the slightly bossy way she talked to this nice, friendly young man who so clearly adored her. But I basked in her protectiveness, even if it did only indicate an elder-sisterly sort of concern.

We reached another larger clearing where there were several gray tent-shaped structures, which turned out to be the roofs of dugout shelters. They were made of sticks and branches and covered with smooth sheets of bark, which I later learned peeled easily away from the local birch trees. It was my first glimpse of the partisan camp, and that evening it presented a peaceful enough picture. An orderly line of about ten people stood by a fire, where an old man was ladling some sort of steaming liquid from a black caldronlike receptacle into their tin plates. Some of them wore dark, baggy overall-type clothes;

others were in an assortment of tattered army uniforms. They greeted Eva and looked curiously at me, but she didn't stop to introduce me, hurrying me instead straight to the leaders' dugout set a little apart from the others.

Dr. Henryk was the second-in-command of this partisan company; he was fair-haired, of medium, very upright stature and with striking, sad gray eyes. He seemed genuinely pleased to see me and actually came forward to embrace me before congratulating Eva on her success in finding and delivering me.

"It's an honor to have one of Dr. Korczak's children among us," he said gravely, as Franek had done. "He was one of my idols, you know. I was actually present at the famous lecture when he used an amplifier to demonstrate what fear does to the heartbeat of a child. It made a great impression on us." He looked at me carefully. "Are you tired?"

"Yes, he is," Eva replied on my behalf. "I think the questions should wait until tomorrow." Almost as an afterthought she added, "If you agree, Henryk."

"Of course I agree." He looked at her with a sort of paternal indulgence. "And Ilya's not here now, anyway. He's investigating an offer of some arms."

"Jan—that's how you will be called from now on, because your Aryan looks mean that we shall be sending you out among the enemy— I'm afraid we're going to have to ask you a great many detailed questions about your experience of things in Warsaw. It'll be painful for you, I know, but the information may be crucial, may save lives, and so we have no alternative."

"I'm not too tired. If you want to start now." I remember feeling I ought to say that. I was also oddly comforted to think that once again a doctor was in charge of me.

"No, Eva's right. You must have something to eat, and then sleep. There'll be plenty of time for debriefing tomorrow."

As we walked back to the supper queue, Eva explained to me.

"It's hard to believe, but there are still Jews living in ghettos and work camps who don't believe what's in store for them. Stories like yours help to persuade them to escape or resist. We've been successful before. Most of the young people fled from Markuszow earlier in the summer because they were warned and persuaded in time. And sometimes detailed information such as you might have helps to track people down, bring families together. Not often, but it has happened."

I was "interrogated" the following day by Henryk and Ilya, who, Eva told me, had been an officer in the Red Army, before being captured and badly tortured by the Nazis after their invasion of the Soviet Union, causing him to go prematurely gray. He had managed to escape during a snowstorm the previous winter. He and some former Red Army comrades had been the original nucleus of the band, before they were joined by Jews. Also in the dugout were a very dark, heavily bearded man called Alexander who never said a word—but who was an engineer, I learned later, the nearest the company had to an arms and explosives expert—and Eva herself. I was quickly coming to realize that Eva enjoyed considerable status in the camp.

I told them everything I possibly could: about the numbers of people being deported every day; which Nazi-owned factories had apparently been given immune status and were still being allowed to operate; about the macabre postcards which some people had allegedly received from their deported loved ones, "assuring" them that they were safe and well; about the efforts of the resistance groups, as far as I was aware of them—the illegal printing press and so on. The effort was unimaginable; beforehand, I myself had no idea what a strain it would be. It forced me to relive every grisly minute of my life over those three weeks since the deportations had begun. I know it's a cliché to talk of rubbing salt in a wound, but this really was the emotional equivalent. I didn't break down, though. I was acutely aware of Eva sitting there cross-legged on the floor (in the forest she abandoned the skirt and cardigan which were her "town mission uniform" for a pair of baggy trousers), and I was determined not to humiliate myself in front of her as I had that first night. I don't know how long it lasted, but it felt like hours.

At the end I was utterly drained but proud—I had provided a lot of information, and I had kept my voice steady, almost all the time. But afterward it was different. Then, once again, it was my wretched body which let me down, as if it had its own will, independent of mine. I remember almost nothing of the following few days because I apparently succumbed to a high fever and had to be isolated in a little dugout of my own, for fear that I had contracted typhus. It wasn't typhus, as it turned out, and Henryk, whose face floated somewhere above me from time to time, told me afterward that I'd almost definitely caught the infection from my trip through the sewers. That made me think with more admiration than ever of my sewer guide, Adziu—and others like him—who made a habit of taking people through those underground tunnels to freedom. When I was recovering, feeling wan and weak, I was very embarrassed by my illness, which I saw as a sort of failure, and I began to apologize and put the blame on my undernourished physical condition. I hoped Eva hadn't told him about the vomiting incident. I was terrified that they'd think my spirit wasn't up to the struggle, that they wouldn't allow me to join them. But as Henryk sat companionably in my dugout despite the fact that he was one of our leaders (it didn't occur to me at the time, but perhaps he had learned such humility in the presence of children from his idol, Korczak), he explained to me that our minds and bodies usually work in unison. He said that my body had collapsed in order to give my mind the respite it needed to start the long healing process. Looking back, I'm sure he was right. After I recovered, I threw myself into the struggle in a way that wouldn't have been possible without that brief period in a sort of limbo. It was as if my emotions simply gave up for a while and sent a jumble of fragmented images to my brain, where at first they careered around in a crazy merry-go-round of fever. Eventually my brain sent them back, but not before separating and sorting them into some degree of order in which, in their time, they would all have to be dealt. And I suppose this document I'm writing for you—whether it's a letter, memoir, peace offering, exercise in self-discovery, or mixture of all four—shows that nearly thirty years later, they are still being dealt with.

My fears of being seen as a weakling newcomer were quickly dispersed. My credentials as one of Dr. Korczak's orphans, together with my age—I was by three years the youngest member of the company—made me into something of an attraction, and everyone was very friendly toward me once the fever had subsided. Piotr, the cook, who was more or less toothless and looked like an old man, though he was actually no older than I am now, appeared several times at the entrance to my dugout with little extra offerings of potato cake, honey, or blueberries, and once a hard-boiled duck's egg. He handed them over with great show of secrecy and much applying of fingers to lips, and in fact, the little conspiracy between us was to last all the time I was in the forest. The first time Franek came to see me he brought me a pocketful of plums stolen from an orchard on the outskirts of Makoszka. I was glad of his and other visits, because Henryk was strict about making me rest quietly for several days after the fever had gone, and I quickly became bored and restless. He told me later that because I'd been so weak and undernourished when the fever struck, it had nearly killed me.

The dugouts were not exactly comfortable. Loose earth was always drifting down into my eyes from between the branches of the makeshift walls, and insects were abundant. I lay there on my straw mattress, swatting flies, sweating, and itching during the long humid daylight hours, trying to think of an innocent-sounding reason for asking Franek about Eva. I ached to know how she was, and every time I heard someone approach I had a moment of leaping hope that it might be Eva coming to see me. But it never was.

I liked Franek more and more. He was easy to talk to, and we found things to laugh about, too. He also gave me a lot of information about the other members of the band. But at the same time I hated to think that the hand that patted my shoulder in greeting stroked Eva's lovely auburn hair, and hated even more to think of his lips and freckled face against her creamy complexion. Such were the thoughts that tortured me as my strength gradually returned.

Eventually the opportunity presented itself. Franek had brought me my ration of "forest" stew, the monotonous watery vegetable soup whose main ingredient was potato, and sat down to eat with me. He began to tell me how desperately frustrated he was that the injury to his leg had left him lame and condemned to almost permanent guard duty. He was in unusually low spirits.

"I just don't feel I'm contributing anything to the struggle."

"But surely guard duty is very important?" I had learned by now that one of the duties of the band was to help guard a growing number of families living about two miles to the southeast, in a settlement which, the following year, was to become a well-organized camp of several hundred families, mostly old people and children.

"Yes, yes, of course. But it's much less dangerous than the errands and missions Eva goes on."

Here was my chance.

"How is Eva?" I asked with long-rehearsed nonchalance.

His face clouded. "We don't know. She's gone to take some false papers, made by a printer in Ostrow who is sympathetic to us, to some Jews in Majdan Tatarski. That's the new ghetto on the outskirts of Lublin. The black guards there are notoriously vicious. If they found the extra papers on her, I can assure you they wouldn't just shoot her . . ." We were silent for a few moments, and my earlier jealousy was now completely overridden by fears for her safety.

I was puzzled, too. "Black guards?"

"That's what we call the Lithuanian and Ukrainian collaborators there. The Nazis keep them in separate units and put them in black uniforms to distinguish them from the regular German Army. For some reason they're particularly enthusiastic when it comes to slaughtering Jews. They have a reputation for seizing on the most trivial thing. The other day, for example, we heard they'd beaten a young man to death for holding out his identity card in the wrong way.''

I wasn't so very shocked, I'm afraid: I'd seen all too many horrors in my two years in Warsaw. But I didn't understand how Eva could cross in and out of this new ghetto so openly. Franek explained that Majdan Tatarski was a cross between a ghetto and a work camp and was inhabited mainly by young Jews between the ages of eighteen and thirty who were employed by Nazi-controlled factories and firms. Eva had ''authorization'' from a firm in Lublin to deliver orders for needlework to certain ghetto residents. That way she had smuggled several lots of false papers in to Aryan-looking Jews who would be able to make use of them.

''The trouble is,'' he went on, ''her looks, though not at all Jewish, are an additional hazard. People notice Eva. Sometimes she plays on that, and it helps her to get away with more than others would; but sooner or later some bastard is going to decide not to let her slip through his fingers.'' I thought of the guard on the train, and of leering Tomasz, and knew he was right. Franek shook his head. ''I used to say that it was unfair, her inheriting all Mother's looks, but now I think they're a sort of curse.''

I was bewildered.

''Sorry? Mother?''

''Yes. Our mother—she was a beauty. She once had her portrait painted by a famous artist who just happened to see her in a restaurant and begged her to sit for him. . . . They took her away to Belzec—''

''You mean . . . you and Eva . . . you're brother and sister?''

Franek drained his mess tin and wiped his mouth with his sleeve. ''Of course we are. Didn't you realize that? Not just brother and sister—we're twins. You look so surprised!''

I felt a wave of relief. Ridiculously I thought, if they're twins, then I can be friends with them both! Do remember that in those conditions age differences didn't count for the same as they do today. You can imagine how stupid I felt! Particularly when I remembered how I'd actually noticed a similarity between them and been struck by Eva's bossy manner toward him—sisterly, now I came to think of it! But the revelation made me think of Rachel and, with a raw tenderness, made me actively miss rather than mourn her, for they are not necessarily the same. I wanted her right there in the dugout, to tell me in her rather hoarse voice how silly I'd been and then, in her favorite hunched-up sitting position, to press her face against her thighs to hide a smile, the way she usually did when I read her a story or when she was pleased about something.

My first assignment was guard duty at the settlement which was later to develop into the Altana family camp. At first I was disappointed not to be paired with Franek, but Ilya had acted wisely in putting me together with his compatriot Vasily, at seventeen the next youngest member of the band.

Vasily Volodimirovich! My Russian friend. Or, to be more accurate, my Ukrainian friend. If you think, Richard, that there is mistrust and suspicion of the Russian people here in England in the 1970s, let me tell you that these feelings are warm and loving compared with the hatred felt in those days by most Poles for their Soviet neighbors. That's the climate I'd grown up in, and nothing I'd seen in the brutality of Ukrainian guards in the ghetto had led me to question that prejudice. For prejudice it was, of the deep-rooted ancestral kind.

There was nothing immediately appealing about Vasily's flat, expressionless Slav face. He had made no approach toward me while I lay convalescing, and Franek had told me that he seldom spoke and never smiled. But he was both a dependable and daring partisan, a good shot who had killed two Germans outright in an attack on an army lorry shortly before I arrived. He'd also carried out several successful food confiscation raids in nearby villages, by intimidating known collaborators at gunpoint while comrades raided cupboards or gardens. So he was respected, though not really liked.

We walked along in silence that first day, and he spoke only when we arrived at the lookout post, to explain the drill to me. There were insufficient weapons for us both to be armed (at that time only two rifles and one pistol for the whole fifteen-strong company), so I had to know how to summon him, if, from my vantage point in a tree over the main approach to the camp, I saw anything suspicious.

We might have gone on like that indefinitely if, after the second day's duty, we hadn't had to go into the family camp to collect flour for Piotr. It was the best hour of the day, before the gnats and mosquitoes became a misery. The clammy air, tempered by a little breeze, would suddenly be filled with the smells of pine resin and woodsmoke, and in our partisan camp the sounds of Piotr preparing our forest stew or *kasza* (a traditional Polish dish made of groats or barley) were always absurdly reassuring. I was looking forward to being back there, and to finding out if Eva had returned, when suddenly the sounds of a violin wafted toward us. Vasily stopped in his tracks, dropping his side of the flour sack and nearly dislocating my arm. I looked at him, startled and cross, and saw to my amazement that his narrow gray-green eyes had lit up with unmistakable delight.

"I used to accompany my father when he played that on the piano."

"You played the violin—that is a violin, isn't it?" I was musically very ignorant.

"Yes, of course it is. Yes, it's my favorite instrument, though I play the piano, too."

"How clever! I wish I could play an instrument." The statement was genuinely admiring and absolutely true, and remains so to this day; but if I had said it merely to please him, I couldn't have chosen a more effective way. I think that, without exaggeration, he became my friend from that moment.

He bent down to pick up his side of the sack again. He said quietly, "God doesn't exist anymore. The Communists have been telling us that for years, and now all the killing and terrible things that are happening in my country—and in yours—prove it. But music is the echo of God's voice; it proves that he existed once."

I don't think I've ever listened to a beautiful piece of music since without thinking of Vasily and those words.

Poor Vasily. Gradually, over the next days and weeks, he told me more of his story, which, put briefly, was this. Shortly after the Nazis invaded the Soviet Union in June 1941 and began their unimaginable atrocities on Soviet Jews and prisoners of war, he took the decision to volunteer, although barely sixteen, for the Red Army. His parents, cultured, professional people in Kiev, had pleaded with him not to, but he had insisted. He had a duty, he'd told them, to fight for his country against the barbarian invaders. "Such grand words for a child of sixteen," he said with a rare and bitter smile. "Just look how I've managed to impede the barbarian progress. . . ." Despite their protests and appeals, his parents had also gambled with *their* lives to contribute to the struggle; they had sheltered a family of Jews in their attic, been denounced by neighbors, and as a consequence, had died in the horror of the Babi Yar ravine outside Kiev, together with 33,771 Jews. I believe that a significant part of Vasily himself died on that last day of September 1941, although he was physically two hundred miles away at the time and didn't hear of his parents' death until the end of the year. He knew, although their farewells had been affectionate and conciliatory, that his action had filled their last weeks with dread, on his, their only child's, account, and he was dogged by relentless self-reproach. And if only, he said to me, if only he'd been there, perhaps he could have saved them.

"No, Vasily, don't torture yourself with that one," I said, trying to comfort him. "Leave that one to me. I *was* there, and I didn't save anyone. That's a worse failure."

When we got back to the others, I looked around eagerly for Eva, but there was still no sign of her. Then I caught sight of Franek and knew for certain that she hadn't returned. He was mooching around, kicking at loose stones and pinecones, his shoulders hunched, his whole demeanor signaling frustration and anxiety. I saw Ilya and Henryk watching him and then exchanging a few words. Later, after the meal, Vasily, Franek, and I, together with two of the other men, Berek and Leon, were all summoned to the bunker which Henryk and Ilya shared. This was in order to receive instructions for my first mission!

The next morning we were to head south, skirting the treacherous Ochoza Marsh, to a village called Rudka. Ilya had made contact with a farmer there belonging to the Orthodox Ukrainian minority who, unlike many of the Polish locals, had some sympathy with Red Army escapees from Nazi prisoner of war camps and who was willing to sell us some pistols and grenades. I should explain that the whole area had been one of the last strongholds of the Polish Army after the Germans invaded us at the beginning of the war, and when the Polish units eventually surrendered after four weeks of bitter fighting, they abandoned a sizable quantity of arms and ammunition which was found and hidden by local peasants. One way or another, a good deal of it found its way into the hands of partisans such as ourselves.

Ilya told us the farmer had agreed to let us have the arms at a price we could afford.

"Either they're totally useless or it's a trap," said Franek skeptically. "Some of this Polish Army stuff that's been buried for three years isn't worth having." All the same, he was in a much better mood, being allowed away from the camp for the first time in weeks.

"I know it's only to take my mind off Eva, but it's nice of the old men all the same." I didn't think twice about his remark at the time; later I was to discover that neither of our leaders was older than thirty-four, but to us, then, they *did* seem like old men!

There were five of us in the party, for a little extra protection in case it was a trap. Only Vasily and I were actually to carry out the transaction—Vasily because he was also Ukrainian (I never discovered why Ilya himself didn't go back with Vasily) and I because of my non-Jewish appearance. The farmer didn't know there were Jews in our band and would almost definitely have refused to help us if he had. Not only that; it was an extremely risky business for Jews to be seen in any of the surrounding villages, for they ran the constant risk of being denounced by a local population which, by and large, was intensely anti-Semitic.

As we walked through the forest, we talked, as always, in low tones or whispers. Those 125 square miles of damp, densely wooded terrain might have seemed eerily silent and empty to me when I first arrived with Eva: the truth was, though, that they hid a good many fugitives of one sort or another, and as she'd warned me, they were by no means all friendly to one another. Although in a few partisan bands like ours Jews and Russians and Poles fought side by side against the Nazis in a spirit of comradeship, there were other escaped and desperate prisoners of war who regularly attacked the bunkers of isolated Jewish refugees, stealing what possessions they could lay hands on and then raping and sometimes murdering the women. It was not only from the Germans that we had to guard and protect the families in the Altana camp. When I first discovered that, it made me admire Eva and her cool daring even more than I had before. Usually when she left the camp, one of the men would escort her to the edge of the forest, but when she and I had arrived from Warsaw, we were, of course, a day later than expected, and no one had been there to meet us. We were extremely vulnerable, for I'd have been of little use if we'd been attacked; what I didn't know until later was that, at Henryk's insistence, Eva had had a knife hidden inside her blouse to give us at least a degree of protection.

But we neither saw nor heard anyone as we made our way toward Rudka. As we drew near the village, Berek became animated. He was the sort of person you couldn't help liking. He'd had a dramatic escape from one of the early deportation trains taking Jews to Sobibor death camp. I knew that from Franek; Berek himself never talked about it. He was the wit of the band, a self-confessed womanizer in his previous life, who always managed to find something positive in any situation. He was good-looking, though years of malnutrition and hardship had ruined his teeth and made him gaunt and hollow-cheeked. But he had wonderfully humorous dark eyes below strong, bushy brows.

"Now, Leon, describe this baker's widow to me again. It sounds too good to be true. All these promises of soft white rolls are giving me a double appetite!"

Leon had identified the baker's widow in Rudka as someone who was likely to help us with essential supplies; he also knew her to be generous in more ways than one, and Henryk and Ilya had immediately selected Berek as the obvious contact. Leon, on the other hand, was of a pessimistic temperament.

"Mmm, I'm not so sure this is a good idea after all. There'll be too many people she whispers to on the pillow. She may be sympathetic, but I doubt she'll be discreet."

Berek laughed and said pleasantly, "You're a miserable old sod, aren't you, Leon? Begrudge anyone a bit of fun." He slapped him genially on the back and turned to wink at me.

Eventually Leon motioned us to stop; he then showed us where Vasily and I had to go and where, armed with one of the band's two rifles, the others would wait for us, out of sight but within earshot in case of trouble. My heart was back in its all-too-familiar position in my throat! My first partisan mission!

The approach to the smallholding was on a broad dirt track which ran along the edge of the forest but was overlooked on the other side by a number of dwellings in small plots of land.

"Just walk normally; don't look as if we're in a hurry," said Vasily under his breath. "Try and laugh and look relaxed."

I couldn't help seeing the incongruous side of that, coming from my tense and taciturn new friend who never looked relaxed and almost never laughed.

"That's fine. I'll just copy you then." For a second I wondered if I'd gone too far; this was after all very early in our relationship. But as I looked sideways at him, I was rewarded by a tiny movement of his lips. I began to repeat some joke Berek had told us a few nights before, just for the sake of talking.

I wondered how many pairs of eyes were watching us from the windows overlooking the track.

Suddenly a dog barked, and I jumped in alarm. An old man outside one of the houses shouted at the dog and then at us. Above us some crows rose clumsily into the air.

"Hey, who are you? Where are you going?"

"You answer," breathed Vasily, whose Polish was heavily accented.

"We have an urgent message for Mikhail Yurkiv over there . . ." and I pointed to our destination.

"Oh, yes?" The old man was too frail to be threatening, but his suspicion was obvious, and his face hostile. I wondered how many other unseen people had been alerted by his shout.

"We don't trust strangers around here," he went on, his hand on the mongrel, which continued to growl menacingly. "These forests are full of bandits. Jews and Russians mostly. What's your business?"

Thank goodness Ilya had thought up a story in case something just like this happened.

"His sister is dangerously ill. He must go to Wlodawa as soon as possible."

I smiled, hoping that my youth and innocent expression would disarm him. Then I added, with a touch of inspiration, "That's why two of us have come, because of all the bandits."

"Well, you'd better hurry then," and he stood and watched us with shameless curiosity as we approached and knocked on the door of Yurkiv's dilapidated farmhouse. We felt his eyes still on us from a hundred yards away as, after a long pause, the door opened.

A young woman stood there, holding a baby girl in her arms.

"Go away," she said sullenly. "You've no business here." She was very pale with fishlike eyes, and it was clear she'd recently been crying. I was just about to tell her we were being watched and must come in when there was a shout from the back of the house.

"Anna, let them in."

"You have no business here," she repeated, but with panic in her voice now, and made to shut the door in our faces.

I was acutely aware that at any moment the old vigilante down the road might summon some more neighbors, and Vasily must have been thinking the same thing, for he rammed his foot decisively in the door.

"We're coming in," he said, and the menace in his voice made her let go of the handle. The baby began to wail. At that moment Yurkiv himself appeared.

"I'm sorry—come in, come in," he muttered, obviously embarrassed. I couldn't help feeling sorry for his wife and for frightening the baby; for all she knew, we could really have had murderous intentions. But her husband said roughly, "I've told you, Anna, I've given my word. Now go to the kitchen and stay there." Before she obeyed, she gave us a look of such venom that I forgot my sympathy.

"She's very frightened," he explained, as he led the way into a small, musty, overfurnished parlor. I noticed Vasily sizing the place up with his narrow Slavic eyes. This could still have been a trap.

"First, the payment," said Yurkiv, watching us carefully.

Vasily handed over a packet of zlotys and several pieces of jewelry wrapped in cloth. The latter were contributions from several of the families in the Altana camp. Then Yurkiv produced the weapons stored in a canvas bag. There were two pistols, a revolver, several grenades, and some ammunition. Vasily inspected each item carefully, and I was impressed that he seemed to know what he was doing. He was only three years older than I was, but he seemed so much more competent, knowledgeable—and brave.

The transaction was completed quickly, and we were almost at the door when Vasily suddenly remembered.

"By the way, your neighbor was very curious. We told him we

were messengers from Wlodawa, where your sister is dangerously ill.''

"I see. So now I have to disappear for a while to support the story.''

"Well, she could just die,'' suggested Vasily. Perhaps it was a helpfully meant suggestion, but the rough edge to his tone made me shiver. In a climate of barbarity it is all too easy for anyone to become a barbarian. Anyone. Even children and very young people.

Then, back in the comparative safety of the woods, we examined our new treasure, and I found myself holding a gun for the first time in my life. The moment when I felt the weight of the pistol in one hand and ran the fingers of the other along its cold, hard metallic bulk was one of self-revelation. The boy Misha—who had mentally survived the horrors in the ghetto because he believed he was on the side of the angels—now Jan Damski, partisan, could use this weapon to kill, would use this weapon to kill if the occasion arose; more, he *wanted* to use this weapon to kill. Misha, alias Jan, could be a murderer, too.

Don't listen to people who say that revenge is sweet. It never is, because it's founded on the crude and essentially inhuman calculation that one life or one loss can compensate for another. For that reason, Richard, I believe that revenge only ever demeans the dead and brutalizes the survivor. But what *is* sweet is the dream of revenge—and such was the dream I dreamed that day in the forest behind Rudka, as I put the pistol tenderly back in its holster.

"We haven't got enough ammunition for proper target practice, but I'll help you with your focus and aim,'' volunteered Vasily, who had had some training in the Red Army.

The gun gave me a totally new sense of power, which frightened and exhilarated me at the same time. It was probably just as well it was only very temporarily in my possession. I saw again my sick, starving mother, I saw again two hundred children marching to their death in the midday sun, headed by Korczak under the orphanage flag, and suddenly, absurdly, it was as if I had within my grasp the means to bring them all back. I'd kill the foreign devils who'd made them die, I vowed—and only later did it occur to me that in so doing, I betrayed everything Korczak had ever tried to teach us.

We left Berek to try his luck with the baker's widow and began to make our way back. Franek wanted to hurry in case Eva had returned in our absence, so he made the pace, despite his bad foot, and after a while he and I found ourselves on our own, ahead of Leon and Vasily, who were carrying most of the ammunition. Presently I stopped and remarked that the path no longer seemed familiar.

"Surely we should have reached the spot where Leon showed us the wolf tracks?"

"Well, perhaps we have without noticing it."

But it soon became obvious that we had taken a wrong turning somewhere along the line. It was a bad mistake, for the path we had followed petered out eventually in Ochoza Marsh. Our progress slowed right down, until we were literally at a standstill.

"Franek, we have to go back," I said ineffectually, as we had little choice about whether to go forward or backward. I had a sudden vision of my career in the partisan movement literally sinking without trace in a bog, before it had properly begun. I felt annoyed with Franek and silently blamed him for getting us lost.

"I'm sorry, Jan—this is my fault," he said, as if reading my thoughts. He looked so miserable that I immediately forgave him.

Suddenly the funny side of our predicament struck us both at the same time. We stood there, submerged to the knees in red ooze, and giggled inanely at each other.

"This is what the fight for freedom is all about, Jan. When people talk of courage and comradeship, don't listen to a word of it. It's about getting stuck in a swamp in the middle of nowhere, being eaten by insects [we had attracted the inevitable cloud of flies], and achieving absolutely nothing."

Seeing the ridiculous side of our situation brought us to our senses, and we started to clamber and grope our way back the way we had come, pulling ourselves along where possible with the aid of bushes and tree trunks. Unaccountably it took us much longer to retreat than it had to get ourselves into the mess in the first place! Eventually Leon and Vasily appeared, having realized what must have happened and come back for us. Vasily undid the canvas bag in which the boxes of ammunition were packed and hurled in our direction the piece of thin rope which had secured it. He then leaned back against a tree and pulled it taut, so helping to drag us both back onto firm ground with relative ease.

Franek thanked them sheepishly and then told us what was uppermost in his mind. "We'll have to clean up before we get back. I don't want Eva to see us like this. In fact, I don't want her hearing anything about it at all." He looked at us all pleadingly.

"Piotr said there'd be rabbit in the stew tonight. And I know a good pool on the way back where you can wash a bit," volunteered Leon. I couldn't quite see the connection between these two comments until Franek laughed.

"All right, Leon, my rabbit portion if you don't breathe a word." They shook hands on the deal, but even at such a moment of triumph, I looked in vain for a smile on Leon's lugubrious face!

I don't suppose Franek and I were ever in *real* danger in Ochoza Marsh, but the incident stands out in my memory—partly, perhaps, because of its symbolic nature and partly because of what it revealed about my new friend Franek: his impetuosity, his readiness to blame himself when things went wrong, and his ability to laugh at himself, except where his beloved twin sister was concerned, whose approval he seemed to crave.

Berek returned from his mission with not only as much flour and oil as he could carry in a sack on his back but also a basket of curd cheese, eggs, and honey. There were sixteen eggs in all.

"That'll be one for each of us tomorrow, and two for Jan," remarked Alexander, the Jew from Lublin with the thick beard, the electrical engineer who'd been present at my debriefing on arrival. I felt myself blushing. So they knew about Piotr's little acts of favoritism toward me! But they all laughed, and amazingly for those hungry days, no one seemed to resent it. And that night, after the rabbit stew and potato cakes, there was even dessert—curd cheese mashed with wild blueberries and a hint of sugar. (Alexander had confiscated a supply at gunpoint from a known collaborator in the village of Bialka.) You can't imagine what a delicious combination that was. Afterward I sat watching the fire, concealed under its roof of branches—we could never allow it to blaze uncovered for fear that it might be spotted by an aircraft—and began to savor a new sense of contentment and comradeship. My stomach was almost full, and I had several new friends. Perhaps life had started to improve at last. There was real satisfaction at the thought that I'd completed my first mission, and successfully. "Dr. Korczak wouldn't have forgiven me for sending you into such danger!" was all Henryk had said on our return, but the relief on his face had been reward enough. It made me realize just what a risk we had run. The thought of Korczak's reproach was one Henryk had to get used to, though, because there were far more dangerous things to come.

Then, with a start of guilt, I remembered Eva. Franek had sat down a little apart from the rest of us, but his face showed that in spirit he was much farther away. How could I even think of my own well-being when Eva was out there among the enemy, possibly . . . ? No, it didn't bear thinking about. I shivered, despite the warmth of the fire.

Then I became aware that Franek was not the only comrade in low spirits. Next to me, Berek, usually so lively and witty, was much quieter than usual. To start a conversation, I mentioned the curd cheese, and almost as if he'd been waiting for a cue, he began to talk.

"She was really nice, that widow. Actually much nicer than Leon had painted her. Blond, plump, shapely, with a lovely smile. She gave me the cheese and eggs and honey free; she said if it weren't for the

Germans, her husband would still be alive instead of being fossilized somewhere in the Soviet mud, and anyone who was fighting them was a friend of hers. Even so, I wanted to thank her—well, you know, in a way that might have brought comfort to us both. You understand? I'm not talking to you as a child, Jan, because no one who has escaped from a ghetto is a child anymore. I tried, but I couldn't, I just couldn't. I kept seeing Maria's face—how it crumpled when we got separated on the platform and she was loaded onto another truck. She held out her arms and called to me in panic, 'Berek, Berek, I'm sorry, I'm sorry.' What did she have to say 'sorry' for, as if it were all her fault?''

I didn't like to look at Berek, for I could hear he fought to keep back the tears.

"The silly thing is, you see, I never told her I loved her. I wasn't sure I was in love with her, but now it's too late, I know I was."

He sat staring into the glowing fire. I laid a hand on his arm, not knowing what else to do or to say, and let it rest there for a while. I think it comforted him because before long he began to talk more about himself and about his own escape from the train to Sobibor. He laughed at himself. "For months I used to dream that she had escaped, too, and that we met again, here in the forest." I knew what he meant; I, too, had had my version of that dream. It was waking up that turned it into a nightmare.

JULY 14 LATE

Dear Katie,

It's only a day since I finished my last letter to you, but somehow it seems much longer. I wish you could read this stuff that Misha has left for me. It's amazing the things he had experienced and seen by the time he was fourteen. Fourteen! I was in the Lower IV at that age, and the greatest challenge I faced then was not to get caught smoking behind the science labs. I can't help wondering whether if he'd told me all this before, it might have made a

*difference to the way we get on. Probably not, though. It wouldn't
have made him any less strict and unreasonable, I suppose. And if
he really fell in love when he was fourteen, like he says, why
couldn't he be more understanding about you and me? It doesn't
really make sense.*

*All the same, I'm not sure how I'm going to handle it if he hears
about the little episode at school. We're due to see the Head
tomorrow. The truth is that all I did was to keep watch, and the
whole thing was only meant as a bit of fun—and well, we did have
a legitimate grievance against the school in my opinion, the way
they expelled Robert like that without a second chance. I don't
suppose the Head will believe me, though. Or Misha, come to that.*

*Tomorrow I'm going to look up "Babi Yar" in the library. I've
never heard of it before. In the forests Misha made friends with a
Russian boy, seventeen—my age—whose parents were massacred
there for sheltering Jews. I'm beginning to wish I was doing the
Second World War for A level—seriously.*

Good night. Write soon.
          Love you. R

I shared my dugout with the two partisans nearest my own age, Vasily
and Franek. Our bunks, set into the walls of earth, were made of
planks and covered with mattresses of sacking and straw.

As you can imagine, they were not very comfortable. But it was
mainly the damp, clammy air in the bunker, the insects, and the loose
earth falling into my face and hair every time Vasily stirred in his
bunk above that prevented me from falling asleep quickly. I seemed
to itch permanently, whether from real or imagined foreign bodies,
and I noticed it most at night when I was lying still. We did wash
ourselves and our clothes from time to time, but the nearest pool was
at least half a mile away.

Once a week Henryk made us check all our clothes for lice, and he
himself personally inspected our heads. If anyone was found to be

"alive," they had their hair shaved and their clothes were treated with precious kerosene. You had to do it meticulously, inch by inch, along the collars and seams. I told him how Korczak used to inspect our heads in the orphanage and how he would make it a pleasant experience for the children to have all their hair removed, by shaving pictures as he worked. Henryk loved to hear stories about the orphanage and the ways which Mister Doctor found to provide his children with some quality of life, despite the unbelievable squalor and brutality which surrounded them. But we had to be especially careful of lice and ticks in the forest, as there was one in particular which could give you tick fever—potentially fatal. Apparently Henryk had been worried for a while that that was what I had caught when I became ill so shortly after my arrival.

Anyway, that night I was finding it particularly difficult to drift into sleep. Vasily was very restless, and the late August weather was still oppressively humid. Suddenly I was startled by raised voices from outside. I soon recognized Franek's voice, tense and angry, Henryk's softer tones, and the occasional contribution from Ilya in his abrupt, heavily accented Polish. They seemed to be arguing about a strategy for the group's operations.

"We should stop putting all our efforts into saving individual Jews," said Franek with passion. He must have just come off guard duty, as he hadn't been to bed at all. "All we do is save one here, one there, and at unacceptable risk to our best fighters. We should be going all out for German targets. We have *got* to get more arms and then fight the devils wherever we have the slightest chance of doing them any harm."

"It's more important to save our families than to kill Germans." That was Henryk's voice. They must have been almost immediately outside the roof of our bunker.

"Not if it means killing our own comrades to do it," insisted Franek. He had waited long enough for his sister, and his patience was clearly at an end.

"Franek, believe me, I understand how you feel about Eva. But what can we do with our three pistols and our two rifles against the might of the German Army? We *can* save lives, though, and the lives of children for whom there may still be a future.''

There was a pause. Maybe I didn't hear everything. Then Ilya said decisively, ''No, I think Franek is right. We should continue to help guard the family camp—it's growing bigger all the time—but we should put a stop to these mercy missions.''

More silence. I heard the trees rustle in a new breeze. I wondered what Henryk was thinking and was glad that it was a decision I didn't have to make. A choice for the doomed: To fight terror, you have to make terrible decisions.

I can't be sure, but I think it was the next day that I was helping Franek chop and file wood for the walls of the winter bunkers. We continually had to stop to wipe the sweat from our faces and make pathetic attempts to swat the infuriating flies. During one such pause I saw Franek's expression change dramatically. I followed his gaze, and there, coming toward us, was Eva.

She raised a hand and smiled wanly, but this was not the bright-eyed Eva who had shaken with silent laughter on the crowded train. Her shoulders drooped, and her hair was totally disheveled; there was no sign of that green ribbon.

Watching her approach, I seriously wondered if hearts can actually burst. I had known her for just two or three days before going down with the fever, but scarcely a waking hour had passed since without my thinking of her. Now, just as our fears for her life were becoming acute, she had miraculously returned to us, but in a state which tempered our, my, joy with tenderness. I longed to do what Franek could do so naturally—to drop the ax and run toward her.

''What is it, Eva, what happened?''

She shook her head without speaking and allowed herself to be led gently to where we had already made a pile of planks. Several of the others who had caught sight of her came up, and someone went off to fetch Henryk and Ilya.

"It was terrible," she said eventually in a small voice, which sounded dry from lack of saliva. "Majdan Tatarski. The things they did. I thought I'd seen it all before, in Lublin, in the spring, but this was even worse. The children, the babies." She stared into the distance and was clearly once again in the middle of whatever horror she had witnessed.

"Try and tell us," coaxed Franek gently.

Gradually the whole grisly account came out. She had been away much longer than expected because there had been complications over photos for the counterfeit papers, and she'd had to stay at the printers for several days. She hadn't thought it worth making the journey back as each day there had been a strong possibility they would be ready. Eventually she had once again got into Majdan Tatarski and had delivered the documents safely. She was talking to another couple with two small children about obtaining false identity papers for them when, without warning, the ghetto had become gripped by a frenzy. People started running along the little dirt roads between the houses, grabbing children and old people by the arm and dragging them along without explanation. Then someone told Eva there was a rumor that the ghetto was about to be partially liquidated, and so everyone was running for the first hiding place he or she could think of. The situation had suddenly become far too tense for her to get back through the gates, despite her apparently flawless papers, so she attached herself to a family as they knocked frantically at the door of a house where they said they had friends. However, they were refused admission there, *and* at the next place, but eventually someone did make room for them in a cellar that was already so crowded that people were quite literally sitting on top of each other. Eva was crammed into a corner beside two children aged about eleven.

Guards with loudspeakers began to march up and down the streets, shouting instructions for all the Jews to come out of their houses and assemble in the square. They announced that farmers were needed in recently "reclaimed" lands, and those people who were selected would be able to work the land and live rewarding lives. This was followed by a house-to-house search. From their hiding place Eva and her companions could hear a great deal of commotion: people screaming, dogs barking, doors banging, shots cracking the air. . . . But their cellar hiding place, which had been skillfully camouflaged with some foresight by the inhabitants of the house, was not discovered, and sometime the next morning, shocked, shaking, and half suffocated, they all emerged alive.

Although it had been a terrifying night, it was only the next day that Eva appreciated the extent of the destruction she had just survived. Many people had been gunned down or beaten to death in the streets— those orderly little dirt streets which ran between white-fenced gardens. Majdan Tatarski was probably the only ghetto in Poland where Jews were allowed to have gardens. But *allowed* is not the right word; with hideous irony they were required to keep their little plots beautiful, to plant and weed them according to rigid rules from which the smallest deviation merited punishment by death. When Eva told me this, I remember thinking that even cruelty can be refined and sophisticated, and be all the more vile for that. Many of the people who'd been killed on the spot—presumably to save the trouble of carting them off to a concentration camp—had been either elderly or very young. It was what she saw in the first pram she looked into that made Eva cry for the first time in that whole bloody operation. I leave the rest to your imagination.

We all sat around, silent. No doubt we were remembering our own versions of what had just happened at Majdan Tatarski; I know I was reliving mine. Eventually Piotr appeared with a mugful of some steaming liquid and handed it to Eva, who carried on with the story.

Dazed as she was, she had suddenly realized that the two children who'd been almost literally on top of her in the cellar, and whom she'd talked to on and off throughout the night, had attached themselves to her. They told her how they'd lost their parents in a previous raid and were now on their own. Eva took their arms and helped them to weave a way around the dead bodies which lay strewn everywhere. She couldn't help noticing that neither of the children, who were called Esther and Moshe, shed a tear: they were in a state of profound shock.

Unconsciously Eva was making for the main gate. Then she suddenly stopped. Looking at the children, whose appearance was as Jewish as their names, she realized that there was absolutely no way she could pass them off as Aryan factory helpers. She had to make a decision then and there. Either she had to use her papers to get out of the ghetto as quickly as possible and say good-bye to her two new friends, leaving them to almost certain eventual death, or she had to find a way of getting them out.

Eva made little of the courageous thing she did then.

"The decision sort of happened to me, rather than me making it," she said. "I knew I had to act quickly, or I'd lose my nerve."

She sipped her drink and turned to thank Piotr. "I don't know what you put in your tea, but it's wonderful, and it's bringing me back to life." She gave him a smile that momentarily stopped my heart, but Piotr just grinned back in his nice toothless way and didn't seem at all excited by it.

Franek showed a hint of brotherly impatience. "Come on, Evi, what did you *do*?"

"I went up to a Ukrainian guard and said that I'd found these two urchins hanging around and looking as if they needed some good hard work. Could I take them back to our factory to clean up the ovens there as no Pole worth his salt was going to do the job?"

Everyone looked at her wide-eyed. Even Leon's usually deadpan face registered interest. Franek's, I thought, managed to show both pride and horror—or perhaps I was just projecting my own reactions onto him.

"Go on," he said tersely.

"Well, I think the guard was as surprised as I was at myself. He looked at me for a moment or two a bit suspiciously as I made to hand him my papers, and then, miracle of miracles, he waved them away without even looking at them, threw back his head, and began to laugh. 'Now that's the best idea I've heard for days. Go on, take 'em and work their dirty little backsides off. And when you bring 'em back, there's plenty more where they came from. Not for much longer, though.' And true as I sit here, he gave me a grotesque wink.'' She looked at the ground and jabbed at the moss with her heel.

"I have to tell you that I actually thanked the monster, and nicely, too. Goodness knows how many people he'd killed, maybe even some of those babies in their prams, that very night, but I actually said thanks to him. What else could I do?"

Despite everything she'd done, Eva could still reproach herself, because she felt that being polite to the murderers represented a sort of betrayal. She looked around the circle of expectant faces, almost apologetically.

"If you hadn't, he'd probably have shot you," Franek reassured her. "They're all bastards—every last one of them. You live or die depending on their whim of the moment; the Ukrainians can be even worse then the Nazis if you ask me."

"I don't think anyone *is* asking you." It was Vasily who spoke up. Nobody else said anything. It was a very awkward moment.

Suddenly I felt a rush of protectiveness toward the normally sullen-seeming Ukrainian boy, who had entrusted me with a glimpse of his private despair.

"Franek, Vasily is Ukrainian, and his parents died helping Jews," I heard my voice protest. It was the first time I had spoken out in front of so many of the band, and I felt myself blush. Vasily looked at me with a funny little frown, and I wondered anxiously if I had broken a confidence. Later, though, he told me he had only been surprised at the unusual support.

"Jan is right." The approval came from Henryk. "Labeling is the business of the enemy, not ours. And don't forget, we've reason to be grateful to quite a few of the Ukrainian minority living around here."

Franek himself had flushed very red. He was impulsive, certainly, and thoughtless sometimes, wearing his heart, as you English nicely put it, on his sleeve. But he was also kindhearted and quick to admit—as I'd seen that day in the bog—when he was wrong.

"Vasily, I'm sorry, I only meant the guards. And I didn't know about your family. I *am* sorry." He held out his hand toward the younger boy and looked at him earnestly. Vasily held his gaze but didn't take his hand immediately, and for a moment I was tempted to interfere again. For some reason I badly wanted them to be friends. But eventually Vasily nodded and then took Franek's hand—briefly, but he took it.

"Perhaps now Eva can be allowed to get on with her story," said Ilya irritably.

"Yes, what happened to the children? Where are they now?" That was Helka's question. I noticed because at that time, before big Roza arrived, she was the only other girl in the band and she hardly ever spoke. She was a very small, shy person, dark with pointed features so that she made me think of the sort of little creatures we sometimes saw in the forest—weasels and polecats. It didn't really occur to me at the time, but looking back, I can see how overshadowed she must have felt by Eva, with her striking good looks and her breathtaking courage. Helka was far too Jewish in appearance to be used as a courier girl.

Eva went on to tell us how being so relieved at getting all three of them through the gate, she was tempted for a moment to relax. But then she realized that the most dangerous part was probably still to come. The children were inescapably Jewish to look at, Eva's papers applied only to herself, and no one would ever believe her story that a ghetto guard had allowed them free exit. She told them to keep their faces down, and with an arm around the shoulders of each one she hurried them along the quickest route to where the suburbs petered out into countryside.

"I fancied I got one or two curious looks, but I made a point of smiling openly at everyone I met, and no one stopped us. The children were marvelous; they didn't complain once though they were both wearing the most awful old shoes, and I knew their feet were killing them.''

"Eventually we got to Tomasz and Zofia's farm. I decided to stay there as I knew we wouldn't make it to the camp before nightfall. We were all exhausted, as you can imagine.''

Franek looked at her keenly.

"And Tomasz?"

"Don't worry. We three slept together; this time *they* protected *me*.''

But Franek protested. "Henryk, Ilya, we cannot go on using that man. He is a disgrace to the struggle.''

"Franek, we don't have any choice." Ilya's tone was impatient, as it often was.

But Henryk said, "And the children, Eva?''

"In the family camp. You know Genia, who has made bread for us a few times? She was the most motherly person I could think of although she has two little ones of her own. I hope she will manage.''

Suddenly she looked exhausted and drained of color. Henryk got to his feet. "Eva, we're proud of you. You've done something truly remarkable. But now you must go to your dugout and sleep. That's an order. Tonight we'll celebrate.''

But before she went, Eva had a special word for me. "So, little brother, you've recovered! But I knew you would; I didn't leave until Henryk said your fever had passed the worst. How are you?''

Fortunately Franek saved me from having to reply!

"He's been fine for several days. And what's more, he's already been on his first mission. He and Vasily picked up some guns and ammunition from a Ukrainian in Rudka. Not bad stuff either considering it had been buried for nearly three years.'' He winked at me, by which I knew he was reminding me not to give anything away about our adventure in Ochoza Marsh.

We did indeed celebrate that night. Berek and Alexander and one or two of the others went fishing and came back with freshwater crab, which many people consider quite a delicacy. They were plentiful in the shallow lakes and pools of the Parczew forests, and sometimes we sold them to local people who were prepared to do business with us. But on special occasions we ate them ourselves together with potatoes baked in the fire, then split open and spread with soured milk or curds, and sprinkled with onion sprouts or fresh mint, which grows prolifically there. That night Piotr hard-boiled the widow's eggs as well, and with moonshine to drink, it was a fitting welcome feast. Moonshine, in case you're wondering, was what we called the vodka which some local people distilled privately and illegally. Ilya always seemed to have a supply; no one ever discovered how he managed to come by it, and it grew to be one of the jokes among the band. Ilya, impatient and inclined to be imperious, was not as popular as the gentler-mannered Henryk.

It was in fact the first time that I had tasted any sort of strong spirit, let alone moonshine, which could be very strong indeed! I still remember the sensation, like an explosion of stars in my throat and chest. Perhaps it was due to the moonshine, but presently I found the courage to offer Eva the extra egg which, as Alexander had predicted, Piotr made sure came my way!

"This is for you—after what you did." The first and only present I would ever offer her.

"Oh, Jan, that's really nice of you, but don't you think we should give it to Helka? She's much stricter about keeping kosher than the rest of us, so she won't eat the crab."

I must have looked crestfallen because she added, "You don't mind, do you?"

"Of course not. It's a good idea." And when I saw the way Helka flushed with pleasure at the unexpected kindness, I was glad.

After the meal Ilya gave permission for us to have real coffee, which was kept for very special occasions, our usual bitter brew being made of chicory or roasted wheat grains. And as we drank, someone started to sing. Soon we were all joining in, even I who had always been rather embarrassed by my indifferent singing voice.

I looked around the circle of flushed, contented faces. Even Vasily was joining in, much less self-conscious in song than in speech. And I noticed Helka watching Eva, wistfulness softening her small, sharp-featured face. It was at such moments, usually in the evenings, usually around the fire, that I felt a new sense of belonging. Life in the forest was often terrifying and deadly dangerous, always uncomfortable and dirty, but it contained moments of happiness as pure and intense as flame.

The Jews of Parczew, on the northernmost edge of our forest, were deported to the death camp at Treblinka on August 19, 1942, less than two weeks after Korczak and the children. Then, in October, the Jewish communities in the villages of Leczna and Ostrow Lubelski, to the south, were liquidated. Inexorably the Nazi net was being drawn more tightly around us. As a result, those autumn weeks saw a significant increase in the number of fugitives who escaped, and it was then not uncommon for us to meet solitary Jews, or little groups of them, wandering aimlessly in the thickets and woods, starving, ragged, and desperate. Several of the younger, fitter ones joined us or other partisan bands operating in the area, but we guided any women, children, or older people to Atanta, where other families had begun to establish a semblance of routine in this strange wooded world. For many it was to be only a brief reprieve, for of those who were not eventually captured in the German raids, hundreds succumbed in due course to hunger, cold, or disease.

As the autumn wore on, I began to wonder when I was to be sent back to Warsaw. I didn't at all relish the thought of traveling back there on my own—in fact, the prospect filled me with dread—but I had thought that the reason for my joining the partisans in the first place had been to acquire some arms which could then be smuggled back to the ghetto. I didn't really want to broach the subject, but I began to feel an uneasy tug—as if I were being in some way disloyal to those who had arranged my escape.

Eventually I mentioned it to Franek, who offered to come to Henryk with me. Characteristically it was Henryk who apologized.

"Jan, I'm sorry, I should have made it plain before this. We have every intention of complying with my cousin Joseph's request and sending you back to Warsaw when the time is right—I'm from Warsaw myself, remember, and my friends there are not forgotten—but the time is not yet right." Did he sound just a little bit defensive then when he said, "I didn't come here to play hide-and-seek in the woods and enjoy myself, whatever Joseph and his Dror friends think. I'm very fond of him, I really am, but he does have a naïve and rosy view of life outside the ghettos; he seems to think that arms and ammunition just drop from the trees. First we have to build up our supply, and when we have some to spare, then you shall go back. I'm sorry."

But I was much more relieved than disappointed, though I'd never have admitted as much to any of them—not even to Franek and certainly not to Vasily. I was ashamed of my fear.

"Jan, if it makes you feel better, we have sent word via the priest in Parczew to the courier in Lubartow—the one who's managed to keep his job on the Warsaw railway line. He will get word to Joseph and the others; no one is going to think you've deserted them." He smiled the kind, tired smile I would come to know so well. All the same, I couldn't help wondering whether by the time we had enough arms to take back to Warsaw, it might not be too late.

But we were gradually and steadily adding to our supply of arms. As well as obtaining them by negotiation with local people, several small-scale but successful sabotage missions during that autumn yielded a crop of guns and uniforms. One particularly windy night Vasily, Ilya, and Alexander went, with Leon as guide, to try and blow up a railway bridge over the river which flowed just to the east of our forests. Although the damage they inflicted on the bridge was only partial, it must temporarily have badly disrupted travel on the main

Lubartow–Sielce–Warsaw route, and perhaps more important for our purposes, the two German guards in the signal box were killed. I'll never forget Vasily returning to us next morning in a pair of their jackboots. They were, in fact, too big for him, and his progress was awkward and uncomfortable, but I could tell that they gave him a satisfaction which outweighed physical discomfort. For him they were a hunter's trophy, for it was he who had killed their owner when, after breaking the window of the signal box with his rifle butt, he had lobbed in a grenade. He had then reached cover only just in time and had been hit and badly cut on the side of the face by flying debris, but he brushed aside concern.

"Never mind that. Henryk will see to my face. Look at my *boots*— and all the *stuff*." And he dropped before us a gleaming black Luger and an entire German uniform whose value to us was potentially beyond price.

There was something pathetically incongruous, grotesque even, about Vasily in those boots—bully boots, as Rachel and I used to call them. To me they were the supreme symbol of the brutality with which so much that I knew and loved had almost literally been stamped out. But none of us in those days could afford to be sentimental for long, and by the end of October boots were becoming a real issue, for no one could survive a winter in the forest without boots.

Winter! It loomed before us like an uncharted wasteland. Those of the band who had lived wild the year before—who included both Ilya and Vasily, who'd escaped from Nazi captivity the previous January— warned us that our foraging expeditions would become even more hazardous. The leaves were already starting to fall from the birches and maples and other deciduous trees so that our cover would soon be much less dense, and we'd be easily visible from the air. And once snow covered the ground, our footprints would lie like written invitations to every potential enemy. It was hard to imagine after those sweltering summer days, but death from exposure was also going to be a real possibility.

We dug deeper bunkers, for paradoxically, deeper meant warmer. I didn't at all like the idea of sleeping any farther underground than we were doing already because as you know, I suffer from acute claustrophobia. I confided that to Franek, who assured me that I'd always be able to see the entrance and that I could have the top bunk. In time I did get sort of used to it, though I never completely lost my unease and would always go to sleep facing in the direction of the entrance. The moonless, starless nights were the worst, for then the dark was impenetrable and I would start to imagine that I lay at the bottom of a deep mine shaft, where I would remain until I decayed into nothing. But once the snow fell and settled, it gave off a ghostly light which seeped down into the little burial chambers we had made for our survival, and except for the night when we heard the howl of wolves in the distance, it kept my more macabre fantasies at bay.

Berek persuaded his widow to lend us a pony and cart so that we could transport sacks of groats and potatoes and other supplies back into the forest, as well as more straw for our bedding. Vasily obtained two goats from one wealthy but unwilling villager, thanks to the persuasive powers of the dead German's Luger. I noticed that Ilya allowed Vasily to treat the gun as his own, though all the other arms were pooled and kept in a special bunker which Ilya himself oversaw.

As we became better armed, we grew braver about our raids, but they were always for food, clothing, or essential supplies. There was an unwritten law that we should never steal anything which we didn't actually need. I suppose that in itself was open to interpretation; perhaps we didn't strictly *need* chicken in our forest soup, for example, though we certainly did remove chickens from farmyards when the opportunity arose. But often we relied on the help of those honorable exceptions to the anti-Semitic rule—people to whom many of us owed our survival, particularly during the bitter winter months. Leon was valuable to us in this. He had been born and brought up in Parczew in a family of blacksmiths; this meant he had an unusually reliable knowledge of many inhabitants of the area. He himself seldom made an appearance in the villages, however, as by the same token, there were all too many people who might recognize him. He was a giant of a man who didn't easily escape notice.

As the days grew shorter and chillier, I had to put my Aryan looks to work by begging in the neighboring villages, together with one or two other Poles (whose names, apart from Piotr's, I have completely forgotten) and one or two neutral-looking Jews. Leon told us which places held markets on which days; it was safer to mingle in market crowds because some of the villages were so small that an unfamiliar beggar could be dangerously conspicuous. Begging was something I had done before, and now, after the first time or two, I became quite brazen, approaching anyone who had a friendly face with a hard-luck orphan story. I managed to acquire quite a lot of things that way; socks, sweaters, a couple of horse blankets, a pair of straw boots of the sort the poorer peasants wore in that area, and usually bits and pieces of food. People clearing up their stalls would throw me rolls going stale or the end piece of a country sausage or mushy fruit. I wasn't fussy in those days! But sometimes I went with Piotr, who would take a little money with him and then drive a hard bargain; he had been a chef before the war and refused to be palmed off with second-class produce. On those occasions I'd watch him out of the corner of my eye, silently egging him on; once he had quite a row over some horsemeat, and I was afraid he'd gone too far and questions would be asked. But that night we sat safely around the fire eating stewed horsemeat!

The times I liked best were when Eva came with me. I know I wasn't the only one who was relieved to hear that the printer in Ostrow had become too frightened to continue producing false documents for us, so Ilya was not tempted to change his mind, and her lone forays farther afield came to an end. In any case Majdan Tatarski was finally liquidated, in November I think it was, and its inhabitants were taken off to Majdanek concentration camp. Several times Eva and I were quite successful in begging as older sister and younger brain-damaged brother, limited in understanding and dependent on her for keeping body and soul together. We did this in different places from where I'd been before and it worked, until one day I was recognized by a butcher with whom I'd once energetically bargained in another village quite some miles away! Perhaps we should have made more of an effort to disguise my looks, but we didn't, and we suffered the consequences! The boy on the stall looked at me suspiciously and whispered something to his boss; I could see what was about to happen moments before it did, but by then it was too late to do anything about it.

"That kid over there," yelled the butcher. "He's no more handicapped than I am. After him!"

Suddenly we were running, chased by a growing crowd of locals, mostly children and young men, it seemed from a quick glance over my shoulder. Our crime wasn't so very great, and perhaps we wouldn't have got more than a thrashing, but we couldn't take the risk. And then there'd have been the questions and the inevitable inspection, perhaps even confiscation, of papers. When we had nearly reached the end of the main village street (I can't actually remember which village it was), Eva panted, "Police!" and, to my horror, out of the corner of my eye I saw two policemen coming out of one of the last buildings.

They were local policemen, not Germans, and luckily for us seemed amused rather than aroused by the sight of two scruffy beggars being chased down the road by a crowd of so many young vigilantes. I was in no condition for this sort of exertion; before long I thought both my lungs and my head were going to burst, and the breath scraped up through my throat like a rasp. In my panic I ran faster than Eva, and as our arms were still linked, she stumbled at one point and almost fell. I slowed down to steady her, tightening my grip through her arm as I did so. I dared not look back, afraid that the gap would now have closed.

But fortunately the village was on the very edge of the forest so that when the road gave way to a dirt track beyond the police station, we were almost immediately surrounded by trees. Then, as suddenly as the commotion had begun, it finished; our pursuers seemed to lose interest in us at the edge of their territory, or perhaps they were afraid of the dangers lurking in the forest in the form of "murderous bandits," for whose capture the Germans offered large rewards. Fortunately it had obviously not occurred to anyone that the pretty young woman and the scruffy teenage boy could belong to a partisan band, with a price on their heads.

When we were sure that we were alone again and there were a couple of dense thickets between us and the village, we stopped and looked at each other. I had never seen Eva so flushed or her eyes so bright; after a moment we fell into a jubilant, laughing embrace. I wanted that moment to last forever, and perhaps, in a way, it did.

She drew away and dug into her trouser pocket.

"Look! I grabbed it off the edge of a stall in all the chaos. I've never stolen anything that wasn't food before. But I've earned this. And I do so badly need to wash my hair before winter sets in." She held up a little tablet of white soap and looked at it lovingly.

To me Eva was always beautiful, but looking back, I suddenly have a vision of how she might have been with sleek, shining hair and pretty, colorful clothes. All that was denied her, along with so much else. In the forest keeping free of lice and disease was the first priority; the second was keeping reasonably clean. There was no chance of anything more frivolous, more cosmetic. I wonder if that was something she missed or ever even though about. The water for washing, which we fetched in buckets from the pool about half a mile away from the bunkers, could hardly have been good for anyone's skin; it had to be boiled before using it for any purpose, for fear of disease-carrying insects.

As we walked back, Eva said, "Thank goodness Franek didn't come. He said he couldn't see why I had to have a pretend cripple for a brother when I have a real one. But Ilya thinks he's too slow to go into the villages in daylight."

"Yes, he'd have been lynched just now. He couldn't possibly have escaped; we only just did."

"Poor Franzi. He feels he's a burden to us and doesn't contribute anything. I wish I could do something about it."

"But that's silly. He does guard duty for the families, and he's been on several of the nighttime raids. *And* he does a lot around the camp. Look how much work he's done on the winter bunkers."

"Yes, but when he goes on the raids, he's always the lookout. And he doesn't really enjoy the carpentry stuff. I think he does it as a sort of penance. It's very hard for him, you see, Jan, because when we were growing up, he was always the strong one. Our father died when we were five, so he was the man of the house. He was devoted to our mother and to me, and we depended on him—too much perhaps. But it makes all this doubly difficult for him."

"I didn't realize that. How did he hurt his leg?"

"He doesn't talk about it because it reminds him of how we failed to protect Mother. On the train to Belzec we were kept overnight in a siding; they opened the doors for some reason or other, and Mother bribed a guard with her wedding ring. He looked the other way while we jumped. Franek stumbled in the rush and broke his ankle, and of course, he couldn't have it set or even rest it. Later Henryk thought it was too risky to break it again for resetting, so he has a crooked foot. Anyway, we made for the woods because we'd heard there were some families taking refuge there, but we wandered around for days looking for them, and then we met Ilya and others who'd decided to form a partisan group. Henryk had just joined them, and it was he who persuaded Ilya to take us on. Ilya would have preferred us to stay with the families, because he thought we wouldn't pull our weight. And I think Franek always remembers that."

"I'm surprised I was allowed to join you in that case," I said.

"You nearly weren't! Ilya and Henryk had quite a row about it while you were ill."

This was news to me. "Didn't Ilya think . . .?"

"No, Jan, it wasn't Ilya. This time it was Henryk. He couldn't bear the thought of subjecting one of Korczak's orphans to more danger than was absolutely necessary. In the end Ilya prevailed. He said we couldn't afford to waste your Aryan looks and that you'd already proved you could be reliable and take risks." I turned away, so she wouldn't see my blush of pride.

I'd often wondered how Joseph, back in the ghetto in Warsaw, had managed to make contact with Henryk and arrange for me to go to the Parczew forest. Now seemed a good time to ask.

"Well, it was through the courier line. That's the priest in Parczew and the railway attendant and probably one or two other links which we're not told about. We're seldom told more than we need to know. Anyway, the courier goes to Warsaw regularly. We've got several messages through that way. There's a place where we can leave things in a grave in the churchyard; you don't have to pass any house to reach it."

"So Henryk never intended me to take arms back to Warsaw?" I know my voice was accusing, for I felt he had lied to me, and already by then I had come to like and trust him a great deal.

"No, I don't think that's so. I believe he agreed in good faith, but when he saw you . . . Jan, you looked like such a child when you arrived, so thin, and you tried so hard to be brave. Henryk had a son of his own—he died of typhus in the ghetto—and if he changed his mind, I don't blame him. Anyway, I think he's right that we have to accumulate more arms before we can start taking any up to Warsaw. I think he *thinks* he'll let you do that in due course!"

The November day had not yet revealed all the surprises it had in store. We had just realized that Alexander, who had accompanied us as far as the village and should have been waiting for us at the other end, would either still be waiting for us, wondering what had happened, or would have heard the rumpus and gone back to the band to alert them that we were in trouble. Then we heard shots, shouts, and the sound of engines in the distance.

"Difficult to be sure, but I think that's coming from the Ostrow road to the south." Despite the distant noise, Eva spoke, as she usually did when we were away from the camp, in lowered tones.

We arrived back as the others were deciding what to do. The Germans had mounted a full-scale attack in the units the size of companies or even battalions; Alexander on the way back from waiting for us had climbed a tall tree and been shocked by the scale of the operation.

"It's one thing to guard the families against small German patrols or groups of Soviet thugs—sorry, Ilya—but quite another to defend them, and ourselves, against an entire battalion." He pulled worriedly at his huge black beard. I don't think I'd ever heard Alexander say so much at once.

"What we must do is try and cause confusion in their ranks—get them to start shooting each other," said Ilya thoughtfully.

"And how do we do that, may I ask?" This was Roza, a recent addition to the band. She was a big, unsmiling, masculine sort of woman, who, it seemed to me, disagreed with almost anything anyone said.

But Ilya asserted his leadership and was curt with her.

"I don't think that's difficult. Those of us who can must climb trees and lob grenades in among them from several directions at once. That'll soon have them running around like rabbits."

"Where's Franek?" asked Eva suddenly.

"He's on guard duty with Berek and Leon."

"On which side of the family camp?"

"The far side."

That meant about a mile and a half away, to the southeast. The noise of the German invasion was coming from the southwest.

"So he's likely to get cut off if the Germans come in from the Jedlanka direction?"

"Yes, Eva, it's possible, likely even."

"And if we start trying to confuse the Germans, our guards aren't going to know what on earth is going on. There are going to be a lot of people killed in the crossfire, including the families.''

"Yes, Eva. But there is no choice." Ilya's tone was firm. "And we have no time to waste. We must get going now."

Eva nodded. "I just wanted to know," she said quietly.

I can't remember the details of who went where then, but Ilya detailed a number of people to head southwest for a little way with him, where they would climb evergreen trees in order to get a picture of what was happening. The rest of us, including Eva and Vasily, were ordered into the bunkers. The largest was Henryk and Ilya's, and several of us crowded in there.

Vasily felt put out that he hadn't been chosen to go and fight the Germans. Henryk explained: "Vasily, you get more than your fair share of missions. With limited arms the risks must be shared out. Ilya is a good leader and you should trust his decisions."

Dear Piotr, who always tried to cheer up anyone in low spirits with something to eat or drink, handed him a baked potato; he'd been cooking them when the German raid had started and had refused to take shelter until they were ready, when he'd piled them into a sack and brought them to us.

"Never mind, Vasily, you've killed more Germans than anyone else in the group," he said to him with his toothless grin. "Must let someone else have a go occasionally."

"In fact, I think it's because of Vasily that they've sent in the reinforcements." Henryk smiled. Vasily didn't smile himself but shrugged in a sort of acquiescence and didn't grumble anymore. I noticed that Eva didn't eat her potato, which she halved between Vasily and myself. She had no appetite.

Suddenly a colossal blast of heavy artillery fire burst through the forest, causing the ground above us to vibrate and loose earth at the end of the dugout to cascade down onto a bunk. The stuffy underground air pulsated with black sound. It was difficult to say how long it lasted because our eardrums ached with the reverberations for some time.

I was terrified. I sat wedged between Eva and Vasily, and after the worst of the blast had subsided, I realized that I'd dropped my potato on my thigh and was clutching Eva's hand.

"Get rid of it all, Jan, or it'll attract the mice—and goodness knows what else." Henryk didn't have to mention rats; we all knew there was a danger of the bunkers' being invaded by rats.

I freed my hand to clear up the mess, but after a while Eva said in a small voice, "Talk to me. Just talk to me—about anything. And don't stop."

And so that's how we passed that endless night. I talked about everything I could possibly think of: about the air raids at the beginning of the war in which my best friend from school had been killed, about Dr. Korczak and the way he ran the orphanage, about the Children's Court, and the weekly gazette, and all the things he had encouraged us to do. I carefully avoided mentioning Rachel and Eli and the deportations, but I told her about my smuggling expeditions outside the ghetto, about my mother and father before the war—in fact, about all sorts of details which I thought might conceivably interest her. I spoke quietly because I didn't think the others would all want to hear, but I know Henryk and Vasily listened because occasionally they would ask a question. Henryk was particularly fascinated by Korczak. But every time I slowed down, Eva would grip my hand as if warning me not to stop.

Eventually, I don't know after how long, I began to run out of things to talk about. For a moment I panicked, guessing that silence would make Eva's agony unbearable. Then I had an inspiration.

"Vasily, tell Eva about your music." I knew that was the one thing that Vasily would be prepared to talk about.

Eva looked at him with interest.

"Do you play an instrument, Vasily?"

"Yes. The violin. And piano."

"Our mother used to play the piano. She taught me and Franek for a while, but neither of us was much good at it—poor Mother, that must have been a big disappointment to her. But she also taught us to love listening to music."

"Who are your favorite composers?" he asked eagerly.

"I'm not sure. Mozart perhaps, maybe Beethoven."

"There's only one thing wrong with Beethoven," said Vasily grimly.

"What?"

"He was German."

We were at last silent for a few moments, digesting the fact of Beethoven's Germanness.

"Do you know, I've never really thought of that before. In fact, so much beautiful music comes from Germany. How is it possible?"

As if to underline the question there was another burst of gunfire, though of small arms and farther away than at first.

"It's possible because there's no connection between beauty and morality—especially in music." That was Henryk. "Who knows? Beethoven might have committed atrocities if he'd had the chance."

"That's a terrible thought," said Vasily, for whom love of music was a sort of religious worship.

"Not really, Vasily. It wouldn't make his music any less wonderful. They are two different things—the creator and the created."

Henryk was a thoughtful man, and I was to become much more familiar with his philosophical reflections. At that time it was all a bit beyond me, but at least the discussion had engaged Eva's interest.

"What bewilders me is not so much what you're saying about the difference between an artist and his art, Henryk, because I find that quite easy to understand. No, it's that sublime and sadistic things can coexist not just in one culture or country, like we're saying about Germany, but in one person even. I mean, we've all heard stories about guards occasionally risking their lives to show mercy, even between the most brutal murders. How is *that* possible?"

"It's easier not to think about it," said Vasily, who was not of a philosophical turn of mind. "Anyway, I shall stick to Tchaikovsky, and Mussorgsky and Borodin—no one captures the spirit of our Russian folk songs better than Borodin.''

They talked on about music, whispering because Roza farther down the bunker was trying to sleep and had complained about the incessant talk. Piotr was actually snoring; his ability to shut his mind to what was going on around him was enviable. I still held on to Eva's hand, but I began to feel very left out. It seemed to me that Eva was more interested in Vasily's silly music than in any of the things I could talk about. I'd been stupid enough to introduce the subject, thinking to help them both, and look where it had left me! I felt tears sting the back of my eyes and was grateful that the light in the bunker was so dim. We were burning a dried fungus called *huba*—I don't know whether there's an English equivalent—which gave off a very slow-burning flame.

I resented listening to Eva and Vasily talking about composers I'd never heard of. Not even Henryk took any notice of me now as he'd begun to doze. I withdrew from the conversation and began to think more about Franek. Had he been killed? Was he lying injured or a prisoner somewhere? I'd grown extremely fond of him in the three months we'd been together; he was easier to talk to than anyone else in the band, and the five-year age gap between us didn't seem to make any difference. And Leon and Berek. Were they dead, too? Berek, who always managed to make us laugh.

I'm not sure that I ever really got over my sense of exclusion that night. Of course, at the time I quickly put it out of my mind—with so many momentous things happening all around us, such feelings were, after all, trivial and self-indulgent—but later, much later, why *did* I spend so much time and effort trying to learn the piano when I clearly didn't have any aptitude? Why do I always feel uneasy or irritated when people talk to each other in my presence about music? I don't resent not being good with my hands or never having been a sportsman, but I do resent—bitterly even—my lack of musical ability. I love listening to music, but I respond to it purely on an emotional level and I can't help suspecting that I'm thereby excluded from one of life's great riches. Perhaps that's why I was so cross with you when you insisted on giving up the flute last year, Richard. You had the opportunity *and* the ability, and you chose to turn away from them both, but I couldn't find the words to explain at the time and you saw it as another example of my "slave-driving." And actually you were right. After all, I shouldn't expect to realize my own ambitions, or make up for my own shortcomings, through you; that, too, is a sort of exploitation. It's strange, but until I came to write this, I'd never seen it like that.

But I digress. Eventually, in the early hours, Eva drifted off to sleep, and she was still asleep when, next morning, weary but unwounded, Franek, Berek, and Leon returned.

Franek was in good spirits. Despite his crooked foot, he had managed to climb quite high up into a thick fir tree and, in the midst of the raid, had shot all four tires of one armored car and a front one of another.

"I couldn't get any of the bastards themselves, unfortunately." He grinned. But the Germans had abandoned the cars, and later, after they had withdrawn, he and Alexander had managed to dismantle one of the radios, which Alexander later adapted, to a limited extent, for our use. The Germans had also left a pair of gloves and some tins of meat in the vehicle.

"I've told you before about staying out too late," said Eva in greeting. Her words hid her relief, but her expression didn't.

"Jan and Vasily kept me going through the night," she told him. "I don't know what I'd have done without them." She gave me one of her wonderful dancing smiles, obviously quite unaware of my fit of pique. Then she asked anxiously about the families and in particular about the twins she had rescued from Majdan Tatarski.

"The twins are fine. I've just checked; in fact, I gave them one of the tins of meat. Genia and all her family survived intact, and everyone living in the bunkers just near her. The thickets are particularly dense just around there, as you know; there's only that one tiny pathway in, so they are about as secure as it's possible to be here. I'm afraid all too many of the others weren't so lucky."

In fact, although we didn't know the extent of it until much later, several hundred Jews hiding in our forests lost their lives during that November raid. Ilya was disappointed that his tactics of confusion hadn't really worked, mainly because he and his men hadn't had time to fan out into the best positions before being forced to take cover. But it did mean that over the next few weeks they worked out a number of contingency plans for responding to assaults, which we knew would be resumed.

And indeed, the next raid, in early December, was even more vicious. This time the German force included infantry, police units, and a Ukrainian unit, too, equipped with machine guns, small cannon, and armed vehicles. Hundreds more refugees lost their lives. It was useless to think of guarding the families against danger on such a scale, and in any case, most of them fled in a vain attempt to escape—only, as later became clear, to run around in circles and end up in the arms of their pursuers. But this time we did succeed in causing some confusion in the invading ranks. At one point Ilya, Vasily, Alexander, and two brothers, whose names I can't remember but who'd joined us after escaping from the Parczew deportations, threw grenades from different directions with the result that one lot of Germans began shooting at another. Ilya personally witnessed one German being killed by a compatriot, and later we discovered that about a dozen Germans had been killed altogether, as we were not the only partisans in action. But one of the Parczew brothers was also killed, literally shot out of a tree, and Alexander was wounded in the shoulder, where a bullet remained lodged. For those of us who were again hiding in the bunkers, the situation seemed entirely chaotic. The noise of small-arms fire approached and receded again and again so that we had no idea how near the enemy was. Once or twice the artillery fire was so deafening that we were afraid we would be blasted out of the earth.

Conditions were cramped and became very uncomfortable after almost three days of continuous confinement. We did emerge very briefly at night, to stretch and relieve ourselves, but it was far too dangerous to make a fire. It was also out of the question for Piotr to cook underground, so what food we did have was cold: hardened *kasza*, onion shoots, and goat's cheese. I remember that because in the confined space, the usual smell of damp earth became mingled with sour sweat and stale oniony, cheesy breath. The highlight of each of those three or four days was the spoonful of honey we were allowed as sugar rations, and on each of the nights, the slug of moonshine. Tempers grew frayed, and by the second night even Berek's store of jokes had dried up. It was so frustrating that because of our lack of ammunition, only about half the band could go into action at a time. Ilya had persuaded Henryk to stay with us: "We can't afford to lose your medical knowledge, Henryk; you are more use to us alive than dead."

Someone suggested that we should pass the time by each telling a story; it seemed a good enough idea until we drew lots to start and began thinking of stories we could tell. Almost simultaneously we each realized that we couldn't do it. It was too hard to make up stories when events we had recently lived through were stranger than any fiction. Every one of us had a tale to tell of violation, terror, or despair, but nevertheless we clung to those very stories as to property that was both private and precious, for did they not link us to the past and the people we had lost? In the telling, or the sharing, we knew that a little more would seep away each time.

When the Nazis eventually withdrew, we had the grim job of looking for survivors and, in most cases, finding only corpses. By now the ground was too hard to bury them, and at first it seemed callous, criminal even, that all we were doing was plundering their clothes, shoes, and any valuables, then covering them with dead leaves and vegetable debris (dressed only in underwear for a shroud) and leaving them with a mumbled and half-remembered prayer in a sheltered place. The awful thing was that I quickly became used to it, and that in itself troubled me almost more than the activity itself.

"You can't care about everyone, Jan." Vasily shrugged, in an attempt at reassurance, as he prized away a bracelet from the arm of a female corpse.

But I suspect Vasily himself felt uneasy. He even admitted that he was glad Helka had told him the Jewish religion didn't allow people to be buried wearing any sort of jewelry or ornament as "it somehow makes what we're doing a bit more legal."

Later we came across the body of a German soldier who'd been shot cleanly through the heart.

"Brilliant—more boots!" cried Vasily with pleasure. The young soldier was blond, and his chin showed a fine dusting of stubble. His identity papers told us he'd been nineteen, the same age as Franek and Eva. We looked through all his pockets and to Vasily's jubilation discovered a sheath knife. There were also some deutsch marks and a wallet containing a couple of photographs. A pretty dark-haired girl smiled up at us out of one; the other showed a middle-aged couple standing in front of an ordinary sort of house, together with a girl of about fifteen. His parents and sister, I suppose. I couldn't help wondering how they would take the news.

We looked from the smiling faces in the photographs to the dead face lying open-eyed on the ground. The body was naked except for its underpants—we had stripped it bare. Suddenly, on an impulse, I knelt down, wrapping the two pictures in the vest we had removed, and laid the little bundle by one stiff hand. Screwing up my own eyes, I then closed his eyelids as I'd seen done often enough in the ghetto streets. As I straightened up, I brushed my hand against my trousers as if to cleanse it. I didn't dare look at Vasily but waited for him to say something angry. To my surprise he said nothing but began to kick some loose leaves and patches of snow onto the body. I helped him, still without a word. When we'd finished, the dead soldier was almost entirely covered, except for the lower part of his face. I can still see in my mind's eye that dusting of blond stubble on the frozen young chin.

We walked away in silence, still not sure whether or not to feel shame. We saw the widespread destruction to the undergrowth caused by the German attack, and I wondered how long it would be before they laid bare all our hiding places. Our winter bunkers were well camouflaged, but they would cave in under the weight of armored cars, and with determination the enemy was probably capable of penetrating the densest thickets.

Suddenly Vasily remembered the sheath knife. He took it out and looked at it rather as Eva had looked at her tablet of soap (which, incidentally she had cut in two, taking one half to the twins and their foster family).

"Jan, I'm not going to give this in." He said it defiantly, for it was a strict rule that anything taken from a dead body, or indeed obtained from our confiscation missions in the villages, should be pooled and shared.

"I think this should be ours. Yours and mine. You never know when we might need it." And as if to put his conscience at rest he added, "After all, you can't really share a knife, like you can a gun or ammunition." I wasn't sure I agreed, but it was obviously so important to him that I didn't object.

"You won't say anything?"

"No, I won't say anything."

"And we'll share it?"

"I don't mind about that. You keep it, Vasily. I don't really know how to use a knife, and well, you never know when you might need it."

When we got back to the camp, we found Henryk worried about Alexander's shoulder. He'd tried to remove the bullet but without success as he didn't have the right instruments. Alexander was very pale but played down the pain.

"What hurts most is wasting good vodka; I think I'd almost rather have an infection!" He grinned valiantly, his teeth showing strikingly white against his dark complexion and curly black hair and beard.

Alexander always reminded me of pictures I'd seen in children's books of pirates on the high seas. I obviously wasn't the only one; I once heard Berek suggesting to him that he ought to wear a gold earring to complete the image!

Before the raids Berek had discovered from his widow that she had a cousin who worked as a nurse at a small Nazi-controlled medical post in the village of Jedlanka. The widow—Irena was her name— thought her cousin would probably be sympathetic to us and might let us have medical supplies should the need arise. Until then there had been no need to endanger either the nurse or any of ourselves in a raid on the clinic. Now, however, the situation had changed. Quite apart from Alexander's injury, there were a lot of people in hiding who had been wounded during the raids and who required urgent medical attention. We also badly needed salve for the scabies which was reaching epidemic proportions among partisan fighters and refugees alike, because of the vitamin shortages.

So the next morning, at first light, Berek and I set off for Rudka. The idea was that we would ask Irena to alert her cousin to the imminent arrival of a boy with an ''injured arm,'' which would then give me a pretext to visit the clinic. There had been a moderately heavy fall of snow in the night, but fortunately a strong wind was blowing now, meaning that drifts would soon obliterate our tracks. All the same, the wind—or gale, as it felt to us—was a mixed blessing, for it deafened us by howling around our ears and blinded us by driving snow into our eyes. We couldn't talk on the way, as we needed all our energies to make progress, bent almost double against its force. That was the first time in the forest that I really felt the cold; it seemed to cut right through the several layers of dead men's clothing which we were wrapped in.

Irena's welcome seemed doubly warm because of the conditions outside her neat, cozy house. She made us sit down and drink hot milk and eat carrot cake while she went off, almost immediately, to see her cousin as we requested. I think that little meal still ranks among the most memorable of my life, like my first breakfast on the other side of the wall with Granny's homemade plum jam.

Berek and I took off our boots and luxuriously warmed our feet in front of the stove. Berek sighed. "Maybe, Jan, maybe it's time to shut the truck door and let that train go to Sobibor at last."

Poor Berek. He was still wrestling with what might have been, or should have been. I felt gratified that he should confide his feelings to me, who was at least ten years his junior. I even felt tempted to tell him about Eva. It would have been such a relief. But by then we'd already been sitting there companionably for an hour and a half, and before I could think of the right words, Irena had reappeared.

"Magda is expecting you. I must say she wasn't as willing as I thought she'd be, but she won't give you away, I'm sure of that."

Berek and I exchanged glances; we hoped she was right. She didn't sound sure. Then Irena set to work. First, she took some old ashes from the bottom of the stove and rubbed them into my arm in several places to make it look bruised; then she folded a large white cloth and helped me bind it around my shoulder as a sling.

"You're to go to the front door like any patient. Tell whoever receives you that you fell off your bicycle and your mother has sent you to see a doctor or a nurse because your arm hurts badly and she wants to make sure it's not broken. If they ask where you're from, just say you've recently moved near Rudka from Warsaw to get away from the city; that'll explain your accent. With any luck Magda will be the one to open the door. You must be out by four o'clock at all costs as that is when the Nazi doctor comes to check that everything is in order. You certainly don't want to get yourself examined by *him*!"

The clinic lay on the Rudka side of Jedlanka, but it had started to snow again after a brief lull, and it took me an hour to get there even though I was now using the ordinary road. With my four o'clock deadline that was running things a little close. I kept my head down to avoid being spoken to and arrived at the clinic without incident before half past three.

The door was opened not, as I'd hoped, by Magda but by a large, severe-looking woman who took my name and asked in a bored way what was wrong with me. If I'd been a genuine patient, I'd have felt I was imposing on her time; as it was, I was relieved by her obvious lack of interest! She made out a record sheet for me and then looked me up and down rather contemptuously.

"Well, if you want to see a doctor, you'll have to wait until four. There's a nurse here who can see you now, though. I should think that'll be good enough."

"That's fine. I'll see the nurse." Immediately I hoped I hadn't sounded too eager!

She called twice for Magda, who eventually came into the hall to collect me. She led me into a small consulting room, closed the door, and told me to sit down. There was one chair placed beside a table. She made no sign that I was expected, but before undoing my sling, she put my canvas shoulder bag on the floor by her feet.

She was a conventionally pretty girl, very pale and slight, with hair drawn tightly back from her face, but I noticed the hardness of her eyes and felt instinctively that she had no real sympathy for my predicament.

She examined my arm thoroughly, if a little roughly, and asked me one or two questions about the fall and whether the arm hurt in certain positions. Anyone watching through the keyhole would have seen nothing untoward. Then, holding my arm up with her right hand, she bent down, opened a drawer in the table with her left, slid out a brown paper package, and dropped it into my bag, all in one flowing and barely perceptible movement.

"It's not broken," she said curtly. She made no attempt at small talk. I was worried by the size of the packet; it didn't look nearly big enough to contain all we needed.

"Well, I've also got some lacerations here," I said, pointing to my leg in case anyone should be listening. "Do you have some ointment? It's very painful." I gestured with my eyes at the package.

"I think you have all you need," she said coldly. "They don't look serious."

At that moment the telephone rang in the office next door, and Magda was called by the receptionist.

"You can go now," she said.

"Well, I did just want—"

"Wait a moment, then. I'll have to see who's on the phone." Her impatience to be rid of me was undisguised.

When Magda went out of the room, she left the door ajar; I looked around quickly, wondering what I could take that would be of most use.

I looked at the clock on the wall. After half past three. It was all too close to the time of the doctor's visit. There was no time to unpack the parcel to see what was already in it. I saw some jars in a glass-fronted cupboard, containing cotton. Useful but not essential. Surely I could do better than that. My heart was drumming right up in my throat, telling me that I mustn't on any account waste this opportunity. I got up and walked over to the window, my bag over my shoulder. I'd noticed a cabinet by the window with little narrow drawers. I opened the top one—a selection of boxes, presumably containing pills, with names that meant nothing. No good. Next drawer. More boxes. Third drawer. Miraculous! A set of gleaming surgical instruments— tweezers, a scalpel, curettes. I knew them from Henryk's descriptions. Even something called a *kulociag* in Polish, a special instrument for extracting bullets. I was really in luck. With panicky, grabbing move- ments I scooped them out of their felt-lined insets and dropped them into my bag. Seven or eight of them. Then I shut the drawer and listened. Magda was having a conversation with the receptionist, so she must have finished with the phone. What else could I take in the few seconds left? Suddenly it occurred to me that Henryk would know what the pills were for—how stupid of me! I opened the top drawer again, scooped out as many of the boxes as I could, and slammed it shut. Too loudly. They must have heard.

I didn't have time to sit down again before Magda came back into the room. She looked at me suspiciously.

"It's snowing again," I said, pointing to the thick flakes whirling outside, almost obscuring the fir trees only about ten yards away.

"It *is* December," she observed. "What else did you want?" I caught sight of the clock. Nearly a quarter to four. All I wanted now was to be out of the building!

"Oh, it's all right. I won't take up any more of your time. Thanks very much." Then, as I was leaving the room, I said so that the receptionist could hear, "Oh, Mother said to ask if I should carry on wearing the sling."

"There's no need. It's only bruising. But try not to use the arm too much for the time being." They were the friendliest words she had addressed to me.

"What's the charge?" the receptionist asked Magda.

"Waived. No treatment."

"Hmm." The big woman looked at me disapprovingly, and I escaped, thankful and relieved, into the driving snow. But just as I walked down the little path a German army vehicle drew up; the driver jumped out and went to open the far back door for his passenger. The doctor was early!

I turned to stone. Supposing he asked me to go in for another examination; after all, there weren't any other patients to look at. There was an agonizingly long moment, while he sat in the back of the car, pulling on his gloves. The driver's shoulders began to turn white.

Somehow I managed to move myself to the side of the path. The doctor was a big, tall man with a mustache. As he approached me, I just smiled and bowed. I was sure my bag must be bulging suspiciously.

But thanks to the snow, his own head was bowed, and he took no notice of me at all. I just kept standing there, looking foolishly at the car. The driver brushed the snow off his shoulders and made a face at me which, if he hadn't been a Nazi, I could have sworn was of the conspiratorial eyes-to-heaven sort!

I was so pleased with myself, once the German car was finally behind me, that I scarcely noticed the weather. It didn't occur to me immediately that my theft might be quickly discovered and that they'd come straight after me. When it did, I veered off the road and took a small roughly parallel path through the trees. But as I got nearer Irena's house, a thought struck me. Whenever it was discovered, how would Magda explain away the disappearance of so many boxes and instruments? Would she blame it on me, and if so, would she be punished for leaving me alone in the room? She had hardly been sympathetic, but she *had* taken a considerable risk in agreeing to see me in the first place and in giving me any supplies at all. Irena tried to reassure me, saying that Magda was well respected as a nurse and wouldn't be blamed. "They'll think it was a break-in at night or something." But I could tell from the look in Irena's eyes that she *was* afraid for her cousin—and perhaps for herself, too. She gave us the rest of the carrot cake to take back with us, and *real* coffee grounds which, she explained, had been used only once before and then mixed with a few fresh ones, but my pleasure in these things was now soured by a sense of unease, even guilt. Had I abused her generous hospitality? I'd quickly lost the sense of euphoria at having achieved what I'd set out to do. I hugged her when we left, wanting but unable to say I was sorry, for how *could* I be sorry? After all, I'd only done what was necessary to save Alexander's arm, maybe even his life.

On the way back Berek said, "Jan, whatever happens back in Rudka now, it is not your fault. Your first loyalty was to us, where you belong. You understand that, don't you?"

The tears in my eyes were only partly induced by the wind, which, contrarily, seemed to have changed direction since we'd set out. It was dark now, and the snow made it very difficult to find the way back to the camp, as many of the familiar landmarks were obscured.

Once we were badly startled by a sound of crashing in the undergrowth. Berek put a hand on my arm, and we stood absolutely still, hearts thumping. A couple of seconds later a stag appeared on the track in front of us. He stared at us for a moment, his bulbous brown eyes registering in our flashlight the alarm we ourselves had felt. Another moment, and he had disappeared into the brushwood on the other side of the track.

"I'm amazed there are any deer left after the uproar of those raids," said Berek. And in fact, although I knew from Leon that elk and deer had been prolific in the area—the town crest of Parczew was actually a stag—that was the only one I ever saw in my year in the forests. Piotr always hoped to be able to cook venison for those of us prepared to eat it, but it never happened.

We got back to find that the others had lit a fire, after building a sort of three-sided igloo around it to hide the smoke. There was great relief at our return, and Henryk's delight when he saw the instruments made me feel better about the circumstances of their theft. The parcel, as I'd suspected, did not contain a great deal: a few cotton bandages, some gauze and cotton, a yellow disinfectant power, and two small tubes of ointment for treating scabies. It hadn't been worth risking my life for.

Alexander had his operation the following morning. We heard a single bellow from the "hospital" bunker, presumably as the bullet was extracted, but afterward he was dismissive about the whole thing. After that, whenever he saw me, he always had a special word or a smile for me.

The next Nazi raid took place on Christmas Eve, just as we were preparing to celebrate our own festival of Hanukkah. Very few of the Jews in our band were religious—some, in fact, were socialist or Communist and actively antireligious—but Hanukkah was an occasion of significance to religious and nonreligious alike. The songs we would have sung might have united us in pride in a common ancestry, but the songs were never sung. For just as we were collecting together our eight bits of candle for the eight-day Festival of Lights, the guns announced the arrival yet again of the Forces of Darkness. We lost poor Leon in that raid, and one or two others I don't remember so well, but somehow that clash of dates was at the time a double cause for despair.

In the period of uneasy but relative calm in January, Berek and Alexander and a new member called Josef went to Rudka to try and replenish some of our supplies. When they eventually reappeared carrying only one sack, we could see from their faces that something was wrong. Berek made straight for me and put his hand on my shoulder, and I knew then what they were going to tell us.

"Irena's gone, and her house has been burned down."

We were all quiet; we knew only too well why. Josef threw down the sack. It was full of carrots, good ones, Irena's legacy to us.

"We found them in an outhouse at the back. Everything else had been ransacked." The thought of Irena's carrot cake made me feel sick. Berek looked at me and shook his head, his eyes—which, despite everything, often shone with laughter—now sad. "Don't blame yourself," they said. Yet how could I not? I'd experienced the deaths of many people by now, but Irena's was the first for which I was directly responsible.

In February the Germans came again, but changing their tactics. This time there were fewer vehicles and heavy arms, but hundreds of police fanned out through the forest, arriving at dawn and leaving only at nightfall. Those Jews who were not gunned down on the spot were taken away to a new ghetto at Wlodawa, slightly to the east, or to one of the smaller camps in the area, but it was a temporary reprieve. Eventually they all ended up in the gas chambers at Sobibor.

Soon after the February operations Eva and I were sent to the village of Makoszka, where we had a sympathetic contact who ran a smallholding. He had been one of Leon's friends. On the way there Eva suddenly tripped and fell. As I helped her to her feet, I noticed what looked horribly like small human fingers sticking up out of the snow. As I knelt down, it didn't take me long to uncover the corpse of a child.

When I'd done so, Eva cried out, "Esther?" And for a moment, as we gazed down, we both mistook the body for that of Esther, the little girl she had brought out of Majdan Tatarski. In fact, it belonged to a younger child, but with coloring and features—already masklike in death—very similar to Esther's.

By now I'd seen Eva in many moods—exhausted, angry, amused, distraught, tender—but I'd never seen her as she was now. She went into a sort of trance, sitting there in the snow by the dead child, stroking the stiff white cheeks, oblivious of her own cold.

Eventually I had to say, "Eva, we should really get on."

"What?" She did look up, but vacantly, not at me. "We must bury her, Jan. You go on to Makoszka and get a spade. Never mind the food, but get a spade. Steal one if necessary." She pulled at her ponytail, a familiar gesture but more frantic than ever before.

"Eva, what good is a spade? The ground is as hard as iron. And the others need food. *Please* come with me."

"It's a sign. I know it's a sign."

"A sign of what?"

"That there's no point in anything we do. Ever again. Pointless. The whole thing."

I was now really alarmed. Eva, my rescuer, who had more spirit, more presence of mind, more zest for life, more—yes, *courage* than anyone else in the world. My beloved Eva was giving up.

I dropped to my knees.

"No, no, no. You mustn't say that. *We're* alive, Eva, I'm alive, you must keep going, we need you, Franek needs you, we, I—love you." There, I'd said them, the words I'd wanted to say so many times in the last six months. I didn't really care anymore if they sounded silly; I just wanted to save her from that despair which I instinctively recognized as fatal.

She looked at me with surprise. I saw with relief that tears were welling in her eyes. They seemed to me much more natural than that earlier weird, absent look. Then, with a sob that almost rent her body in two, she leaned forward and took me in her arms. She clung to me, rocking to and fro, and I held her as close as my strength would allow.

Eventually we drew apart, and together we performed the pathetic makeshift ritual that was becoming all too familiar; we could do nothing but heap loose bits of the forest floor around the little body, which was too rigid for us to fold her hands across her chest. "We can't even leave her with dignity in the right position," said Eva, shaking her head in distress.

When we got back, neither of us for some reason felt like telling the others what had happened, and it remained our secret. But we never again referred to my avowal of love.

Maybe Eva was right in interpreting our discovery of the child's body as a sign, because soon afterward we learned that Esther, her brother, and her foster family had disappeared from Altana during the February raids. We never discovered what happened to them, but for all the signs to the contrary, I like to think that they evaded their pursuers and were among the two hundred or so civilians who, despite everything, managed to survive the entire war in the forests of Parczew.

JULY 15

Dearest Katie,

If only you could read this story of Misha's. It's beginning to defy belief. And for all sorts of reasons.

One, it's just amazing, mind-boggling that he survived all the things he did. They say that truth is stranger than fiction, and I'm beginning to believe it. How can Leonie in the IVth form get killed by a car when she's walking along a pavement, and Misha, who at the same age was exposed to every danger imaginable, come through unscathed?

Well, perhaps not unscathed. That brings me to another reason for finding it all so unbelievable. They were terrible days he lived through, Katie, really terrible, and what I want to know is, How can someone who has lived through so much not talk about it at all for years on end to the people he lives with? I mean, in the six years I've known him he's never given me an inkling of all this. And then again, how can someone who's looked death in the face as he has mind about trivial things like when I come in at night, how many pints I drink, whether I get my homework done on time, and all the rest? I find it all more rather than less puzzling than before.

By the way, isn't it just typical? The Head's been called away because his father is very ill. No one's been delegated to sort out our bit of trouble, so it just drags on. Perhaps I ought to tell Mum before they do. I was hoping it wouldn't come to that, but everyone I've spoken to says they're bound to send us a bill for my share of the damage. But I really don't want Misha to hear about it—especially not now.

Good night, Katie. No other news, I'm afraid. I hope all this isn't tantalizing you too much because you don't really know what I'm talking about, but Misha's past is beginning to dominate my life. I tend to read a bit, and then reread it, trying to imagine the Misha I know now as a teenage partisan at risk of losing his life every single minute of the night and day. Just because he happened to be Jewish. Crazy, really. Why did everyone loathe the Jews so much? It strikes me that other people's hatreds always seem faintly absurd or ridiculous, but that doesn't stop us having our own. Odd, that. Must see what happens to him next. Maybe one day soon, when he's back from Australia, he'll let you read it, too.

Love you. R

During that winter and the following spring our partisan group under-went a number of changes. At the end of 1942 a few Jews led by a man called Yechiel Greenshpan (for some reason we *were* allowed to use his surname) came to our forests and began to organize several of the separate bands operating there into one unit. Henryk seemed reasonably content with the changes, but at first Ilya was not so happy to have his leadership questioned, particularly as Greenshpan was illiterate, uneducated, and, at twenty-four, a much younger man. But he quickly gained a reputation as clever and reliable, and like Leon, whom we had lost, he had a great deal of local knowledge. His family had also been in the horse business, though as dealers rather than blacksmiths, and some of his contacts proved very valuable. Soon after his arrival, a large cache of arms from the September '39 battles was found through one of them, adding significantly to our arsenal. This helped to reconcile Ilya, who was in any case thinking of leaving us to make for the Pripet marshes beyond the river Bug, where he knew there was a great deal of Soviet partisan activity. He tried to persuade Vasily to return "home" with him; I knew that Vasily was torn, for part of him longed to go back to "my country," as he always wistfully referred to the Soviet Union, yet he had also in his quiet, undemonstrative way become very attached to several of us, and with no parents left across the border it must have been hard to think of leaving.

I wasn't really affected by the changes, particularly as Greenshpan spent little time in any one camp and we still thought of Ilya as our leader. But when the thaws began at the end of March, we started to think again of how best to attack the enemy and of activity beyond the basic tasks of immediate survival. It was then that Henryk collected a message via the graveyard in Parczew that some sort of uprising was being planned in the ghetto in Warsaw.

"I think the time has come for us to honor our commitment. Thanks to Greenshpan, we now have some arms to spare, and the time seems right." He looked at me sadly, and with stomach-melting certainty I knew why. He doubted that I could get back alive.

By now I had no wish whatsoever to leave the forest. It was a harsh, hazardous existence, and during that winter I had known extremes of hunger, cold, and fear. But one night, unable to get to sleep on our board bunks, Franek had whispered to me from the one below, "Jan, which did you find harder, the ghetto or this?"

Unhesitatingly I had answered, "The ghetto, definitely." When he asked why, I couldn't immediately explain why I was so sure and felt a pang of guilt. Had I been disloyal to Korczak, who had done so much to make ghetto life bearable for all his charges? But eventually I said, "Because in the ghetto everyone loses in the end. Here in the forests there's at least the chance to make a little difference; we do have a sort of freedom."

Henryk and Ilya had another of their arguments, this time about whether I should take grenades as well as pistols to Warsaw. Henryk was against it, fearing that their age might make them unstable, but Ilya felt it was worth the risk, as they would be one of the most effective weapons in any ghetto warfare. Given the pitiful number of arms the Jews of Warsaw had during the Ghetto Uprising, he was certainly right. As usual, Ilya was able to put the good of the cause before the good of individuals; he had never treated me any differently on account of my age. That's probably why he was an effective leader. I can see now that Henryk was too kind a man to take the sort of general overview that leadership at such a time demands.

Everyone said good-bye to me in an affectionate but matter-of-fact way. Eva's parting words to me were "Good luck, little brother. No giggling on the train this time, mind." I could have been forgiven for thinking that she wasn't really bothered about my leaving on such a risky mission. I hoped I wasn't going to let myself down by showing how much I minded her lightheartedness. Then she leaned forward to embrace me and, as she drew away, reached out and touched the side of my face with the back of her hand. It was the tenderest gesture; my mother was the only other person who'd ever done that to me. I turned away quickly, for now I knew I would cry.

Vasily and Franek took me as far as the outskirts of Parczew, where

I collected the name and address of my Warsaw contact from the courier's "postbox." I wasn't alone in the churchyard; I had a sudden fright when I caught sight of the priest on his knees at a freshly dug grave. But he took no notice of me, for he was well used to not seeing or hearing unusual visitors to this little sanctuary on the edge of the forest. There would come a time when he would be obliged to notice me and when I would most urgently need his help. But it's a mercy that one can't see into the future, and that day it was the immediate future which preoccupied me.

I carried my cargo of death and destruction in my usual old canvas bag, the one I'd taken to the medical post. In case I needed to explain its considerable weight, I'd been given a few books to lay on the top, books which someone had left buried by the grave under a pile of evergreen cuttings. Perhaps they had belonged to the priest himself; we were seldom told how things like that came about. The less we knew, the safer our helpers were. My cover story was that I'd been ill and sent by my parents to convalesce in the country with relatives, where I was supposed to catch up with the schoolwork I'd missed. The trouble was that the books now made my bag very heavy indeed, and I had to carry it as if I scarcely noticed!

I sat in the corner of the carriage with one of the textbooks open on my knees, my face pressed against the misted pane, watching the desolate end-of-winter landscape roll by under a steely sky. The snow still lay in gray patches on the fields, but where it had thawed it seemed to have sucked all the color out of the ground. At times the track ran through thick woods, and I wondered how many other partisans and refugees were out there hiding.

The first part of the journey was uneventful. I shared a carriage with two young lovers who were absorbed in each other and an old woman. But all three, unfortunately, left the train at about the third stop. It didn't do to be alone in a carriage because you never knew who might get in and try to make conversation with you. Vasily had reminded me of that when he said good-bye. I was just wondering whether I had time to get out and into another carriage when, to my horror, the door opened and its space was filled with the black bulk of a very unwelcome figure indeed: an SS officer.

As he turned around to put his cap with its skull and crossbones insignia on the rack above, I went through my usual repertoire of physiological responses to fear, by now all too familiar: high-drumming heart, a liquid sensation in my thighs and stomach, nausea.

But then an extraordinary thing happened. I became aware of a strange rush of exhilaration. After all, I could, perhaps, control what was to happen. This was to be a test of my cunning, my presence of mind, my wits. I knew only too well that a Jewish life could hang on the momentary whim of any Aryan citizen, let alone of a full-blown officer in the SS. But as far as this man was concerned, I was not, after all, a Jew: I was an ordinary Polish boy who had done nothing to be ashamed of.

To begin with, he took no notice of me. I pretended to be absorbed in the meaningless blur of figures on the page in front of me. I didn't dare even glance in his direction. In my head I went over and over my cover story, so that it would be word perfect if he started to ask me questions. It suddenly seemed a very thin story, and I wondered how much extra I ought to invent to make it ring more true.

"Never say too much. Liars need good memories, and when you're scared, your memory is one of the first things to go." Henryk's advice had been sound. He suggested that my illness should be glandular fever, as the symptoms were suitably vague and diffuse. But suppose he asked me about my treatment! We hadn't thought about that. And my "relatives"! We'd agreed that to make it sound precise, I should describe an actual farm near Makowska, but I'd say it was on the far side of Parczew, away from the forest, to avoid any hint of association with "bandits." I had it all perfectly rehearsed.

But my preparation turned out to be in vain. The approach, when it came, was of a very different kind. I was suddenly aware that there was something else on my knee besides my book. I watched, frozen in a sort of fascinated horror as four long, well-manicured fingers traveled slowly up my thigh as far as the book. Another hand, with a gold ring on the fourth finger, removed the book and threw it onto the seat beside me. All I could do was stare, transfixed, at the silver death's-head motif on his black cuff bands.

"Look at me," he said, quite gently. I could understand some German because of my Yiddish, and Franek and Eva, who'd learned it at school, had taught me a little during the long winter evenings for just such an eventuality. Obediently I looked up and took in the first SS face I had ever seen at close quarters. He was a good-looking man, I suppose: fair hair, with an uncompromisingly straight part, pale ice-blue eyes, high cheekbones, and a dimple in his chin. I can see him now. His lower lip was damp, and my instinctive reaction was to shudder and push the obnoxious prying hands away. But I dared not. I knew I had to play him along.

"What's your name?"

"Jan, *mein Herr!*" I couldn't interpret the rank badge on his collar, so I didn't know the proper form of address and hoped that would do.

"How old are you, Jan?"

"Thirteen." I thought it as well to err on the side of childhood. Then I thought of my papers and wished I'd told the truth.

"How nice." His hands rested at the side of my thighs, and both thumbs massaged the tops of them in a rhythmic circular movement. "How nice," he repeated.

"Come and sit by me here, Jan." The menace was not in his voice itself, which remained gentle, but in his identity. He took his hands from my legs and patted the seat beside him.

I played for time.

"Krank-ich, krank gewesen."

I felt the bulk of my bag pressed tightly between me and the side of the carriage. There was no way I could reach for one of the pistols, buried beneath the books, before he saw what I was doing. Besides, I had a mission to complete. I had enough ammunition to blow up the entire train, and it was totally useless to me in my moment of need!

My "friend" was in no hurry. I understood he was asking what was wrong with me.

I began to speak rapidly, in Polish, in an agitated way, pointing to different parts of my body as I did so. A terrifying thought had just struck me. Not only was I at imminent risk of being raped, but if he started making me take my clothes off, he would see that I was circumcised, and the game would be up. He'd probably shoot me on the spot or beat me to a pulp on the carriage floor. Like the things Eva had seen in Majdan Tatarski.

I stopped my Polish gibberish as he was beginning to look less interested and pointed to the math book. In a voice which I hoped sounded suitably flirtatious I said in halting German, *"Sie klug."* You—clever. *"Sie . . . mir . . . helfen."* You help me.

I waited with trepidation. Would the idea enrage him? He was, after all, an officer in the SS; would he see me as intolerably impudent? But I was lucky. The idea seemed to amuse, even flatter, him.

I handed him the book and my stub of pencil, which he threw with contempt on the floor, pulling out a gold mechanical pencil from his inside pocket instead. And I watched, mesmerized by what was certainly the most incongruous image of my entire war. An officer in Hitler's elite SS doing a little Jewish boy's homework!

That math book almost certainly saved my life, but it had some help from another incongruous source. I was thinking frantically how to prolong this stage of the proceedings when to my overwhelming relief the train began to slow down. I'd not really taken notice of the stations we were due to stop at—in those days there were often unscheduled stops, anyway—but hadn't expected to be rescued so soon. Barely had the train lurched to a halt and my companion looked out of the window when the door was torn open, there was a shout of *"Klaus, Mensch, due hier!,"* and two other SS men piled on board. Amid the general laughing and slapping of backs, I got up quietly, put my bag under my arm, and murmuring, *"Danke, danke vielmals,"* slipped out onto the platform, ungraciously abandoning my book to the enemy. I expected to be shot in the back at any moment. Instead I heard guffaws of renewed laughter, of which I may well have been the object, for who knows what story Klaus was fabricating, and then the guard—the wonderful, wonderful guard—blew his whistle and the train moved slowly away. I staggered to a seat, my legs unable to support me. It was one of the most spectacular instances of that extraordinary good luck which on so many occasions has singled me out for survival.

My contact in Warsaw, which I reached by the next train without further incident that evening, couldn't believe her ears when I told her what had happened. It was, in fact, Tosiah, whom I'd met before in Leon's kitchen in the ghetto. She was a frightening, severe-looking young woman whose intense blue eyes stared through you unflinchingly. I knew she was a revered member of the resistance and that she had a reputation for great daring, but I felt uncomfortable in her presence. She was much less approachable than my Eva.

We met in some anonymous house not far from the station, which the owners had vacated for reasons not shared with me. Tosiah was not particularly pleased with the contents of the bag.

"We've waited a long time for these," she said disapprovingly. I remembered Henryk remarking that in Warsaw they seemed to expect arms to fall from trees at the partisans' feet, and I wanted to tell her that life in the forest wasn't one long party either. But of course, I said nothing.

"Still, you did well, Mish—Jan . . ." Tosiah had known me before as Misha, but I was surprised at her slip; it seemed out of character. "It all helps. We need every single gun and grenade we can get hold of." Food had been left for us, and we talked for an hour or two, exchanging news. "Little" Leon had sent his "kindest regards" to me—typical of the formal, undemonstrative manner I remembered. I sent my love to him. I added—and it was difficult for me to say anything so intimate in the full glare of Tosiah's unsmiling blue eyes— that I would never forget how he had given my mother a home for her last weeks. I couldn't remember if I'd ever really thanked him at the time, and I knew this was very likely to be my last chance. As events turned out, it was, and I've sometimes wondered whether Leon ever got the message.

"He'll be glad I've seen you." Even then she didn't smile. But she asked me a lot of questions about our activities in the forests and seemed to be impatient when I explained how the weather and the large-scale Nazi manhunts caused us to suspend "military" operations during the winter months.

"The struggle must never stop."

That sounded unfair to me. I thought of Eva sitting in tears in the snow beside a child's corpse and said firmly, "It doesn't."

Tosiah had a lot of information for me to take back about the new spirit of resistance in the ghetto. The Nazis had attempted to liquidate it finally in January, to complete the work they had begun in the summer of 1942 with the mass deportations to Treblinka. But they did not succeed. "It's the first time," Tosiah told me with triumph, "that the Germans have been thwarted by Jewish armed resistance."

But Jewish losses had been crippling, with one of the groups, the Jewish Fighting Organization, losing four-fifths of its members. Because they had no firearms, ammunition, or grenades, the Jews had adopted partisan tactics, using homemade bombs, crowbars, knives, and clubs, attacking individual German soldiers who pursued them into their hiding places in houses and cellars. "It was a turning point," she told me proudly. "No longer will Jews go to their slaughter, unquestioning as sheep."

During February and March the influence of the resistance groups in the ghetto had steadily increased: Workers were refusing to obey repeated calls to line up for "resettlement"; SS warehouses and a train were set on fire with petrol bombs. Savage retaliation on the part of the enemy had killed about two hundred people in the streets, but this, Tosiah assured me, had served only to inflame the spirit of resistance among both combat groups and ordinary workers.

"When they come to cart us away to our death next time, there'll be no submission as in those shameful days last July and August. We shall barricade the doors, arm ourselves with hammers and axes, and wait for them in the cellars. Woe betide any of them that dares to enter my house. He'll not emerge alive, I promise you that."

My meeting with Tosiah took place during the first week of April. She had hoped I'd be able to get back to Warsaw with more guns, and at the time I really hoped so, too. It seemed right that I should do all in my power to help save lives in the city where I had been born and brought up. But it wasn't to be. Less than two weeks later her defiant words were put to the test.

When I returned, spring was coming even to the forests of the Parczew region; somehow, despite the ravages caused by recurrent shelling and shooting and frequent invasions of jackboots and bushbeaters, the trees and bushes managed to turn green again. By some miracle, undaunted little birds which I never learned to identify sang each morning to the new day. There was a corresponding surge of activity on the part of our enlarged unit: We took several police posts in the area, killing a number of German sentries and adding to our supply of arms and uniforms.

Then, as my thoughts were returning to Warsaw and Tosiah's urgent request, over the radio which Alexander had repaired we gleaned the information that something drastic was happening to "the treacherous Jewish troublemakers in the capital."

At five in the morning, on April 19. 1943, the Nazis, together with units of Ukrainian, Lithuanian, Latvian, and Polish police, invaded the ghetto; the famous Ghetto Uprising—one of the most heroic of all the resistance struggles against the Nazis—had begun.

The Germans were well prepared for the liquidation of the seventy thousand Jews left in Warsaw, having all the weapons they required, from heavy machine guns to many hundreds of rifles, as well as huge stocks of ammunition and mortars. Of those seventy thousand Jews left (in 1941 the ghetto had held eight times that number), perhaps only three and a half thousand belonged to a combat group, and there were nowhere near enough arms and ammunition to go around even this tiny percentage. Every pistol, every revolver, every grenade was desperately needed, so my three pistols and the grenades did, I suppose, make a contribution to the revolt. But of course, it wasn't enough.

Then, three days later, on April 22, the Germans launched their largest offensive yet against both fighters and fugitives in our forests. It was the Thursday before Easter, and later we learned that, with grotesque irony, they had called the assault *Unternehmen Ostersegen*—Operation Easter Blessing.

Since the previous raids there had been a steady reconvergence of refugee families on Altana, and we had resumed our guard duties there. On that morning of April 22 a number of us from the "old" group were walking toward Altana when, suddenly, we heard the sounds of a Nazi raid. No shots as yet, only the distant but unmistakable drone of motor engines. We had just reached a particularly tall oak which we had often used as a lookout post as it was also easy to climb; with my help, Vasily heaved himself up onto the lowest branch and then scrambled quickly to the top, from where he commanded a view of three separate approach tracks.

When he got back down to us, he reported breathlessly that whole companies of German soldiers in camouflage dress were advancing toward us from all three visible directions. There was no knowing how many others were approaching along countless hidden pathways. Vasily thought they seemed to be congregating in a clearing by the "tadpole pool," which was a well-known landmark for us. The previous autumn he and I had a heated discussion about the teeming mass of tadpoles and baby frogs we'd found there; he had thought that Piotr could use them to make some sort of nourishing soup for us, and I had been revolted by the idea. Although at the time Helka was the only Jew among us to keep kosher, there were certain traditionally forbidden foods which the thought of eating made a sort of primeval revulsion rise up inside me, and I felt sure that it would be the same for the other Jews in the group. Eventually Vasily had given in with one of his characteristic shrugs; it wasn't after all that important to him. Anyway, if the Germans were now at our tadpole pond, it meant they were probably nearer to us than they had ever been.

Vasily took command, although Berek and Josef and one or two older men were with us.

"Go back to the others and warn them. The Germans will soon be between our camp and the families. They're approaching from the east as well as the north and south, and it's too risky to stay where we are. They must leave by the path we made going due west, in the direction of Buradow."

"And you?" I asked.

"I have to go to Altana and warn at least a few families. If I go now, some of them may still be able to get away. I'll meet you at that lake just east of Buradow."

"Vasily, I'm coming, too."

"No, Jan, it only needs one. The others will want you to help carry the food. Go—go now, *quickly*. There's not a minute to lose."

It was only after I'd obeyed and we'd started running back the way we'd come that I realized I'd not even wished Vasily good luck.

When we got back, there was a brief debate about whether it might be safer to stay put and hope that the camouflage of our bunkers would save us. Then some small-arms fire started, and we were shocked to realize how close it was.

"Vasily was right. We must go. Now." That was Ilya; Henryk was already in the stores bunker, throwing out German uniforms onto the ground. Ilya went on. "As many people as possible put one on. Start with the jackets."

I shuddered as I donned the German jacket and was glad there were no mirrors. But looking across at Eva as she struggled into one that was far too big for her, I thought, ludicrous though it sounds at such a moment, how well its particular shade of green suited her auburn coloring. Then, when she scraped her hair back and put on the cap, I felt my heart give a lurch and my cheeks begin to burn; she looked so horribly stunning in what I had come to see as the clothes of the devil.

We left the camp carrying a few blankets and other essential belongings and with potatoes stuffed into our pockets. The firing was sporadic and seemed to come from all directions; it confusing and very frightening. I felt sure we were completely surrounded. But Ilya was calm. He ordered complete silence, and in single file we entered the narrow overhung path leading west which we ourselves had cut through the undergrowth before the frosts at the end of the previous year. I remember seeing a squirrel dart out of our way, hardly an unusual sight in such territory as you can imagine, but on that occasion I envied the fleet agility with which it escaped up one tree and then, as if on wings, across to another.

I felt terrible about leaving Vasily behind, even though he had ordered it himself. Not for the first time I wondered whether part of him actually *wanted* to die. He did seem to court additional hazards in situations already fraught with risk and danger. But, then, he had a very developed sense of duty or obligation. Warning the Jewish families in Altana was perhaps just one more way of doing penance for that other family he had not been able to warn or save. By now it was obvious that the enemy was between us and Altana, and I was convinced that Vasily would be cut off and slaughtered. All I could think was, I never even said good-bye, I never even said good-bye, and the words seemed to keep rhythm with my footsteps.

To begin with, the tiny path was more difficult to negotiate than most, with low-hanging branches reaching out to slap and scratch our faces, and bramble fronds grabbing at our stolen uniforms as if to impede and punish us. Our boots made too much noise squelching in the peaty, rain-softened ground, and once or twice large magpies flapped treacherously into the air at our approach.

But despite all that, we were by now used to moving around the forests with stealth and speed, and we made steady progress, although Franek, Eva, and I were a little slower than the others because of Franek's limp. After a while the path widened into an older track, and the undergrowth became a little less obstructive. Eva was immediately in front of me, and I was just noticing how some strands of that dark red hair had started to escape from the German cap, when all of a sudden I was pounced on from behind and pinned viciously to the ground.

Everything happened so quickly: Two shots rang out, and Eva and the others in front dropped instantly onto their stomachs. I was almost suffocated by whoever was on top of me, and in the panic and the confusion of strange uniforms it wasn't until he said, "Are you all right, Jan?" that I realized my assailant was Franek! He lessened his grip on my arms, and I followed the direction of his gaze. There, to the left of our path, where the underbrush was a little less dense, some sunlight had filtered through the canopy of foliage and irradiated, almost like a searchlight, the body of a Red Army soldier. A black pistol glinted under his outstretched hand, and a little dribble of blood oozed from the side of his mouth.

Franek was breathing very hard with the shock.

"I saw him just in time. He was crouching there with his pants down; he must have thought we were Germans, and he was taking aim and . . ."

The others had stopped in their tracks and then came back. We were now standing in a small, tightly knit group.

"Franzi, there were two shots. Were they both yours?"

Franek shook his head at Eva, and under the barbarian's uniform it felt as if someone were running a brush the wrong way against the hairs on my arms. So the first shot had been fired by the Russian, and I had been in the line of that fire. The second would almost definitely have reached its target: Franek had saved my life! My throat was dry, and I couldn't say anything, but for a moment I leaned against him and put the top of my head against his shoulder. An awkward gesture, but what do you do or say to thank someone for saving your life?

"All right, little brother?" No, I wasn't all right! I wanted to sink into Eva's arms and weep a sea of tears. But there was no time for any such luxury.

"We can't be sure he was on his own. It shows we need to be even quicker and quieter. Come on, everyone." But neither Ilya's caution nor his impatience stopped him from running the twenty or so yards across to the dead man and prizing the gun out from under his splayed fingers.

We re-formed, this time Henryk taking up the position behind me. Berek was now immediately in front. After a while I heard him chuckle. "Poor devil! What a way to go—literally caught with his pants down!" I glanced back over my shoulder to see if Henryk had heard. He put a finger to his lips and passed me his personal flask of moonshine. I took a greedy draft and felt the warm flood of neat alcohol smooth away the shock.

We made a temporary camp near the western edge of the forest, due east of Buradow by the shore of the lake where Vasily had hoped to meet us. Piotr was, for once, in poor spirits.

"I shan't be able to cook you anything worth having. I knew I should have brought the pot. I shouldn't have listened to you, Ilya."

"It was too heavy. You couldn't have managed it."

"*You* could have," retorted Piotr, looking Ilya's more powerful frame up and down.

Then Ilya did something I'd never heard him do before: He actually apologized. "I'm sorry, Piotr. Don't worry, we'll find something else to use.'' And Piotr said that he certainly hoped so. I don't think Ilya would have been as tolerant with any of the rest of us, with the possible exception of his compatriot, Vasily. For a fleeting moment, after overhearing the little exchange, I did wonder whether the fact that Piotr wasn't Jewish might have something to do with it. . . . But no, it was probably only due to Piotr's special status in all our affections as our chief cook.

We set about obtaining some supplies, and Eva and Franek went together to an isolated farm not far away, having first removed their uniforms. It was not a successful expedition! They had been turned away by people before, had been insulted before—as indeed, we all had—but this time they both came back burning with anger. The farmer's wife had said to them, ''If you're begging food, you must be Jewish scum. Go to Majdanek, where you belong.'' And the door had been slammed in their faces.

''At least she didn't give chase or call the police,'' said Henryk, trying to comfort them. But an hour or two after her return I saw how Eva's eyes still glittered an almost metallic green. Majdanek! It was a name I was to hear a great deal more before very long.

On the second night in our temporary new home I was sitting with Franek, our backs against a tree trunk, when we noticed a great pall of smoke drifting toward us from the east, across the forest roof.

''I dread to think what's happened to Vasily,'' said Franek, echoing my own thoughts. He was smoking his quarter share of a cigarette from a small supply which Alexander had been given by one of the Altana refugees, in return for fixing their radio. He offered me a puff, but I declined; I'd never forgotten the nausea my first drag had produced when Vasily shared a cigarette with me soon after we became friends. The evening light was failing, and the mosquitoes and midges were returning in full force.

''That's one thing about the winter: We didn't have these wretched things to contend with.'' I already had two huge mosquito bites on my leg, which I was desperate to scratch. Suddenly, to our amazement, into the little clearing in front of our shallow makeshift bunkers strolled Vasily.

Everyone jumped to his feet and crowded around him. I guessed he'd rehearsed the next moment, for he heaved from his shoulder Piotr's beloved cooking pot, dropped it on the ground with a dull thud, and said, "Careless of you to leave this behind!"

As he did so, I noticed that his lower arm and wrist were red and raw and beginning to blister.

After warning a few of the nearest families about the German approach, Vasily had led one or two of them to our escape route along the hidden path. He had then decided to return to Altana for more people, but before he reached them, he became aware from the shooting and a loudspeaker that he was more or less surrounded. He decided that the safest thing to do was to wait in our camp and hide in one of the dugouts, reckoning that as a single individual he stood a chance of being missed even if the camp was discovered, as now seemed all too likely. He'd taken refuge in the stores bunker as that was set apart from the others. He'd stayed down there for over twenty-four hours, listening to the shooting alternately approach and recede, just as we had on previous occasions. Eventually the noise subsided, and he must have fallen into a deep sleep. When he awoke, he was just wondering whether it was safe to emerge when he heard a strange new noise, a sort of dull, thunderous roar. Thinking it must be a squadron of bombers, he left the bunker to look up, and it was then that he first saw that cloud of black smoke spreading like a stain across the spring sky. At the same time he became aware of a pungent smell of burning wood and overheated resin and realized that he was in the path of a raging forest fire!

Now he could see the flames, to the east and south, being blown by a steady breeze from the direction of Altana, and he knew he had to run. He'd actually entered the westward-leading path through the thicket when he remembered that he'd seen Piotr's cooking pot lying on the ground, abandoned, and that he'd intended to bring it to us. Should he go back? After all, the fire was surely several minutes away, if not more. And being Vasily, he did go back.

What's more, he decided to dash down into the stores bunker again and fill his pockets with food. That was his big mistake, because it cost him several precious minutes. By the time he got back to the pot, at the far end of the camp nearest the fire, the smell of it was overpowering. It hadn't yet reached the little clearing—in fact, it looked as if it might just miss it altogether—but Vasily had bargained without the wind. Suddenly the air was full of flying and falling debris, and it was then that a large flap of red-hot bark had fallen onto his lower arm and rested there for a moment or two like a burning sleeve. Vasily had shaken it off almost immediately but not before it had given him a burn which rose in an ugly red ridge from the inside of his elbow to below his wrist. He was fortunate that he hadn't been wearing a long-sleeved jacket at the time or the damage might have been much more serious, but it was clearly very painful as it was.

Vasily looked at Ilya. "I saw one of our Red Army soldiers; he'd obviously been shot having a shit."

"He knows. It was me," said Franek. Vasily looked very taken aback.

"He did it to save my life. He'd already taken one shot at me; we were in German uniforms, remember."

Vasily shrugged. It wasn't that important to him that an unknown compatriot had died. I thought he might have said something to Franek—about saving my life, I mean—but he didn't. I suppose that wasn't his way. Later, though, when Henryk had treated his arm with the last of the salve I'd stolen from Rudka and bandaged it, and Alexander had given him a cigarette in recompense for his injury, I noticed that he shared it only with Franek.

The weeks and months merge into one another in my memory, and though the well-documented German raids help to punctuate them and therefore pinpoint the chronology of certain events, the sequence of some of the others may be unreliable. It's of no consequence to you in any case. But I think it was soon after we returned to our former camp, which mercifully had been spared by the fire—unlike a good many of the fugitives, some of whose pitifully charred bodies we had to bury—that we were joined by more newcomers, among whom was a man called David, a former inmate of Majdanek concentration camp. He had not escaped from the camp itself; that would have been virtually impossible, surrounded as it was by a double row of formidable wood and barbed-wire fences and overlooked at frequent intervals by heavily armed guards in watchtowers just as you see in films. He and other prisoners had been escorted each day to work in the fields of a nearby estate, producing food for their captors, and he had got away from there by hiding under sacks in the bottom of a cart, in which a local peasant had delivered some sort of farm supplies. He'd been very lucky indeed that the owner of the cart happened to be an acquaintance of Greenshpan's and on discovering him had been sympathetic enough to give him some old clothes so that he could discard his camp pajamas, as well as bread and cheese to take away with him.

I don't know whom the idea originally came from, but I do know that Eva had smarted for a long time from that callous injunction of the farmer's wife to go to Majdanek and that the idea of going there to rescue prisoners rather than be taken prisoner appealed to her enormously as a sort of silent yet resounding retort! In any case a rescue attempt from the estate near Majdanek was precisely what was now being proposed.

The plan was a relatively simple one but would involve quite a few members of the unit in one way or another. One or two rescue attempts in the region had reputedly failed because of unprepared prisoners running amok and not escaping quickly enough or by the shortest route; for this reason Greenshpan and Ilya were keen that the prisoners should be alerted beforehand. A hundred weak and starving men attempting to run in all directions at the crucial moment could easily result in a bloodbath.

It fell to Vasily and me with our non-Jewish looks not only to carry out reconnaissance of the area but also to get some sort of message to the prisoners. We were to borrow a peasant's cart with sacks of manure or fertilizer and deliver them to the entrance of the estate. There would be some confusion, of course, as the delivery would be unexpected, but Vasily and I would use the confusion to start trying to unload some sacks ourselves. We would be very slow, finding them cumbersome and heavy, and would politely ask the guards if some of the inmates could come and help us; that way we hoped to get close enough to at least one prisoner to whisper a message. That was the most we could hope for; after the recent escape of one prisoner we would no doubt be regarded with suspicion and certainly not be allowed within the perimeter fence, even if the actual method of David's escape—in just such a supply cart—had never been discovered.

Tension mounted once the plan had been conceived, and while we waited for the practical arrangements to be made, I tried not to think of the role I was to play in case I lost my nerve. Vasily, as usual, seemed unperturbed by the prospect of heightened danger. Refusing to make any concessions to the pain from his raw, blistered arm, he even went off on his own one day and came back having shot a huge hare for Piotr, who showed him how to skin it. Vasily's knife, the one he'd taken from the dead German with the family photographs, was the best we had, and he lent it to Piotr on such occasions with a certain show of ceremony.

"All right then, here you are—as long as you don't blunt it," I heard him say more than once. And no one ever asked him where he got it from.

Finally the day arrived. Yechiel Greenshpan had negotiated with a local farmer to supply a pony and cart, with enough sacks of fertilizer and some animal feed—pigs were reared on the estate—to make the exercise look plausible.

Our contacts were a nice young couple, recently married, who seemed concerned for our safety and took time to show me how to steer the pony. (There had been talk of using Tomasz, the lecher, and I'd been very relieved when Ilya and Greenshpan decided he lived too far away from the estate for safety.) Once I was driving the pony, I felt the fresh breeze in my face and was aware of being oddly light-headed, exhilarated even. It felt good to be trotting along the narrow country lanes several feet off the ground, good to be out of the gloom of the forest and under a wide blue sky for a change, and, yes, good to feel that we had been entrusted with such an important task. All those things helped to balance the apprehension—no, the *fear*—of what might possibly happen to us.

A Ukrainian guard, a burly fellow with a rifle, greeted me. "Yes?"

I gabbled the reason for our arrival in fast, ungrammatical, indistinct Polish, hoping that he would find me hard to follow. Ukrainians and Poles can each understand what the other says—otherwise Vasily and I would not have been able to talk to each other so easily, for Vasily's Polish was quite elementary—but their speech has to be clear. Vasily could of course have addressed him in his own language, but he didn't want any questions asked, as he didn't have the right papers to pass as a member of the local Ukrainian minority. Anyway, the safest thing was to try and pass ourselves off as uneducated delivery boys intent on carrying out one simple task. I followed up my speech with what I judged to be one of my nicest smiles, to show that our intentions were entirely honorable.

He looked puzzled, as predicted. He told me to wait; we weren't expected; he'd go and ask. He disappeared inside a small shack and was joined by a colleague, equally large, but without a rifle. Instead my eyes rested for a moment on the wooden handle protruding from a holster at his belt. The second guard shook his head and began to tell me, in broken Polish, to go away as there was obviously some mistake.

I became very agitated. After all, a young farm boy who has been charged with an important delivery for his employer could not be put off so easily. I jumped up and down in my seat, speaking even faster, looking worried—that part certainly wasn't sham!—and pointing repeatedly back in the direction we'd come from, then at the gates behind the guards.

The guards looked at each other. The boy seemed pretty certain of his orders! Perhaps someone had forgotten to tell them he was expected. They spoke between themselves, too quietly for me to catch any of it. As they talked, Vasily and I got down from the cart, walked around to the back, and let the rear flap down. I looked toward the guards and, smiling again as if taking their acquiescence for granted, began trying to heave one of the sacks down. Vasily did the same. We made very heavy weather of it, as the two huge Ukrainians watched us, apparently resigned now to our presence.

As if the idea suddenly struck me, I gestured toward the field behind the gates where some figures could be seen bent almost double over the ground.

"Prisoners—help—carry," I suggested, clearly this time.

The second guard, who seemed to have more authority than the first, said something to his comrade, who went back through the gate in the direction of the prisoners. Glancing after him, I noticed other black uniforms standing around keeping careful watch over the inmates. We were going to be very lucky to get close enough to whisper anything to any of them.

Vasily and I stopped working, and we all three waited. The guard began to pace up and down impatiently. At one point he stopped and, to my amazement, patted the pony's muzzle. It seemed an incongruous thing for a concentration camp guard to do. But then I read somewhere after the war that Himmler himself was very fond of animals. In fact, what I find most amazing is not that extreme cruelty can exist but that as Eva had said that night in the bunker, it can cohabit with tenderness and kindness, that human beings appear to have an infinite capacity to split their behavior into different compartments. Should such mysteries give us hope—or dread? Is a good act less good because it is performed by someone who the day before committed a brutal murder? I am no nearer answering these things than I was the day that guard gently patted my pony's nose, nearly thirty years ago. And as you may imagine, Richard, they weren't questions I was brooding on at the time!

After some moments he said almost companionably, "Taking their time, the lazy bastards." I nodded in agreement and produced another charming smile. I bent over the cart, pretending to busy myself with something and managed a casual remark to Vasily about the smell of the fertilizer.

Eventually a few prisoners appeared by the outhouses on the inside of the gate.

"Get back," barked the first guard, who was with them. He motioned me to reverse the cart and then began to swing open the gate. Another two guards had appeared with guns cocked; any prisoner who had attempted to use the moment to escape would have been dead within a second. The pony didn't like the idea of reversing, so we had to abandon it, and instead, with a lot of shouting, the prisoners were pushed through to where we stood, covered at point-blank range by all four guards. I quickly realized that my only hope of passing on my message was to get at least one of them up on the cart with us. I jumped up, followed by Vasily, and, in trying to move one of the sacks, pretended it was much heavier than it was. I beckoned to the nearest prisoner who happened to be looking at me. My heart, banging away mercilessly, missed a beat at the close-up sight of him. He was so emaciated it was hard to see how he could do work of any kind, let alone toil in the fields and carry loads. His eyes were huge and dark and glowed with unnatural brightness, as if with fever. His head, of course, was shaved. We bent down simultaneously, and I put my head as close to his as possible, acutely aware that the guards were only feet away. Vasily, seeing what I was doing, began making a commotion to distract attention. One of the sacks started spilling foul-smelling fertilizer all over the place. I only realized afterward that he had surreptitiously cut a hole in it with his knife, while pulling another toward him to conceal what he was doing. The result was that the second bag scraped awkwardly along his burned arm, making even stoic Vasily yelp with pain. One of the guards lashed out at the prisoners indiscriminately, for of course, they had to be punished for the mess.

"Monday morning—rescue—German uniform—on way to farm. Do as you're told—keep together."

I was hardly moving my lips and couldn't believe that my prisoner had heard me. He certainly didn't give any indication that he had. Then I realized he was pushing the bag back into the corner of the cart, away from the lowered flap. Playing for time. Vasily was now standing behind us, pushing bags along to the end.

The prisoner murmured to me in Yiddish, "I don't understand. I'm French. Can you speak Yiddish?"

My heart sank. I should have thought to speak Yiddish in the first place, for of course, there were Jews from all over Europe in Majdanek.

I repeated what I'd said in uncertain Yiddish. Then I remembered to add as I'd promised, "David is well; he's with us." That was really to help their morale. I then swore as I began heaving again, to show the guards how fed up I was with the whole thing. My prisoner jumped down and turned to pull the last sack toward him. As he did so, the first guard hit him across the back with the butt of his rifle, shouting at him to hurry. He staggered, but Vasily, who was standing next to him, saved him from falling. The guard then swore at Vasily in Ukrainian, and for a terrible moment I could see how tempted Vasily was to give as good as he got. I intervened by calling to him to close the flap, and to my intense relief he turned away to do so. I took one last look at my prisoner; he was gazing at me with an expression which told me that my message had indeed been received and understood the second time. It wasn't hope on his face so much as an expression of profound yearning.

I gave the senior guard the "official" delivery note to sign, to prove to my employer that the goods had reached their destination! As he took it into the hut, I watched the prisoners struggling with their loads and was glad that we'd purposely not made them too heavy. It was just as well the guards had been too lazy to lift any themselves! After they shut the gate, one of the guards cracked a whip behind the little cluster of men in their black-and-white-striped pajamas; one of them jumped, startled, and dropped the sack from his shoulder. The guards all laughed, one of them gave the prisoner a hefty kick on the behind, and another cracked the whip again. It was a sight to make you want to vomit and oddly enough upset me more than that of the many pitiful corpses I'd helped to bury over the previous few months.

But even so, it couldn't quite stifle our sense of elation as we drove our pony and cart away from the dreadful place. We had accomplished our task! We had fooled the guards, alerted the prisoners, and obtained an up-to-date picture of the lay of the land. Vasily looked back as we were leaving and noticed a guard letting two Alsatian dogs out of a shack to the right of the main gate; that was information the escapee, David, had not given us and which could be very useful indeed.

There was a good deal of competition in the unit to be included in the mission to rescue prisoners from Majdanek. There had already been attempts by Greenshpan to rescue Jews from other smaller labor camps in the region, though neither I nor any of my immediate friends had been involved in those, but the very name Majdanek had a particular ring to it. Polish soil is littered with names which testify that the devil is alive and well and stalks our earth, never mind some unlocated hell. Majdanek! Treblinka! Sobibor! Belzec! Auschwitz! And there is no better illustration of the inability of human beings to learn from the experience of the past than the blank looks on the faces of many of your generation, Richard, when most of those names are mentioned. But everyone has heard of Auschwitz. Auschwitz, it has been said, "was the scene of the greatest crime in the history of mankind." Well, perhaps Auschwitz may be used as a collective term for all the horrors that took place in all the concentration camps, all the ghettos and all the death pits, horrors which I hope are beyond your imagination and which it is neither my intention nor my place to dwell on here. Suffice it to say that Majdanek alone is thought to have accounted for the deaths of half a million victims, from starvation, disease, epidemics, inhuman conditions, and overwork—as well as from all the gassing and shooting.

Our plan was for several of the band to pose as members of the Inspectorate of Concentration Camps. Although this required more detailed preparation than a straightforward ambush, we felt that it made a shoot-out, and thus partisan and prisoner casualties, less likely— especially as there was very little cover along the approach road to the estate. We would have to gamble on the Ukrainian guards' having no better idea than ourselves as to the exact uniform the inspectors would wear; we did have one SS death's-head unit uniform, and several belonging to assorted police units which were all under the general command of the SS, so we would have to hope that these would be convincing enough.

Knowledge of German was the chief criterion for selection, coupled with looks that weren't too obviously Jewish. Franek, who had studied German, fulfilled both requirements, and as they outweighed the disadvantage of his crooked foot, he was intensely delighted.

"*My* turn this time," I heard him saying, or even crowing, to Eva. Henryk, who was usually ordered to stay in the background in case medical attention should be needed, was to lead this expedition as he had an excellent command of German. I was included in the group delegated to wait at the southern edge of the forest, to receive th escapees and guide them in the right direction.

It was with intense excitement and anxiety that we watch

group set off on the route which Vasily and I had spied out, from the cover of the forest to the estate: Henryk, Franek, Ilya, who'd picked up a smattering of German when he was a prisoner of war, Greenshpan himself, and several of the less Jewish-looking newcomers. Vasily was not included, much to his chagrin, in case he was recognized.

This, briefly, is what happened. They spent most of the night hiding by a granary in cornfields bordering the road from Majdanek, forcing themselves to stay awake so as not to crumple their uniforms. Our young farmer contacts had told us that the prisoners were usually escorted to the estate—or driven like cattle, might be a better expression—between five-thirty and six o'clock. Sure enough, soon after daybreak they heard the distant clatter of a hundred pairs of heavy wooden clogs on the paved road. It was a pathetic noise, made eerie by the morning mist.

The band was waiting for the Jews and their Ukrainian guards just beyond a bend in the road, the only place in the deserted part of the approach to the estate which offered any sort of cover or chance to surprise. The guards stopped in their tracks, taken aback, and meekly obeyed when Henryk stepped forward and in fluent, well-rehearsed German asked to see their identity cards. The others quickly got into position, so that each guard was marked by a partisan with a drawn gun, under the pretense of waiting to see the documents.

Henryk told them there had been reports of corruption and sloppiness at Majdanek, and in particular on the estates which produced food for the camp, and that there was to be a general tightening up of procedures. He spoke fast, banking on the Ukrainians' probably not understanding everything and certainly not picking up any mistakes. Franek told us with glee how Henryk actually seemed to change character: He narrowed his eyes and glowered in such a way that the guards grew noticeably more cowed. Henryk himself later admitted to having enjoyed his own performance once it got started!

Franek took the card he was meant to be inspecting up to Henryk, and together they frowned at it as if it contained some irregularity.

Franek said something to that effect so that those in the front of the group could hear; Henryk then ordered Franek curtly back to his post, as if he were a lowly subordinate, and gazed coldly at the offending guard. Then, after ensuring with a quick glance that all the Ukrainians were covered, he put his hand to his mouth and coughed. That was the sign for the shooting to start.

It all happened very quickly. The guards, taken by surprise and with no time to become suspicious of their "inspectors," were relatively easy to deal with. Only one of our men, one of the new ones, was injured by returned fire, and that slightly. All the guards were killed though "it took three bullets to kill mine," our injured comrade said sadly, obviously regretting the wasted ammunition.

Henryk, who had not had to deal with a guard, ordered the prisoners to follow him along the dirt track through the fields, while the others scattered poisoned meat in case the dogs were sent after us, and moved the bodies off the road into the high corn to delay their discovery. This part of the exercise was every bit as crucial as the first, for the prisoners had a good mile to run across exposed country before reaching the relative safety of the forest. They were so wasted and weak that their pace was maddeningly, tantalizingly slow. Although the road ended at the estate and was used by very few people, Henryk and the others knew they couldn't rely on the raid's not being discovered until the next change of shift, so they had to be brutal in hurrying the prisoners along.

"There was one who was obviously completely confused by what was happening. He just stood there, rooted to the spot. He was so thin you could actually see his ribs through his pajama jacket, but I had to threaten him by sticking my gun in his back, to get him to move. I had to. A single prisoner wandering around could have given the whole game away." That was Franek, shaking his head in disbelief; several hours later he was still visibly shaken by the condition of the prisoners they had rescued.

Once they reached the forests, some of the prisoners broke away, hoping to escape independently, but most of them were glad to be guided to the comparative haven of the family camp, where the food, though erratic and meager, was of banquetlike proportions compared with that of Majdanek. Franek took personal responsibility for helping the prisoner he had threatened to reach Altana, but having seen him, I doubt whether he lasted very long. My prisoner, however, the one I had managed to forewarn, a Frenchman called Vidal, joined our fighting unit after a couple of weeks of "rest" at Altana, but even then his eyes still glowed with an unhealthy brightness. When we met again, we embraced and greeted each other in Yiddish.

"If we hadn't been warned, we would have rushed off in all directions when your men killed our guards, and perhaps none of us would have reached the forest." That was probably an exaggeration, but Vasily and I smiled at each other, feeling very proud of ourselves. I knew that for Vasily it made up a little for not having been part of the main rescue, and I put my arm through his in a gesture of affection, before realizing I'd chosen his bad arm.

I apologized profusely, but he answered me so strangely that I remember it exactly: "Don't worry, Jan, the pain is good for me; it makes me strong." For one brief moment I couldn't help suspecting that the burning sleeve of bark which had caused his injury had not after all been blown there by the wind. But it *was* only a suspicion, and I could never have mentioned it to him.

A few nights later Piotr cooked one of the best meals I ever had as a partisan. Yet the occasion was both sad and joyful. On the one hand, we were celebrating the successful rescue of nearly a hundred Jews from the Majdanek farm; on the other, we were saying farewell to Ilya and Vasily and another Russian Jew who had recently joined us. Vasily had finally given in to Ilya's persuasion to go back across the river Bug, to Volhynia and the Pripet Marshes, where they knew that Soviet partisans were numerous and very active.

For once there was no shortage of food as there had been a recent raid on a cattle farm led by Alexander. So we had herb-flavored *kasza* with a wonderful hot pot of beef and root vegetables and Piotr's special potato cakes, which I loved. It was one of those soft, warm pine-scented and midge-filled nights, when the moon seemed to float just above the tops of the trees, almost as if you could reach up and touch it. I traced the dark continents etched on its surface like ghostly prophecies and wondered what this world still had in store for us. As if in answer there came, faint but clear from the far distance, an eerie yearning howl: wolves in the night! It was only the second or third time I'd heard them in a year; now, as before, the melancholy wail cast a brief spell of silence on the listeners, and we looked at one another with unease and foreboding.

But then we resumed the festivities with even more determination. We sang songs around the fire until late into the night; perhaps we were imprudently loud, for everyone's emotions were at a very high pitch. I remember the last song we sang—or if it wasn't the last it's the one that made the most impression on me—with Vasily, who had drunk a good deal of farewell moonshine, repetitiously going through the motions of playing an imaginary fiddle!

"Maybe one day," he said breathlessly, "I'll teach you how to play an instrument. Who knows? But I think it would be easier for you to start with the piano than the fiddle."

I translated for him the Yiddish words of the song:

> This is not the end of the road
> Though the clouds conceal the sun
> The day will come when light will shine again
> And our marching feet proclaim, "We have come."

It does lose somewhat in the translation into English!

The Russians left the next day. Franek and I went eastward with them for the first three or four miles, in the direction of Sosnowica. When the time came to part, Ilya, with whom I had never felt really at ease, began to shake me solemnly by the hand. Then, to my surprise, he thought better of it and took me in his arms; I couldn't be sure, but I thought there were tears in his eyes. Vasily, on the other hand, now that he was no longer under the influence of moonshine, characteristically displayed very little emotion. Instead he fumbled in his belt and took out his prized sheath knife in its leather case.

"This is for you," he said gruffly. I was really taken aback; I think I quite literally took a step away from him.

"No, Vasily, you can't do that. You treasure that knife. Besides, you may well need it."

"I've nothing else to leave you," he said simply. "I want you to have it, Jan. Anyway, *you* may need it, too, and after all, it's really yours as much as mine. We found it together."

But I saw him looking at it and could see how much it cost him to give it away. Suddenly I relived the panic I'd had back in the ghetto the day I smuggled my baby sister Eli out to the other side, when I realized that I had nothing to give her, nothing of me to take into her new life.

"But I've nothing for you."

"You've given it to me already," he said matter-of-factly, and went on to show me how he'd written his grandmother's address on a scrap of paper and stuffed it down into the bottom of the sheath.

"She'll know where I am if I'm still alive. And if we both are, after the war, we'll meet again, Jan." He embraced me very quickly and lightly then and, before I knew it, had followed the others along the path to the east and to the Soviet border, several days' walk away. He looked back only once to wave.

Franek and I stood at the fork in the track, tears running unashamedly down my cheeks. I knew I didn't have to hide them from Franek, who put his arm around me. "He's right, you know, Jan. You gave him a lot. None of us had seen him smile before you arrived."

Vasily and I never did meet again. After the war I wrote to his grandmother, who did know where he was, approximately: in a shallow grave somewhere in the Pripet Marshes, killed there in a partisan action in 1944. He'd been highly commended by his comrades for his courage. I know how much that would have pleased him.

They buried him near a place called Pinsk. I sometimes thought I'd like to go there in an absurd attempt to find the exact place where he fell, but of course, I never did. It was touching, though, how pleased his grandmother was to hear from me; we maintained a correspondence until she died well into her eighties, and I told her all I could remember of the things Vasily and I had done together, though, of course, leaving out much of the detail I have told you. I had to get help with translating her letters, and no doubt she with mine, but I think that although we never met and didn't speak the same language, it meant a lot to both of us to be in contact: she, an old lady who'd lost everyone close to her and was waiting to die; I, a young man who had also lost everyone close to me, living alone in a very foreign country and waiting for life to begin again. And I still have the knife sheath; it survived, miraculously, and remains one of my most treasured possessions. Of the knife itself, more in a moment.

By that summer of 1943 both partisans and refugees hiding in the forests around Parczew had become much more experienced and skilled in evading the Nazi manhunts. Whereas in the winter hundreds died in every German raid, the number of casualties during the summer months could be counted, as it seemed to us, in dozens. So it was ironic that at a time when the German threat was dwindling, my career as a partisan should come to such an abrupt and savage ending. But the Germans were not the only enemy to be reckoned with. Around this time there were more attacks against Jews by members of Polish extremist groups. It wasn't a straightforward struggle between Poles, Russians, and Jews on the one hand and Nazis on the other; anti-Semitism and fear of communism made it a very much more complicated and fragmented picture than that.

One day we made a pleasant, relaxed expedition back to near where our temporary camp had been by Lake Obradowskie, as we knew that was a rich fishing ground. Perhaps we were too relaxed, after the recent success of the Majdanek and other missions, for we began the journey back in lively and not particularly quiet discussion. Roza, who usually kept kosher, was expressing disgust that we intended to eat freshwater crabs and was even refusing to take them to Buradow to sell; she didn't want to have anything to do with them. I'm afraid Franek and I, and I think Berek, too, then started trying to annoy her even more, to "wind her up," as you would put it! She was easily riled and rather funny when she was cross. Eva walked on ahead with her as she was the only person who ever managed to placate her; I think, in retrospect, that Roza disliked males on principle. Anyway, all that is irrelevant and totally trivial compared with what happened next. All I am doing is putting off the moment when I have to describe what that was.

Eva and Roza were out of sight when we heard the shouts, and then a shot brought us to an abrupt halt. Only for an instant, though; almost immediately we were running in the direction the women had taken. In a small clearing a grim scene met our eyes. Two men in camouflage jackets and wearing the sword and plow badge of the fanatically anti-Semitic and anti-Communist National Armed Force had overpowered Roza and Eva; one of them, the larger, held Roza clasped to him with his arm across her chest, the gun in his other hand hovering around her temples. Meanwhile, his friend, also brandishing a pistol in one hand, had pinned Eva against a tree and was tearing at her clothes.

"You don't look Jewish, so you're probably Communist scum! But you've got a nice body. Resist, and your friend is dead." I remember his words ringing out, crisp and clear, presumably so that Roza could hear them. Then everything started happening at once. There were shouts and suddenly more people running around, more men in a hodgepodge of uniforms. I was transfixed where I stood, not knowing what to do, as I wasn't armed.

But Franek was. As if in slow motion, I saw him trying to jump onto a tree stump at the edge of the clearing, stumble, but succeed in getting onto it at the second attempt. And then came the last and most abiding image of my friend Franek; I can see him now, sunlight on his mass of curly hair, the tilt of his chin as, upright and steady, he took aim and shot the enemy who had dared to molest his beloved sister. Simultaneously I heard Alexander cry, "Franek, get down." The cry was too late; Franek's bullet had met its target, but he in turn had made all too easy a target for one of the other terrorists. He fell heavily from the tree stump to the ground, where he lay inert on his stomach, a pool of blood spreading out from under him.

Alexander took aim, and then shooting seemed to come from all directions, disorientating and deafening us. Roza was knocked to the ground, and her head kicked by the brute who had been holding her hostage; then he and two others converged on Eva, who stood as if paralyzed against the tree, staring down at Franek's bleeding body.

Then I remembered that I was armed. *Vasily's knife!* It was the work of a second to draw and hurl it at the back of one of Eva's assailants, who presumably hadn't realized in the confusion how many of us there were. I had taken good aim, and the passion of my hatred propelled it across the clearing and clean between the enemy's shoulder blades. With a horrible rattling, gurgling cry the man staggered and collapsed as his companion reeled around, shooting indiscriminately.

Eva took advantage of the diversion to rush across to where Franek's body lay in the sodden, darkening moss. As she knelt by him and bent over to put her head beside his, I do remember—I think—a glimpse of that dear green ribbon in her hair. But then there was an explosion of red-hot pain somewhere in my hip area, and Eva disappeared in a sort of milky mist, as I myself fell to the ground and then lost consciousness.

Later, when I was recovering from my wounds, Henryk told me that she had been shot in the head, right there, on top of her brother's body. If I saw it happen, then the sight is mercifully hidden forever behind a curtain of amnesia.

That's it, Richard. I can't write any more now. Tomorrow, or maybe later, I'll find the strength to tell you about the next stage of my charmed—or accursed—life. For many many years I was unable to cry about these things. But now, more healthily and despite the distance of time, I am unable to think of the horrors of that forest clearing except through a veil of tears. Tears of heartbreak, tears of rage at such senseless waste and brutality, but also tears of pride—pride that I once knew and loved, and, I think, was loved by, people with such vitality of spirit. Eva and Franek died aged just twenty, that's only three years older than you, but I think that in the one year I was with them they lived more intensely, more fully, more generously than many of us who may live to acquire the so-called wisdom of age. Of course, how they would have coped with the business of growing old slowly in an era of safety and plenty, I can only speculate. But there is a sense in which they, and Vasily, too, in a slightly different way, gave to life more than they received from it. And perhaps that's the nearest I'll ever come to defining what people insist on calling the quality of courage, as if it were some undifferentiated, consistent, stable thing.

JULY 16

Dearest Kate,

I've come to the end of the partisan part of Misha's story. Judging by how it's made me feel, I'm beginning to see why he left it so long to write. It must have felt like going through it all, all over again. Imagine that instead of you moving up north, you'd been murdered right in front of me, and I'd been totally powerless to do anything about it. That's what happened to Eva, the girl he was in love with.

I did look up Babi Yar—the place where the parents of Misha's friend Vasily were murdered, in the Ukraine. I found an eyewitness account in a book in the library. I've never read anything so disgusting in my life. Of course, everyone knows that the Nazis committed atrocities in the war, but they've always sounded very distant—in time and place. Misha's story makes them all seem very close to home. It does make you wonder . . . I mean, that exchange I went on two years ago in Freiburg. It was a nice family, but the father and the grandfather would both have been adults in the war. I never wondered before what they did. There again, perhaps it's wrong to keep suspicions like that alive. I don't suppose they did anything at all—except stand by with millions of others and let it happen. But then there are all these awful things happening in different parts of the world now, which Dad writes about. I think Misha's right about one thing at least: We don't seem to be able to learn from the past.

Misha talks a lot about courage; he seems uncertain about what it means. Well, one thing is for certain: I didn't show much of it today. I told Mum about the trouble at school, as I said I was going to. She had to know something because they're bound to send her a bill. But I chickened out of telling her everything and maybe, with any luck, they won't go into detail either. I wish I'd never got mixed up in it—even just as an accessory to the crime, as it were.

After school today I went and looked at some of our old photo albums. I don't know why, I just felt nostalgic for some reason. Perhaps because I had another card from Dad in Uruguay this morning. It occurred to me looking at the ones of me as a baby with Mum and Dad that Misha can't do that. All he's got is one little photo of his parents that's so creased and faded it's almost worthless. And he hasn't even got that much of his two sisters. It must be weird to be so cut off from your own past. I looked at the ones of him when he first got to know us. He looks so sort of—young—in them, and they were only taken about six years ago. I liked him then, I liked him a lot. He liked me, too, I think. What on earth went wrong? Whatever it was, it did go very wrong.

No more news, Katiegirl. School is boring as hell. I've got a *history essay for tomorrow and I'd rather be reading the next bit of Misha's story. Oh, there have been one or two pieces by Dad about the Tupamaros guerrillas in the press recently—I wonder if you've seen them? I'll keep them to show you, anyway. I still think he's really gutsy, taking the sort of risks he does. Even if Mum does think it's just because he gets a kick out of it.*

    Write soon. Love you,
            Richard

PART 2

RESISTANCE—
IN HIDING

You who will emerge from the flood
In which we have gone under
Remember
When you speak of our failings
The dark time too
Which you have escaped.

BERTOLT BRECHT,
"TO THOSE BORN LATER"

When I came to, I didn't immediately recall what had happened and couldn't understand why I was being transported through the forest on a board, a makeshift stretcher. Henryk's face bobbed up and down in a blur in front of me. Then, suddenly, I saw again the scene in the clearing and must have groaned, for my "bearers," Alexander and Henryk, stopped and apologized for jolting me. They lowered me carefully to the ground, and Henryk explained what was happening.

"Jan, you've been shot in the upper arm and at the top of your thigh. You've lost a lot of blood, but you're not going to die. We're taking you to Parczew and the priest; Berek has gone on ahead to warn him. He'll be able to get someone reliable from the local hospital to come and attend to you. There's nothing I can do for you in the forest, because we've scarcely any supplies left. We're nearly there, so bear with us if the ride is bumpy for a bit longer."

"And Eva? Franek?" Henryk shook his head slowly, confirming the worst. I must have drifted into unconsciousness again, because the next thing I knew I was in a bedroom upstairs in the priest's little house, with the twin spires of a church filling the view through the window. It was a bare room with no other furniture except the narrow bed and an upturned box beside it, on which were a candle and a glass of water. The only decoration in the room was a huge crucifix on one of the walls.

The priest, who wore big, thick-lensed spectacles, muttered a prayer as I came to and said gently, "The doctor's coming, the doctor's coming."

I wondered if he meant Henryk and desperately hoped so, needing to see a familiar face in that strange, bare room. My whole body was a mass of pain; I couldn't have told you where the wounds were.

But the doctor who appeared soon afterward was neither Henryk nor familiar. I remember thinking that he seemed rough and unfriendly, but he must have given me some sort of anesthetic because I drifted off again soon after. Later when I awoke in the middle of the night, completely disoriented as to time and place, the priest told me that I'd had a bullet extracted from my upper thigh and the bad flesh wound in my arm excised and treated.

Everything throbbed in a sort of ghastly rhythm, and I felt very sick. When day broke, I remember pathetically trying to push at the light with my good arm, in an attempt to make it turn back and leave me in merciful darkness again. Although neither of my wounds was in itself immediately life-threatening, I had lost about two pints of blood and had given the back of my head a severe bump when I fell after first being hit. That probably accounted for my dreadful headache. My recollections of the next day or two are almost nonexistent, and I think I spent most of them asleep. I just have a vague visual image of those twin spires filling the square of window and a church bell tolling at certain intervals. Prophetically, perhaps, for the next stage of my war was to be dominated by a twin-spired sort of religious dilemma.

Dr. Klyza, the priest, who had given a lot of help to various people in the resistance, was afraid that the local German garrison had begun to have suspicions about him. They had started visiting him unexpectedly and hanging around for no obvious reason. He was therefore anxious that I should move on, as soon as I was well enough to be moved. So, a couple of days later, I found myself driving along in a small pony and trap beside Stefan, one of the priest's parishioners, who had called to see the father on "routine" church business. The priest pressed a small Bible into my hand as I left and patted my head. "My prayers will be with you," he said, and although I was standing up for the first time since being shot and was concentrating on not passing out from either weakness or the infernal headache, I am glad, in view of what happened later, that I managed to thank the old man for all he had done. And I was genuinely grateful for the Bible, not, I must confess, for scriptural reasons but because even in the state I was in, I realized it could be a nice refinement to my Aryan disguise.

The months I spent under Stefan and Fela's roof were probably the safest of the war in that they were the period in which I was least likely to be detected as a Jew. It was known that Fela had an extended family in southern Poland, so no one was likely to question the sudden appearance of a new young "cousin." In any case there were no near neighbors as their little farm was in the countryside and I never accompanied either of them into Parczew or the other villages in case I should be recognized from one of our food confiscation raids. I hadn't forgotten the frantic escape which Eva and I were forced to make that time in November. But if the months with Stefan and Fela were the safest, they were also the saddest and, from an emotional point of view, gave me the greatest struggle.

Although I was better nourished than at the time of my fever about a year before, this time I was much slower to regain my strength. And although the rough doctor from the hospital thought one of the bullets had probably chipped or fractured a bone, I wasn't forbidden to walk after about the first week. It was just that I simply lost the inclination to get up. I lay on my bed, staring at the wooden ceiling for hours, probably days on end. All I did was eat the meals which Fela brought me but without enjoyment, without interest. I'm not sure that I even appreciated the luxury of soft, smooth sheets after the itchy straw and horse blankets which had been my bedding in the dugouts. Out of action, and unable to make the smallest contribution to the struggle in the forest, I had nothing to do but reflect. And reflect was the last thing I wanted to do.

I began to be tortured by guilt in all sorts of guises. How could I bear to be alive when all the people of any real value had already perished? And by this time in 1943 I was becoming aware that the people I personally had lost were but the tiniest fraction of a colossal tragedy. What I had before seen as my luck, the charm which preserved my existence, came to feel more like a burden or a curse. I can't hide from you, Richard, that once or twice at my lowest ebb I even considered suicide. But somehow such a step demanded a resolve and an energy which I no longer possessed. I eyed the knife which Fela put on my meal tray and handled it thoughtfully once or twice, but each time it only reminded me of Vasily's knife and the blood-soaked scene in the forest clearing. I know it sounds silly, but I actually thought of the mess it would make for Fela, who was being so kind, making all sorts of special things to tempt my appetite. It seemed a discourteous way of repaying her hospitality. And then, when I thought of my parents, and Rachel, and Dr. Korczak, and Eva, I knew deep down that I could never put an end to my own life, for I owed it to them to keep going, to make their sacrifices worthwhile. And once it occurred to me, with a sadness as piercing as any knife, that it was when *I* died *they* would finally die, for their memories would live as long as I did. It was in those long, melancholy hours that I began to think again about my baby sister Eli: to wonder if she was still living, and, if so, where and with whom, and whether she still had in her possession the story of the beginning of her life, which Rachel had taken such care to write for her before I smuggled her out of the ghetto. I wondered whether "they" had told her that she had once had a brother and sister, who had died at Treblinka along with hundreds of thousands of others, and whether despite it all, we might one day meet again.

I agonized about my own father and the fact that my memory of him had grown less distinct than it should have done since his death from typhus in 1941. Had I been disloyal to him by being so fond of Dr. Korczak? Would my father have liked what I had become? Would he have approved of his fifteen-year-old son, like most of his generation so prematurely arrived at adulthood? Had I done anything at all that

I could tell him about with pride, if in some distant afterlife we again came face-to-face?

I had no interest in whether it was night or day, sunny or wet, no interest in whether my little patch of sky was blue or gray. It was all the same to me. I couldn't bear to think of Eva or Franek, but I did think of Vasily a lot and wished he were there to help me convert my anguish into anger, as he had so successfully done. I felt abandoned by the other partisans, particularly by Henryk, and was convinced that they had forgotten me. I was very lonely, and no one came, except Fela with my meals.

When the wound in my arm became infected, I knew a sort of grim satisfaction. At least I didn't have to make the effort to get up and about again; Fela had started making noises about dressing and going downstairs.

Then, one day, Henryk came. I was surprised when he told me he had been before while I was still at Father Klyza's house and semiconscious. No one had remembered to tell me. Henryk had always treated me with gentleness and respect, but he had never obviously shown any favoritism toward me. That day, though, he made no attempt to be detached. He must have seen my despair from my general manner—I didn't even sit up to greet him—and no doubt Fela had told him how I was behaving. Anyway, he just sat down on the bed beside me, took me in his arms, and held me silently, for a long time. I clung to him, wanting so badly to cry, but the well was dry.

Eventually he laid me back against the pillows and asked if he could inspect my injuries. He grimaced at the evidence of infection, and I flinched as he probed the edges of the inflamed area.

"Has the doctor been again?"

"Yes, he brought some sulfonamide cream, but it doesn't seem to have done much good. Fela changes my dressings; she's more careful, anyway."

For the first time since being away from the forest, I felt a spark of energy and interest, and I asked after the others. Piotr, Alexander,

Berek, and even Roza, now recovered from her brutal treatment, had sent messages; in fact, they had wanted to take turns in coming to see me, but Henryk had dissuaded them, for too many strange visitors to the house might have alerted suspicion somewhere, despite the fact that there were no immediate neighbors. And of course, Alexander's physical appearance was an instant giveaway. Dear old Piotr had sent me two potato cakes. They hadn't improved being wrapped up in Henryk's pocket, and Fela made a face when he asked her to warm them through; I think she felt it was some sort of insult to her cooking. To me they tasted wonderful. And for once there was good news. Envoys from our enlarged unit had been sent eastward to fetch arms and equipment from a Soviet partisan unit operating in Polesie, beyond the river Bug, north of where Ilya and Vasily had headed, and one of the men had stayed on to be trained in sabotage techniques. Meanwhile, Alexander and Berek had been in a group led by Greenshpan in a successful mission against a tar factory outside Wlodawa which served the Germans. All the installations and stock had been destroyed, and it was being viewed as a major victory which would seriously impede the Germans' road- and bridge-building program. Two bridges on the Parczew–Wiszince road had also been blown up. We really were beginning to make progress at last. *Of course*, I was pleased, but there was just a little bit of me that resented it all happening without Eva, Franek, Vasily, even Ilya—and yes, myself. Perhaps Henryk guessed what I was thinking because he said, "We miss you, Jan. And the others. It isn't the same anymore."

I thought he said it just to please me and didn't realize until much later that Henryk himself was by then wondering whether he had come to the end of his usefulness as a forest fighter. He was not, and never had been, a natural partisan; he was first and foremost a healer, not a soldier, and although his common sense, his calm, and the sort of natural authority which emanated from him had made him a good second-in-command of a small band, he had been only too willing to relinquish his power to Greenshpan, and then for that larger unit to merge with the Communist People's Guard, who also began to operate in our area in the summer of 1943. He had no interest in the inevitable politicking which takes place when smaller groups become absorbed into a larger one. And the departure of his sparring partner Ilya and of Vasily and the deaths of the twins together with my own removal had, as he later put it, "taken the electricity out of forest life." In the meantime, though, he managed to visit me, faithfully, every week. And slowly, very slowly, my wounds began to heal. After about a month I was able to help with small tasks around the house, though it still hurt to walk for long.

By that late summer of 1943 I could say with some confidence that my life had been saved by at least eight different people: Dr. Korczak; Adziu, the sewer guide; Eva; Granny; Henryk; Franek; Alexander (who, I later learned, killed the man who'd shot me); Father Klyza—and there were probably others. All the peasants who helped supply us with food and clothing, for a start. But the one who found the role of rescuer the hardest, who had the greatest struggle within himself, and to whom I should therefore, perhaps, be the most grateful despite my reservations, was Stefan.

Stefan was a devout man, uneducated but very thoughtful. He spent a lot of time in the evenings reading the Scriptures. When I began to emerge from my deepest depression and to look around for something to do, he suggested that I should read a little piece each day from the Bible which Father Klyza had given me and then discuss with him every evening after supper what I had read. I liked that idea; it was the sort of thing we had done at the orphanage, though not, of course, in relation to the Bible. I've tried it with you, if you remember, though you weren't exactly enthusiastic after the age of about fourteen! But it soon became clear during those evening sessions that Stefan had more on his mind than my Christian education. Or rather, he was attending to my Christian education in the hope of earning himself pardon in heaven for harboring an enemy of Christ. He was a man of conscience and was troubled by what he saw as a fundamental conflict of religious values. On the one hand, he believed that because Jews had killed Christ, they were a marked or cursed people and as such probably deserved whatever came their way. All the same, the Scriptures told him quite clearly that all human beings are made in the image of God, and the Second Commandment enjoined him to love his neighbor as himself. He would puzzle this out openly in front of me, but oddly enough, perhaps because of the earnestness with which he so obviously tried to do what was morally right, I never felt angered by his confusion. It did make me feel very vulnerable and threatened, though, and never more so than after his return from church on Sundays.

I need to explain that Father Klyza, the elderly priest who had acted as intermediary for the partisans and other resistance workers since the German invasion, was eventually arrested. His cleaner, cowering in the cupboard under the stairs, had been in the house at the time. One of the arresting soldiers had torn the priest's thick-lensed spectacles from his face and jeered, "You've been shortsighted in more ways than one. And you won't need these where *you're* going." Peeping out from behind the cupboard door, she had seen how they dragged him across the hall, and how, bereft of his spectacles, he had stumbled over the threshold.

Well, Father Klyza was replaced by a very different sort of man of God—or so I understood from the state in which poor Stefan would return from his weekly attendance at church. Normally quiet-spoken and thoughtful, he would come home swearing and shouting, "I'm sure to lose out every way. They'll kill me in this world for keeping Jews, and then I'll be turned away at the gates of heaven for helping them, too."

I'd retire to my room, or later, when I could anticipate these moods, I'd simply not come downstairs until he was calmer. The kitchen was underneath my bedroom, and I'd hear Fela telling him off in no uncertain terms. Later, at lunchtime, he would apologize to me and to make amends would bring out his homemade plum brandy and drink several glasses with me.

But although these explosions were short-lived and became predictable, they upset me; they reinforced my growing sense of being a curse to everyone I came into contact with. The point had, after all, been recently reinforced, this time by Father Klyza's arrest. I began to dread Sundays and on Saturday evenings would sometimes consider leaving of my own volition. But in those moments I became more acutely aware than ever of just how vulnerable I was, for in truth there was nowhere to go.

Stefan's outbursts were not the only thing that made me uneasy in that house, despite the fact that I was well cared for and certainly much better fed than at any other time in the war. It was the relationship between Stefan and Fela which made me uncomfortable. I quickly noticed that they seldom spoke to each other, except to make practical arrangements. At the table they would both make an effort to talk to me but hardly ever addressed a word to each other. In fact, the Sunday scoldings which Fela delivered in my defense were almost the only direct exchanges I heard between them. Sometimes Fela's mother visited; she was a sour-faced old woman who clearly resented my presence and made a point of ignoring me. On those occasions Fela seemed to collapse into herself, speaking to no one and only nodding and responding in monosyllables to her mother's remarks. Stefan would be more attentive than ever toward me and ignore his mother-in-law completely. I was always thankful to escape to my room, which, oddly, merges in my memory with the one in Father Klyza's house, though I spent months in the former and only two or three semiconscious days in the latter.

Fela was neat and dark-eyed, and I'm sure had once been very pretty, but now her face was disfigured by an almost permanent frown. I realized as I got to know her better that the frown indicated worry, rather than disapproval, but it still had a rather off-putting, distancing

effect on me. In three months she never did or said anything unkind
or impolite to me, she persevered gallantly with the stubborn infections
of my arm wound without a single complaint, and she was always
making cakes and extras that she thought I'd enjoy, and yet it may
sound ungrateful but for all that I never came really close to her.
Perhaps it was me, needing time and space when I wasn't called upon
to be close to anyone, but somehow I don't think it was entirely due
to me. It's difficult to explain, because I did—or hope I did—show
my appreciation of all her attentions, particularly, as you may imagine,
of the food, yet for all the enforced intimacy of our contact we remained
strangers. Sometimes I sensed that she would have liked to take me
into her confidence, but she never made the leap. Instinctively I knew
that some profound sorrow had alienated her from her husband and
that though I was, most of the time, a welcome distraction in the
house, I could do nothing to help this brave, generous, troubled,
childless couple. For all Stefan's misgivings, for all his weekly ranting
and raving and, I believe, totally misguided interpretation of the Scriptures, he and his wife risked their lives to help a stranger who was
nothing to them. How many of us would do that, Richard, if put to
the test?

More than anything I looked forward to Henryk's visits, though
each time he arrived I couldn't prevent a little jolt of hope that Eva
and Franek might be close behind him. Absurd, but perhaps my brain
had not yet fully convinced my heart that they were both irredeemably
dead. As the autumn progressed, there was more good news about the
success of our operations. In early October there were three spectacular
sabotage missions against railway lines, with one of them actually
running a troop train off the track. This particular train carried an
entire Waffen-SS unit. At the end of October twelve prisoners who
had escaped after the rebellion at Sobibor death camp about thirty
miles to the southeast managed to reach our part of the forest, despite
pursuit for part of the way by German police and army units.

"We gave them a good welcome. But it wasn't the same for us

personally as the Majdanek escape. I still think that was our greatest triumph, Jan.'' We smiled at each other in shared pleasure at the memory, and though neither of us knew how many of the prisoners we'd helped to escape were still alive, I agreed wholeheartedly. It was at that moment that I knew, intuitively, that I would never go back to the woods and also that Henryk's days as a partisan were nearing their end. I didn't realize how near, however!

A few days later I was helping Fela by doing some jobs in the garden; I tried to do as much as I could around the place once I began to feel better, so as to earn my keep. After making a pile of dead plants, I walked over to fetch the wheelbarrow, upturned against the wall of the house near the kitchen window. It was a lovely, still late-autumn afternoon, and in the distance the edge of the forest glowed gold. The kitchen window was open. As I reached for the handles of the wheelbarrow, I stopped, suddenly hearing Fela's voice raised in anger.

"Now take it and go. I have no more."

"That's all right. That's enough. Until next month."

Something made me stand back in the shadow of the wall, hidden by the shutter which had not been properly pinned back. I heard the back door slam, and footsteps, and whoever the visitor was walked away out of sight around the corner of the building. Then I heard a familiar whistle and recognized the favorite tune of Zygmunt, a laborer who helped Stefan on the farm.

I recognized the voice of old sour face, Fela's mother.

"You're a fool, a silly little fool. This month five hundred zlotys, next month seven hundred. What will happen when you can't afford to pay anymore?"

"What else can I do, Mother? He's a child. No more than a child."

"But a Jewish child, Fela, a Jewish child. What's happening to the Jews—men, women, and children, too—is only God's will."

I held my breath. I had a desperate need to hear everything that was said. After all, it sounded as if my life depended on it. I wondered if my heartbeat would actually make me deaf to the next exchange. Instead there was a rattle of plates, and I crept as close to the shutter as I dared.

Fela said, quite calmly, "Then, Mother, I am glad I am no longer a Christian." I felt a rush of tenderness; I'd never heard her stand up to the old woman before.

"That's wicked, my girl, and you will surely be punished. You need to examine your conscience and go and see that new priest; he will sort you out."

"I wouldn't go anywhere near him. I've seen what he does for Stefan." Fela's tone was more bitter now.

"Well, that's your decision. But my advice to you as your mother is to get rid of that Jewish boy. He will ruin you; he has no place here. First you'll pay with your money, then with your lives."

"Mother, when Jan is well enough to leave and stand conditions in the forest, then we will let him go. Until then he stays. That's final—and for once Stefan agrees with me."

"I can't understand you. I simply can't understand you. To me it's so clear. If God takes no pity on their people, how can they expect pity from other human beings? An eternal curse is on them."

I heard a door slam, and the conversation came to an end.

You can imagine the state of agitation I was in by then. I suppose I must have realized before that my very presence was a danger to Stefan and Fela, but perhaps because I needed to believe that the "cover story" of the sickly cousin was plausible and because I never ventured beyond the garden wall, I had convinced myself that the risks they ran were relatively small. Of course, I had absolutely no idea how the laborer had found out who I was—perhaps he had just guessed—or when the blackmail had started, but I did know that now I would have to leave immediately. I also knew that as Henryk and the others had recently changed the location of the camp, the old one having become infested with rats, I was unlikely to find them on my own. Once again, after three months of a sort of numbness, I was literally sick with fear.

I couldn't eat that evening, even though Fela's mother had left, and made the excuse of a stomach upset. Unusually neither Fela nor Stefan talked to me, and I felt a new tension in the air. Lying awake later, I decided that the best thing I could do was to wait for Henryk's next visit and then go back to the forest with him. I was slower than I had been as my upper thigh and hip area could still be painful, so I'd not be much use for a while, but at least I was independent and could help prepare the winter bunkers again. I worked all this out on one level, despite the intuitive knowledge on another that I would never return to the forest.

I went through agonies during those next few days, rehearsing all the only-too-probable things that could happen to prevent Henryk from ever coming back. I was so preoccupied that I forgot to register when Sunday came around. In fact, Stefan returned from church as docile as a lamb. There was no outburst, no shouting—but no plum brandy after lunch either.

"Better not finish the stocks, Jan; you never know when we might need them."

His manner toward me hadn't really changed, yet the different routine made me uneasy. I would wake up in the middle of the night and wait for that famous dreaded knock on the door, all the while working out improbable methods of escape for when it actually came. In the daytime I was tempted to ask Fela if I could have a fallback hiding place in the cellar or the loft, but somehow I never dared broach the subject. It was as if by so doing, I would make the eventuality more real, and Fela and Stefan were after all carrying on as if nothing had happened. By not acknowledging the new threat, I could almost, at least by day, pretend it would go away. But at night it haunted me so closely that it was like having another living person clinging to me. And once I actually discovered the meaning of the cliché "I nearly died of fright."

It was very light, the moon almost full; I was just drifting into a merciful sleep when the night was filled with a harsh, strangled cry.

What's more, it seemed to come from immediately below my window. I couldn't get out of bed because my legs had turned to lead; I just lay there, my heart beating so fast that I was afraid to move a single muscle in case it overreached itself and gave up.

The sound came again, maybe a little more distant but still wild and tortured. Someone, surely, was being murdered, and it *must* have something to do with me and my illegal presence at the farm. Silence; then to my horror it came again, farther away still. Suddenly I remembered. It was the cry of a fox; I'd heard it once, early on, in the forest, and Franek had enjoyed my startled expression.

"That's one of the few things you don't have to be afraid of out here," he'd reassured me. And as my heartbeat slowed down, I felt myself blush in the darkness, ashamed of my panic, certain that my friends would have laughed at me.

When the knock on the door finally came, it was only Henryk—a day later than I'd hoped, but with some important news. After Father Klyza's arrest, another contact, who I later learned was a post office clerk, acted as a vital link in the communication chain with Warsaw. From our usual place in the graveyard Henryk had picked up a message from his cousin Joseph, who, miraculously, had escaped the Ghetto Uprising and was then in hiding in Aryan Warsaw, continuing the struggle with the remnants of the Jewish Fighting Organization. Henryk, with his medical knowledge, his neutral looks, and his flawless Polish, was needed back in Warsaw, where couriers to take papers, supplies, and treatment to Jews in hiding all over the city were in urgent demand.

"And you, with your 'good' looks [that expression was used to mean non-Jewish, you understand!] will come with me. It was always intended that you should be a courier, but you became a partisan instead because we didn't want to let you go." We smiled at each other, remembering other reasons he'd given for not sending me regularly back to Warsaw. We were leaning against the garden gate behind the house, only one field stretching between us and the woods. It was safer to have this sort of conversation outdoors.

Then I told him my news and watched the smile disappear from his face.

"So we must leave even sooner than expected. You shouldn't stay here another night," he said gravely. "The blackmail could go on for months, but we can't be sure, and we don't know how many other people he might have told. Vodka loosens tongues."

Henryk had to go back to the others, not only to tell them what we planned to do in case they assumed he'd been captured or killed but also to collect some small arms and grenades to take back to Warsaw. The five-hour walk there and back would probably have been beyond me, so I had to spend that night in a disused stable suggested by Stefan (to whom I could now admit I knew about the blackmail), an outhouse belonging to a deserted farm off the Makowska road. Henryk had brought me on one of his visits my old schoolbag, the one I'd used to steal the medical supplies and later fooled the SS officer with. I rather vainly liked to think of it as my "Uprising" bag, as it made me feel I had played a tiny part in that struggle! Anyway, this time Fela filled it with nice things to eat: some of her delicious yeast rolls with carrot filling, pierogi filled with buckwheat and mint-flavored cottage cheese, and *sekacz*—that's a sort of tree-trunk–shaped cake which is wrapped around a rod and cooked by rotation over a fire. It's very dry and keeps for a long time, so it was just right for a fugitive's picnic bag. She put in a bottle of her cloudy apple juice, and cheese and sausage and honey; she went on and on until my bag was overflowing and very heavy. I didn't try to stop her, for I had no idea where the next lot of food would come from; in any case I sensed that all this frantic preparation of supplies was her way of saying how sorry she was. When we parted, I kissed her for the first time—a little awkwardly, because of that odd distance between us, but for all that there was a definite lump in my throat, and I found it very hard to find the words to thank her. Fela frowned her worried frown; indeed, it had seldom left her face in recent weeks.

Private and rather formal to the last, she gave me only a perfunctory kiss. But then she said, "Don't thank us, Jan. We've enjoyed having you. The house will seem empty without you." And I knew that that, for her at least, was all too true.

Stefan, who'd made an earlier journey across the damp fields to the stable with blankets for me—we were now well into November, and the nights were getting very cold again—was confused to the last. He kissed me on both cheeks, but then he growled, "You keep reading the Bible, Jan. If I can claim to have turned one Jew into a Christian when I get to the gates of heaven, then maybe I'll be allowed in. But you've been a good lad, even though you're a Jew. It's hard to see how God might punish me for helping you."

Fela unashamedly raised her eyes to those much-discussed heavens. I thanked them again and then was on my way with a mixture of relief, regret, excitement, and dread.

Henryk was late at our rendezvous next morning. A thick mist lay on the fields, and he'd mistaken the way, so that by the time he arrived at the bus stop near the station I was already very agitated, fearing the worst and wondering what on earth I would do if he never arrived. We had to take a later train than planned; apart from that the journey was without incident. Very different from my previous trip to Warsaw! The railway carriage was packed, but no one said a word to anyone else. In those days it was safer, even for ordinary Polish citizens, to remain silent among strangers. And this time there was no small child to break the rules.

Warsaw, in the autumn of 1943, was officially *Judenrein* or "free of Jews." In July, after what must be one of the greatest urban blood-baths of the twentieth century, the Nazis systematically blew up the mountains of ruin and rubble to which the ghetto had been reduced, despite superhuman attempts on the part of Jewish survivors to fight a rearguard action. Only a few hundred had eventually escaped and made their way, mainly through the sewers, to the Aryan parts of the city. I think perhaps I should give you some figures so that you can see for yourself the scale of the slaughter.

On the day of the German invasion on September 1, 1939, Jews living in Warsaw represented one-third of the capital's population. Only in New York were there more Jews in a single city. When Henryk and I got back to our home city at the end of November 1943, only one person in ninety was Jewish as opposed to one in three, and all of these in hiding. It seems to me that only one conclusion emerges: Everything is possible. That is the everlasting legacy of all those things to which may be given the collective term *Auschwitz*. In the realm of human ruthlessness, the only limits are those of human imagination; everything imaginable is possible.

We spent the first couple of nights in Warsaw sleeping on the floor of the flat which Joseph shared with other resistance workers. But Henryk and I were soon able to find lodgings of our own, for our Aryan looks, our good counterfeit papers, and our excellent Polish gave little cause for suspicion. Henryk grew a mustache and took to wearing spectacles, for he ran the constant risk of bumping into old friends or acquaintances who might recognize and give him away— intentionally or otherwise. It wasn't a perfect disguise by any means, but anyone who hadn't seen him for a while would have had to look twice to be sure it was him. His medical skills were in constant demand; all too many of the ten thousand Jews in hiding were sick, wounded, or starving. He would return to our flat in the evening, his face gray and haggard from the suffering he was forced to witness day after day. And from the fear, too. Because you couldn't escape that. You never knew when you were being followed, when you might get caught in a roundup, when a German soldier might ask to see your papers or the contents of your bag, when you might be walking into a trap because the address you'd been given to visit had already been betrayed, or "burned," as we used to call it. I woke up every morning with butterflies in my stomach, and they stayed with me until we had both safely returned to the flat around dusk. I was no stranger to fear by this time, but there was a particular quality about the menace which stalked us during those months in Warsaw. Perhaps it was because we were constantly living a lie, which we hadn't had to do either in the ghetto or the forests except when on food-foraging missions. Even with Stefan and Fela I had been more or less myself within their four walls. The danger seemed somehow more concentrated and unrelieved than in the forests, where despite a thousand threats, both hidden and obvious, we did have days of relaxation and enjoyment.

On the surface, life in Warsaw seemed to go on largely as normal. People shopped, traveled around the city, made appointments, and ran businesses despite the grim ubiquitous presence of the Germans. I had known the city quite well before we were forced into the ghetto when I was twelve, but now there was a continual sense of not knowing what lay underneath commonplace everyday exteriors. Was the nice-looking man who politely asked me the way a German spy? A member of the Polish resistance? An ordinary Polish citizen? Or, like me perhaps, a Jew "passing" as such? Was the kindly-faced priest on the park bench one of those who on Sundays preached venomous sermons against those archenemies of Christianity, those murderers of Christ, the Jews? Or was he, like Father Klyza, among those who did all they could to help victims of this appalling persecution? So did he turn a blind eye to the resistance broadsheets folded into missals in the pews of his church? For that was one of the ways in which we used to find out what was happening to the German armies, and as 1944 progressed, the news of their increasing defeats brought comfort and hope.

I spent about nine months as a courier in Warsaw, and much of what I did was repetitive, so perhaps I'll describe a typical day in my life at that time. I would wake, as I've said, with those butterflies in my stomach. I never got out of bed without wondering if I'd ever feel the comfort of my sheets again. For there was proper bed linen in our rented accommodation although the bedspreads were the sort you often

saw in the war, made of layers of strong paper. On the wall above
the chest of drawers was not a crucifix this time but a picture of the
Virgin Mary, and I found her oddly comforting. It sounds silly, I
know, but perhaps it'll demonstrate my frame of mind if I tell you
that before I left the room each morning I invariably said good-bye to
her. I never felt like eating in the mornings, but Henryk always made
tea and insisted that I have a piece of bread. That was usually all there
was in any case!

I would then go to one of my bosses' addresses. Another house on
Miodowa or one on Senatorska Street usually, where I would fetch
the money I was to distribute or the false documents or sometimes,
though less often, guns. Sometimes the money would be in large wads,
even as many as two thousand five-hundred-zloty notes, so I always
wore two shirts, the under one tucked in tightly at the waist to conceal
the notes which I wore wrapped around me as evenly as possible. One
of the courier girls in Senatorska Street sewed a false bottom into my
"Ghetto Uprising" bag, and I carried guns around in that. Sometimes
I would meet contacts in cafés, where I would hand over photographs
for new identity cards, and then make a rendezvous in a different café
to collect the finished product. I had a certain number of addresses of
people in hiding to whom I was responsible for deliveries of money,
newspapers, and documents, and I had to learn them by heart as nothing
was to be recorded in writing. I also had to find out how to get to
each one without asking directions, not as easy as it sounds as there
were countless different stairways leading off countless courtyards all
looking almost identical. And to call on the wrong address could quite
literally be fatal.

As you may imagine, now that I was back in Warsaw, I was anxious
to make contact with Eli's foster parents. The address Korczak had
given me was in the southern suburb of Ochota. I was very tempted
to go there in the first few days, yet something held me back. Caution
was now becoming second nature to me. So I gave the name and
address to one of my bosses, and she promised to make inquiries for

me. I heard nothing for some time and didn't like to pester her; everyone was so busy and in such a constant state of high tension. But I was left with a certain degree of hope which gave me a pleasant little shock every time I thought of it.

We messengers were not supposed to use public transport because the Germans had a habit of carrying out random searches on the buses and trams. Sometimes the drivers would slow down between stops to warn passengers that a patrol was approaching or waiting at the next stop, though there wasn't usually much anyone could do about it anyway. The Germans would often check not only identity cards but also written evidence of one's current address and employment, to ascertain that everyone was helping the German war effort. Henryk had managed to obtain such evidence for me in the course of his travels, from a Communist in the People's Guard, who was sympathetic to Jews and who ran a laundry. All the same, I should have known better than to risk public transport; I had been warned.

But one day I was weary from a lot of walking and my hip injury was beginning to ache, so I decided to risk it. The bus was crowded, and I had to stand, crammed in tight between the other passengers. I had one more visit to make, and then there would be just enough time to get home before dark. After about two stops there was a sudden shout, and turning around, I saw that three German soldiers were standing on the pavement, hailing the bus. It stopped. They climbed onto the rear platform, packing the crowd in tighter still. Under my two shirts I was acutely aware of the false identity papers, which I was taking to an address in the Old Town, against my skin. I hoped the sweat wouldn't make the ink run. Fear descended on the interior of the bus; you could almost *touch* the silence. I was convinced that the documents would rustle treacherously if I so much as shivered, so I stood as still as I could, clutching the overhead support ring with an iron grip. When we got to the next stop, I heard the dreaded " '*Raus*" repeated several times. Darting a quick glance over my shoulder, I saw that three or four of the passengers unlucky enough to be nearest the platform were being ordered out onto the pavement. Then one of the Germans shouted, "*Fahren Sie weiter*," and the bus lurched forward. You could actually hear the collective breath of relief! But I'd learned my lesson, and I never used public transport in Warsaw again— at least not until long after the war.

This is not turning out to be one typical day at all, as I promised, but rather a random collection of memories. They'll give you an idea of my life as a courier, anyway. Another day I had a much closer shave with the Germans, and this time it was the Gestapo. I was just entering a courtyard on my way to one of the families I liked to visit best; they were always very friendly and so pitifully grateful to see me with their allocation of zlotys that I usually stopped to have a game of chess with their eleven-year-old son, Reb (I had learned chess from Dr. Korczak himself), while his mother made me a cup of tea. It became a sort of social occasion which we all enjoyed. I can see them now in that one cramped room, becoming paler and thinner every time I visited, but I have completely forgotten the names of the adults. I was just turning the corner when I heard the familiar dreaded sound of boots and shouted orders, and there, being marched toward me, was my nice, friendly family—father, who'd been a lawyer, mother, and two sons aged eleven and eight. I stood there paralyzed. Would the boys show that they recognized me? Their mother must have registered the danger at the same moment, for she put her hand around her younger son's head and turned his face in toward her. A natural gesture of maternal protectiveness under the circumstances, but one which undoubtedly saved my life. How long was my extraordinary luck going to last? Eleven-year-old Reb, to his eternal credit, showed no sign of recognition. It was terrible, having to let them pass like that—without a word of farewell, without the smallest gesture of solidarity. I later discovered that they had been given away by their landlord's sister, after a family quarrel.

It haunted me for a very long time, that scene; I can even remember that Reb was wearing a blue sweater and a woolly hat. I've never really shed the feeling that I let them down when they most needed me. Absurd really, given the circumstances, but there you are. By this stage of the war it was becoming an all-too-familiar feeling. . . .

Henryk was, as always, a comfort. On that occasion I remember his saying that the family would have gone with a sense of satisfaction that at least they had managed to outwit the Germans by saving my life at the very moment of their own capture. He was probably right. But I dreamed about it for weeks afterward.

And that was another thing. The dreams. My sleep became shallow and fitful and disturbed again, as it had been in the ghetto. For all the claustrophobic and clammy, itchy conditions of the bunker, on the whole I had managed to sleep surprisingly well in the forests. Now every night was plagued by nightmares. There would be a jumble of faces, some of the dearest, but somehow fragmented and only half familiar. There was my mother, who had died in her bed, dying, like Eva, from a bullet and bleeding to death on the ground. Stefan would raise a glass and turn into a grinning SS officer. Franek would acquire spectacles and gradually merge with Korczak, and then Korczak would raise a huge butcher's knife and—oh, travesty of the dreamworld!— use it to murder Vasily. I would wake up more tired than when I went to sleep and began to feel more ill than when I was first recuperating from my bullet wounds.

One night our landlord appeared at the door. He exchanged a few whispered words with Henryk, who seemed to be hesitating. The landlord then ran downstairs but came back immediately, flushed and out of breath and triumphantly bearing aloft a large bottle of vodka. Perhaps the reason that our landlord, Mr. Galeski, had been so conveniently lacking in curiosity about us was that he himself was heavily involved with the black market and didn't want us to ask *him* too many searching questions. He never queried the fact that we were both "laundry workers," though we were afraid that Henryk's obviously well-educated speech would make him suspicious. Henryk made up a story about a recurrent digestive illness that had not only disqualified him from the army but also prevented him from following a proper career! If he had admitted to being an unemployed doctor, the game would have been up immediately.

Anyway, by the night in question Galeski had obviously decided that we could be trusted. He wondered if we'd care to have a drink with him! Henryk decided it would be dangerous to refuse; we couldn't risk offending him. "But we must take great care not to get drunk," he said when Galeski had disappeared for a second time to fetch glasses. "Vodka loosens tongues. One glass for you—and two for me," he added with a smile.

The vodka offered solace, and I slept dreamlessly that night, better than I had for weeks. But it was the start, I'm afraid, of a habit. Partly to please Galeski but partly, I suspect, because the alcohol gave blessed, if temporary, relief from the constant dragging fear, Henryk bought a regular supply. Galeski had a friend who owned one of the illegal stills, and this vodka, or moonshine, was every bit as strong as the rough stuff Ilya had got hold of in the forest. Henryk was careful to watch my intake but less careful with his own—except, that is, when Galeski visited us, and then he never had more than two glasses, pleading the useful alibi of his digestive weakness!

After a while we developed a little domestic routine. The first one home would lay the table with the plates and glasses, put the potatoes on to boil, and sweep the floor. Occasionally we'd have eggs or a piece of meat to stew, though often the meal just consisted of potatoes and carrots or pea soup and bread. We didn't need to sweep the floor every day, but there was a certain comfort in the regularity of these little rituals.

Sometimes Henryk would pour himself a drink before we sat down to eat. Every day he was witnessing desperate situations and with only a few drugs smuggled to him by sympathizers or bought on the black market, and no equipment at his disposal, there was more often than not nothing he could do. The worst cases, he told me, were the children, particularly those who were never allowed to see the light of day.

Pitiful little cases of malnutrition, rickets, chronic chest infections, moldering away in cellars or shut away in lofts. Once a nine-year-old child said to him, "Today isn't so bad because it's raining. It doesn't hurt so much not being able to go out." The particular safe house where he was staying with his parents overlooked a playground which must have intensified the little boy's torture. The anecdote made me wonder about Eli again.

Then, soon after that, I had news of her—for what it was worth. My caution in not going straight to her last-known address had been well advised. My courier boss, a nice plump girl called Marysia, had discovered from a contact on the grapevine that Eli's foster parents had started to receive blackmail threats from someone who must have guessed the truth about her—or perhaps from someone close to them who actually knew the truth. They had moved away from the area and for obvious reasons had left no forwarding address. Now the thought of her was no longer followed by that pleasant little leap of hope which had become rather familiar. Henryk listened, as always, with attention and patience. "After the war, Jan, I'll help you find her. We'll manage it, you see." Empty words, as we both knew, but comforting all the same. Only much later in the evening, perhaps so as not to compete with my sadness, did he tell me what had happened to him that day.

"I saw something this morning that would have broken Korczak's heart. A baby, accidentally smothered to death by her mother; there were Germans in the shop above, and she was afraid the crying would give them all away." I saw the tears in his eyes, but mine were dry. There were times, many of them, when I thought I'd come to the end of my capacity to care.

The quiet evenings with Henryk sipping tea and listening to a few old records on a gramophone which Galeski had lent us, were the best thing about those months in the underground movement in Warsaw. Sitting on our beds, with our backs against the peeling yellow walls, we talked for hours about everything as, in the background and between scratches, the passages of melancholy and longing in Tchaikovsky's piano concertos echoed and magnified our own. Our cover story was that Henryk was my uncle, my mother's younger brother, to explain the connection and the difference in our ages and names. My mother had died tragically young of TB. That at least was no lie. Though in my own mother's case, of course, the end had been hastened by gross malnutrition. And I really came to think of Henryk as my uncle. He talked to me freely about his wife and son, who both died in the ghetto of the typhus epidemic which had also claimed my father.

"I loved Stasia very much." He got up to put some water on to boil. "As much, perhaps, as you loved Eva."

"Did it show so clearly?"

He replied gently, "Yes, Jan, it showed." We were silent for a few moments while he went across to our one chest of drawers and opened the top drawer. He handed me a crumpled little paper bag. I looked at it, puzzled, and then opened it. Inside was a coil of green velvet ribbon. Eva's.

"I've been waiting for the right moment to give you this. It was Berek's idea to save it for you. When we buried her, together with Franek, in the same grave."

I didn't know what to say, and if I had, I wouldn't have been able to say it. Suddenly she was there before me, shaking with silent laughter as she had that first day in the train. All I could do was lay the ribbon over the palm of my hand and stroke its soft texture. I must have given Henryk a helpless look because he came over and sat on the bed and put a hand briefly on my shoulder. Somehow Henryk's support was always just right: there when I needed it but never intrusive. The sort of support I have so manifestly failed to give you, Richard.

"She was so brave and so beautiful," I managed to say at last, almost choking with pride as well as grief.

Henryk said thoughtfully, "And always will be. A formidable rival for future loves." I couldn't have known then how acutely prophetic those words were to prove.

* * *

Henryk and I came to rely solely on each other for support, and I know that I couldn't have survived those nine months as a courier without him. But because we were always worried for each other's safety, I doubt whether we told each other everything about the risks we ran and the close escapes we had. I didn't, for example, tell him about the time when, with two precious guns to deliver, I slipped on a film of ice and dropped my bag, spilling the cover of potatoes all over the pavement. Two nice old ladies helped me pick them up, and if they noticed that the "empty" bag was extremely heavy, they gave no sign. Afterward I had to sit on the steps of a building for a few moments, pretending to nurse a bruised knee but in reality waiting for my poor heart to stop pounding!

One dreadful evening Henryk had still not arrived home by curfew, which was long after dark. I was quite convinced that that was the end; I'd never see him again. I couldn't sit still and kept looking for jobs to do in those two small rooms, which were already perfectly clean and tidy. I decided to move all the furniture, pretending that the floor needed a really thorough sweep. Moving Henryk's bed away from the wall, I found underneath it a small bottle containing clear liquid. A quick sniff confirmed my suspicion. Vodka. So Henryk had started to have a surreptitious drink, probably in the mornings before going out on his helpless rounds. I pushed the bed back, leaving the bottle exactly where I'd found it. Apart from occasionally falling asleep in the middle of a conversation in the evenings, Henryk had never shown evidence of having drunk too much, and if he wanted this to be a secret, then that was his right. I confess that on the evening in question I myself had had several swigs of vodka, as well as boiled dry two pans of water, burning the potatoes beyond redemption, before Henryk finally appeared in the doorway.

He had, in fact, been only a few blocks away for the past two hours, hiding in a deserted courtyard. After leaving his last patient, he'd become aware of being followed. Torn between openly confronting his pursuer and giving him the slip, he had chosen the latter. He thought, but wasn't certain, that the man had been in the year above him at medical school.

"Rather a nice person as far as I remember. If it's the same one. But he'd probably have known that I was a Jew, and I could only deduce the worst from the fact that he was following me."

As it happened, that particular experience had a happy sequel. Henryk bumped into the man again, this time when I was with him. It was in a restaurant run by nuns in an old community center in a quiet side street which, as it was never visited by Germans, had developed into a meeting place for resistance workers of all kinds, Polish and Jewish. On that second occasion the man, who was called Anton, introduced himself properly; he was indeed a former fellow student of Henryk's and, knowing he was Jewish, had wanted to make contact to offer help. He had followed him for some time that earlier evening, under the mistaken impression that Henryk was leading him to a safe place where they could talk. It was only after Henryk's disappearance in the shadows that Anton realized his mistake.

"I'm really sorry, I must have scared you," he apologized, holding out his hand to each of us in turn. And to make amends he bought us both a meal, for, as a member of the Communist People's Guard, he had more money than we did. I remember it well: roast loin of horse, which was quite a luxury after weeks of potatoes and pea or cabbage soup! Talking of money, I never discovered exactly where the money I had to distribute came from or how it reached us. We weren't told anything we didn't strictly need to know, for obvious reasons, but I believe there was a fund set up and administered by the official Polish underground in London, specifically for the purpose of helping Jews in hiding, and that this was bolstered by foreign Jewish interests. Also, some of the Jews remaining in Warsaw took extra risks by engaging in black-market business, which could be lucrative.

As Henryk did, in a minor way. We were very lucky with our friendly and incurious landlord, but the trouble was that he became rather too friendly! He couldn't understand why we were so reluctant to take his moonshine to the laundry where he thought we worked and after a while tried instead to persuade us to set up a trade in saccharine, another black-market commodity which was very popular in those sugarless days. To save too many questions' being asked, Henryk gave in over the saccharine, which was at least easier to secrete and carry. But he put his foot down when Galeski tried to persuade me to take some, too.

"I can't endanger the boy. I'd never forgive myself; my sister would rise from the grave," he argued. Even I was nearly convinced!

But Henryk's "commercial" activities made a little extra cash for us, which was extremely welcome, and we did eat rather better after that. Once or twice he even brought home cakes from a patisserie—not as delicious as the things you can buy now, as most necessary ingredients were, of course, either synthetic and second-rate or simply unavailable. All the same, to my palate—used to Piotr's *kasza* and "forest" stew and then, in Warsaw, endless bread, potatoes, and watery soup—they were a luxury indeed!

But unfortunately Galeski's attentions didn't stop there. He then started trying to get us to go to church with him! Henryk made up something about having had a crisis of faith when his sister, my "mother," died, but Galeski made up his mind that he'd be saving our soul if he persuaded us to return to the fold. Again, in order to escape suspicion, Henryk gave in.

Galeski chose a church near the cathedral for our "reintroduction" to the faith, and he chose Good Friday for the timing. Easter fell earlier that year than in 1943, so it wasn't the precise anniversary of Operation Easter Blessing in the forests of Parczew, or of the early days of the Ghetto Uprising in Warsaw, but you may imagine that those were the events which the Christian festival brought all too vividly to mind.

The Easter sermon taught me a lot. It did not teach me, as the priest intended it should, about the sins of the Pharisees, the Jews who betrayed Jesus and handed him over to the Roman authorities, who resisted Pontius Pilate's pleas for clemency and insisted that he be killed in the slow agony of crucifixion, who later compounded their sins against Christianity by murdering Christian children for their Passover feast, which often coincides with Easter itself. Not at all. What it did teach me was that Jesus' great and universally valid second commandment is of no consequence to some of Jesus' most ardent and faithful followers.

And more even than that. I learned that some men claiming to possess spiritual power can, with their strident certainties, pervert and devalue the essence of the things they stand for. It was a bewildering and lasting lesson. A paradox which confirmed my growing conviction that in mankind everything is possible. The anti-Semitic message of hatred that rang out in clarion tones that Good Friday in the Old Town in Warsaw was the very antithesis of what Jesus died for. Yet elsewhere in Poland—and across Europe, although of course, I didn't know that at the time—Christians were giving their lives in isolated and desperate attempts to halt the deadly consequences of that message. Father Klyza had been one of them; without his courage I probably wouldn't even have been alive to hear that sermon. It occurs to me that in a way the Church failed its own members almost more than it failed the Jews.

And if there were among the Christians some spiritual leaders who dressed up self-satisfaction and hatred in showy religious exhortation, then, conversely, there were among the brutes who occupied our country some individuals who were not slavish followers of the evil ideology they had come to enforce. I know, because I came across one.

It was in Nowiniarska Street, which ran right up to the ghetto wall and was almost always virtually empty. I used to visit a grocer's shop there because the prices were reasonable, the service obliging, and you could linger as long as you liked over a cup of tea or coffee, or what passed for coffee in those days, without being urged to buy more. After a while I came to be on quite friendly terms with Igor, the proprietor, and, though I never gave him any cause to believe that I was Jewish, he began gradually to confide in me, perhaps because my youth and innocent appearance made me seem trustworthy. He kept an illegal radio hidden in his dog's kennel in the backyard, so he would give me up-to-date information about the war situation, which I would then gleefully report back to Henryk. By the summer of 1944 it really did seem as if the end were approaching. The eastern front was moving closer almost every day.

But Igor had disturbing ideas about Stalin and the Soviets. Henryk and I, and, indeed, all the Jews we came into contact with, saw Stalin as our potential liberator. Our only hope, we thought, was the successful conclusion of the Soviet campaign. Igor, on the other hand, likened Stalin to Hitler and hadn't a good word to say for him. Igor had been in the upper house of the Polish parliament before the war and was an experienced politician. An astute one in his judgment of Stalin, too, as events were to prove.

The little coffee shop was on the first floor of the building, up a long, steep flight of stairs, and from there I could see Jewish slave workers clearing away the rubble of the ruined ghetto; Igor told me they had been brought from Auschwitz to do the job. Wagonloads of bricks and metal were being carted away on specially laid tracks. So great was the devastation that I could see clear across to the other side, to the site of the old Jewish cemetery. There, in June 1942, Dr. Korczak had obtained through bribes a tiny space for us to bury our mother, and my sister Rachel had planted her tribute of two bloodred geraniums, lovingly nurtured in time for Mother's birthday a few weeks before her death. Poor little Rachel. Barely ten at the time, and with only six more weeks to live! What strange accident of birth had given *me* the Aryan features and therefore the chance to live? Did I have any right at all to this advantage? Would I ever be worthy of the fact that I had gone on and on surviving when so many others, so many betters, had not?

But it didn't do to gaze too long or too intently at the haunted desolation that had once been my home. It might easily make someone suspicious.

From the coffee shop Igor had had little option but to witness the carnage of the Ghetto Uprising over a year before. He told me how outraged he'd been by the way many of his compatriots had come to stare at the slaughter, making callous or flippant remarks as they did so—often on their way to the fair the Nazis had set up, just the other side of the wall on Krasinski Square. "There were occasions when they made me ashamed to be Polish," he told me. Did his gaze linger on me for an extra moment or two? Was he half expecting a confession?

One day a German officer came into the shop. He exchanged some razor blades for bread and then looked through the window, out over the remains of the ghetto. He told Igor that he hadn't heard from his wife and sons since the British had started bombing Hamburg, his home city. He was very worried, he said. "It makes you realize what some of those poor devils over there had to go through. That should never have happened; there was no reason for wholesale murder and cruelty like that."

Only the German, Igor, and myself were in the shop at the time. Whenever a German appeared, which wasn't frequent but had happened before, I pretended to be engrossed in the newspaper as I drank my tea. But when I heard these remarks, I was so amazed I looked up at him with a spontaneous, involuntary movement of the head. Too late I realized my mistake.

He must have noticed the movement out of the corner of his eye, for he turned his own head, and for one long moment we stared at each other. I knew without any shadow of doubt that at that instant he realized I was a Jew. Don't ask me how I knew, but I did; the certainty stood between us, palpable, like a third person. Then I remembered some advice Henryk had given me. "In an awkward situation, smile your nice smile. No German would ever expect a Jew to smile at them."

Accordingly I gave him what I hoped was both a sweet and respectful smile before returning to the German-language propaganda sheet which passed for a newspaper in those days. But not before he had returned the smile, as if to seal our fleeting conspiracy of silence.

When he had gone, Igor said to me, "At least one German with a bit of human feeling. I was tempted to say, but didn't quite dare, that the Nazis won't succeed in wiping out a whole people. One day out of those ashes over the wall there, the phoenix will surely rise."

I nodded wisely, though not having had any classical education, I really didn't know what he meant. Later I repeated his words to Henryk. I remember that we were standing at the window, watching huge raindrops explode on the gray street two stories below.

He explained to me about the mythical bird whose own funeral ashes were supposed to give birth to its young. Then Henryk said thoughtfully, "Yes, Igor is right. Certainly we have to believe that; otherwise there would be no point in this struggle or in going on at all. But is that enough? Can the phoenix sing, Jan? That's what I would like to know. That's another question altogether."

It was to be a long time before I understood Henryk's question. Now, nearly thirty years later, I still don't really have the answer.

JULY 18

Dear Katie,

After the last bit of Misha's story, I was ashamed to keep my secret to myself any longer. I couldn't—not after I'd read about babies' being suffocated by their mothers to stop them crying and revealing their hiding place. Because they had committed the crime of being Jewish. And all the other things—you're going to have to read all this when you come (which I hope will be soon).

So I told Mum the whole story. The Head is due back any moment now, they say, so it'll all come out then, anyway. But I didn't want her to hear from anyone else. Not now. And I did actually want her to know that I was sorry and that I just hadn't realized the implications of what we were doing. Because after all it wasn't only me. I just kept watch. Just. That's what a lot of people did in Warsaw while others died in their thousands in the ghetto right there under their noses. Just kept watch. And in hundreds of other places, too—not just Poland.

When I told Mum, she was surprisingly calm about the whole thing. I think part of me wanted her to make a fuss and beat the hell out of me, but she just said, "Well, I'm glad you realize how serious it was now." And that was that. In a way, that's a worse reaction than going over the top, and more than ever I wonder what Misha would say. Or will say, because he'll sure as hell find out. And if he doesn't, I think I have to tell him. I think I owe him that now, at the very least.

I just felt like writing, though I haven't said much, I know! I'll add more later on tomorrow.

For now, kisses.

> *Rich*

One day toward the end of July I had a nice surprise. I was given documents to take to a new address, which didn't mean anything to me until I got there; it turned out to be Granny's. As I approached the house, I remembered so clearly my previous journey, darting after Eva through the shadows of deserted, ruined buildings, my clothes caked and stinking of sewage. My first night of freedom! And a strange sort of freedom it had turned out to be.

Granny was touchingly pleased to see me still alive. The kitchen was just as I remembered, but it did give me a pang to see someone else's clothes drying over the range. She was hiding a survivor from the Ghetto Uprising who had come back to Warsaw after many months in nearby forests. Her youngest grandson, who was a little older than I was, was there, too. Antek, whom I was to get to know very well indeed.

I had to tell Granny about Eva, of course, though not in any detail, because I couldn't bring myself to do that. She left the room for a few minutes after I'd broken the news, and Antek said, "Eva was her favorite. I think she was everyone's favorite."

So Antek had known her, too. For some reason I resented that. I was happy for her to have been Granny's favorite, but I resented her being everyone's. Eva belonged to me—and to Franek and Henryk and Vasily—and there was now no room for newcomers in the enclosed world we had shared.

I was very relieved when he added, as an afterthought, "Not that I met her more than once. But she *was* pretty striking."

Talk turned, inevitably, to liberation. By that time the distant thud of artillery fire to the east of the Vistula could be heard almost constantly, and processions of weary, bedraggled German deserters, retreating from the front, were now a familiar sight. Occasionally Soviet planes flew over the city, which was in a state of tense expectancy. Everyone knew "something" was about to happen.

Antek, who had just joined a unit of the Home Army, was excited and eager. "It'll be time to fight any moment now. It surely can't be much longer."

Granny shook her head and said nothing as she laid the table with warm new bread and cake and, yes, a pot of plum jam!

Nearly a quarter of a million civilians and soldiers died in the sixty-five days of fighting which were called the Warsaw Uprising and which began on August 1, 1944. There is disagreement as to how many Jews took part, as those who joined the ranks of the Home Army almost invariably concealed their identity, fearful of the unknown consequences of anti-Semitism among their cofighters; the number, however, has been estimated as between one and two thousand.

On the afternoon of August 1, I was in the southern suburb of Mokotow, where I'd had to take ammunition and messages to a group of Jews in hiding there. I had started on my way back when I grew suddenly aware that the streets had become unusually quiet and deserted. An eerie silence had descended on the suburb. I stopped and looked around, immediately understanding that whatever it was that had been going to happen was starting—now. I heard again Henryk's anxious parting. "Come straight back. And after today I don't want them sending you beyond the Old Town. Anything could happen anytime now." The Old Town! Now a remote hour's walk away—under normal conditions. In the distance some rifle shots punctured the unnatural silence; then, after a pause, machine-gun fire. I didn't know what to do. If I continued walking home, in the direction of the gunfire, goodness knows what I might walk into the middle of. On the other hand, I knew no one in Mokotow except the Jews I had just visited, and I couldn't really impose myself on them as they were cramped enough already. To put off the moment of decision, I made for a small park I knew where I thought I might be able to sit and consider my options for a few minutes.

To my surprise, however, the park was full of people. I hovered, diffidently, again unsure what to do next. They were mostly boys and young men, not much older than I was. I watched for a little while and presently saw a taxi draw up with a red and white flag on the bonnet. A girl got out and immediately began distributing similar red-and-white armbands. Some of the men stepped forward and helped to unload submachine guns and rifles. I had realized by now that all these young people must be a company of the Home Army, assembling for the long-awaited Uprising against the Germans. An idea was just formulating in my mind when I heard someone call softly, "Jan?" At first I didn't look around, accustomed as I was to extreme caution.

"Jan." The call came again, louder this time. And then I saw Antek, Granny's fourth grandson, crossing the road toward me. He came up and embraced me warmly.

"Come and join us, my *Polish* friend," he whispered in my ear, making it clear that I should not attempt to reveal my true identity.

"I ought to go back—the others—Henryk—waiting," I stammered. He stepped back and shook his head.

"Jan, it's too late for that. Don't you realize, the Uprising has begun? I'm afraid you're stuck here—with us."

I felt the panic twist deep down in my gut. At that moment I wanted

more than anything else to be sitting on my bed in our room in Miodowa Street. Would I ever get back there? Would I ever see Henryk
again?

Antek introduced me to his platoon commander, who welcomed me
without query, despite my obvious youthfulness. As he spoke, he took
out a pistol and pushed it into the belt over his jacket. That struck me
as a symbolic gesture; it meant that now the Uprising was open and
declared, no longer a conspiracy discussed in whispers and awaited in
secret. And that, quite simply, is how I became a member of the Polish
Home Army.

I was among the lucky half of the company who were given enough
ammunition and grenades to go into action almost immediately. We
tried, two or three times, to assault a heavily guarded SS barracks
which before the war had been a school. We fought all night, but the
German fire was intense, and by dawn we were forced to retreat and
prepare for an expected German counterattack. By this time, however,
despite our disappointment, more encouraging news was beginning to
filter through from other sectors of Mokotow and the rest of Warsaw.
Large areas had been cleared of the enemy, we heard, and all that
remained was for the rebel forces to link up with one another, eliminat-
ing Germans from the key streets and buildings which separated them.
Soon, very soon, reinforcements would arrive from the west by air
and the Soviet army would cross the Vistula and help rid us, finally,
of Nazi oppression.

Or so we thought. But as everyone now knows, that never happened.
I think it is generally acknowledged that the decision to launch the
Uprising was a tragic mistake. Although no doubt taken for honorable
motives, it was fundamentally unrealistic. It underestimated not only
the residual strength of the German Army but also the political cynicism
of Stalin, who was more than happy to stand aside and watch the
Germans use up their remaining energy in disposing of his political
opponents—or, if you like, smoothing his way for him.

But all that belongs to hindsight, luxuries not afforded at the time to the participants of such shattering events. All I knew was that we were fighting to rid our city of the oppressors and that I was glad to do with all my heart—as both Pole and Jew.

The next few weeks were spent either attacking positions occupied by Germans or "resting" in deserted buildings while our comrades used the rifles and machine guns, for there were only enough arms for half our company at a time. Our ranks became swollen by men, women, and children—some as young as twelve—begging to be taken on as couriers or to help in any way possible. The couriers did a marvelous job delivering messages and progress reports through the sewers to companies in other parts of the city. I had to admire them in silence, for of course, I remembered all too vividly the horror of those tunnels though I couldn't admit to having used them as an escape route from the ghetto. I felt, humbly, that my own job as a courier over the previous eight or nine months had been easy by comparison.

Our suburb of Mokotow changed character. Polish-language newspapers and broadsheets were distributed regularly, placards with patriotic slogans and orders made sudden appearances overnight, an insurgent radio station began to broadcast, and the Home Army even issued its own stamps for a while during the Uprising! Polish flags replaced swastikas, and former street names started to reappear. It really did begin to feel as if the old times might be returning, despite the constant sound of gunfire, which was never far away, and the ever-present smell of smoke.

The thought of Henryk was a constant torture. Sometimes I wondered if I had it in me to go down into the sewers again, to try and reach the Old Town where the fighting was fiercest and where I guessed he would be with the remnants of the Jewish resistance. But of course, I had no real idea of his whereabouts. And even if I found him, would I be able to contribute more than I was doing at the moment? Would I be able to help him? I might easily get killed on a totally fruitless mission. And after it was all over, when he found out what had happened, how bitterly he would regret my pointless gesture. Or perhaps he would never find out and would always wonder what had happened to me. Or was all this a way of rationalizing my blinding terror of going down into the sewers again? Was it a way of concealing from myself the fact that my fear was stronger than my love for Henryk? But I could have died for him, I honestly believe that, just not that way—not in the sewers.

One day, toward the end of August, something happened which banished even Henryk from my mind—at least for a short time. I was off duty after a particularly intense burst of fighting on the front line. In my house alone two comrades had been killed, and another had had his arm blown off. From a first-floor window I had thrown a grenade at an armored car, which had burst into flame. They were the first—and only—Germans I ever killed, and I don't even know how many of them there were. Even at the time I didn't care to think of how those men died. Today I shudder at the thought. But if I tell you that in Mokotow a third of all the insurgents died, and almost as many were badly wounded, you'll understand that this was a battle for survival, where squeamish sentiment had no place.

Anyway, afterward I was walking along a quiet street well behind the front line with Antek when all of a sudden the dive bombers appeared. They were regular visitors those days, and there was no defense against them. You just darted into the nearest shelter and hoped for the best. Together with a lot of other people, Antek and I rushed for cover into the basement of a large house. I remember the frightened shriek of a baby before the roar of the Stuka engines blotted out the sound. Then there was a single moment's silence. I think "deathly" silence is the phrase. And then an ear-shattering crash, as the house collapsed around us.

Can you imagine the effect of being buried under three floors of rubble on a boy already prone to acute claustrophobia? Fortunately, for the first few minutes I was numb with shock. Then I became aware of Antek shivering—no, shuddering—beside me.

"Jan, what's happened, what's happened?" I looked around the tiny space we were filling.

"We seem to have been saved by two huge beams," I heard myself say matter-of-factly, as if the words were coming from someone else. I noticed that they echoed strangely, too.

Just as my life had already been saved by many people, Antek now saved my sanity. But he did it in a very unconscious way—by being even more terrified than I was! It wasn't so much the sense of being confined and buried that frightened him as the certainty that no one would ever find us and that we'd die a slow, anguished death, forgotten beneath the ruins. It was a well-founded fear, although I knew that strenuous efforts were always made to find survivors.

I spent the next few hours—I've no idea exactly how long it was—trying to keep us both above the level of panic. I have no doubt that the burden of having to be strong for Antek saved me quite literally from going mad. Every so often he would clasp my arm in an iron grip and say, "We're going to die, we'll never get out of here," and I would stroke his stretched white knuckles and mutter soothing, meaningless words. Remembering that night in the dugout when Vasily and I had calmed Eva with an incessant flow of chatter, I now talked about anything and everything that came into my head. I talked about the orphanage, the ghetto, and the forest, about the German raids and our rescue of the prisoners from Majdanek, about Father Klyza and Stefan. I recited poetry I'd learned as a young child at school and thought, until that moment, I'd forgotten, and I even began to teach him one of the partisan songs, for once unembarrassed by my poor singing voice. Eva and Franek and Vasily and Henryk—they were all there with us in that infernal cavity under the rubble. We had no way of knowing how many of the other people who'd been with us in the basement had been killed, but an intense silence surrounded us.

Then, suddenly, we clearly heard a shout and a scraping sound. Was it a shovel? Then it came again. The joy and the relief were overwhelming. Then the noises stopped, and our renewed terror was worse to bear than at the beginning. Had they given up hope of finding anyone alive? Would they leave us to die from slow and agonizing suffocation?

"It's getting hotter. I think we're running out of oxygen," wailed Antek, gripping my arm once more.

But the scraping sounds began again. We shouted at the top of our lungs, heedless of possible lack of oxygen. There was a pause, and we heard an answering shout, and someone beat out a little tune with a spade. They had heard us! Antek and I embraced and wept with relief. After that it must have taken about half an hour for them to dig us out, but they talked or shouted to us continuously, and after a while we began to see patches of blue sky.

"You were very lucky," said the blond young man who seemed in charge of the rescue, as he wiped away the sweat of his efforts with the sleeve of his gray overalls. "No one else survived in that house." I followed his gaze and saw a pathetic little line of half-crushed corpses laid out in a row on the pavement. Among them were several small children and a baby.

We were slightly injured, though I suspect we both looked worse than we really were. Antek had some nasty cuts, and I had a dislocated ankle and the scar tissue of my upper arm wound had reopened, probably caused by my fall under the impact of the blast or maybe by pieces of falling masonry. We were taken to an improvised field hospital for a few days. It was in the basement of another house, and as the Stuka bombers returned every day, you may imagine how petrified we were that we might be buried alive a second time. As it was, the worst that happened was that two windows in the floor above us were blown out by a nearby blast.

I remember that at the time I was trying to watch one of the doctors performing an operation. Such was his concentration that he never even looked up. I thought of Henryk—well, in fact, I thought of him constantly—but at that moment I wondered, with a sharp, tender pride, whether he was also operating on wounded people under similar conditions in another part of the beleaguered city. So near and yet so very far.

When we got back to our unit, we found that their earlier buoyant mood had changed. The Germans had brought reinforcements from the Russian front and were stepping up the pressure. On September 2 the Home Army finally had to evacuate the Old Town after the most deadly struggle. We heard that survivors carrying some five hundred casualties on stretchers found their way down one single manhole into the sewers and then through four miles of waist-deep sewage to comparative and temporary safety in the center of the city. Quarter after quarter fell to the Germans. Hunger was mounting, and I began to feel that old familiar ache in the pit of my stomach as rations dropped lower every day. In the middle of September a daylight mission by British and American planes attempted to bring in supplies and arms for the rebels—but in vain, for the vast majority of them were taken by Germans. Even in Mokotow, which had not seen the worst of the fighting, cellars were overflowing with the wounded, of whom there were now far too many for the makeshift hospitals. Medicine and bandages were in any case virtually unobtainable by then. No stray dog or cat was safe from being killed and eaten, and at nights we took it in turns to raid some allotments in the no-man's-land between the two front lines for potatoes or anything else we could find. I went twice on these armed expeditions and after the second occasion enjoyed extreme popularity for a brief moment as I had come across two laden tomato plants.

Toward the end of September the Germans began their final assault on Mokotow. It was a Sunday morning, I remember, because some of my comrades-in-arms had held an improvised Mass with two of the last candles in the house we had temporarily taken over. We were suddenly deafened by an onslaught of shells and rockets, which then continued remorselessly until nightfall. Toward evening my platoon was sent to the rear to strengthen the Polish defenses, but despite the fact that we put up a spirited defense of one house after another, killing plenty of Germans in the process, we were pushed steadily backward. It was two or three days later, with half our men killed or severely wounded, when we held less than a square mile of Mokotow, that we were totally surrounded by enemy tanks and troops. It was clear that we couldn't last more than another couple of hours, and so the order came to evacuate and make for the last remaining stronghold of resistance in the central district of the city. The evacuation, needless to say, would have to take place through the sewers.

To begin with, I followed orders and waited meekly in the long queue which quickly formed by the selected manhole. By now it was the early hours of the next morning. Moonshine was passed from mouth to mouth; a lot of people were getting drunk, and I began to drink, too, in the vain hope of drumming up an illusion of courage. Part of me was glad that the queue moved with such agonizing slowness as it helped me to defer the decision I would have to make. But looking back, I don't think I was ever in any real doubt about what I personally would decide to do. Perhaps it was the sight of the moon, hanging low in the sky as it had on Vasily's last night in the forest, when we had gazed at it as if in supplication, half expecting some prophecy or message to give us heart and hope for another sort of freedom. Whatever it was, I suddenly found the strength to lower the bottle and look Antek in the eye.

"I'm not going to do it," I said, with finality.

"Jan, it's the only way. We've got to. We survived the collapsed house; we survived the shelling; we can survive this. You *must*."

It was not for Antek to tell me what I must do.

"I'm sorry, Antek. Enough is enough. You go, and good luck to you."

I moved out of the queue and walked away, without looking back. I didn't want Antek or any of the others I'd fought alongside to ask me questions or try to persuade me. I knew, quite simply, that to go back into those infernal tunnels was beyond me.

But Antek came after me. Perhaps I had underestimated the sense of allegiance he had toward me, after those few shared hours of hell under the bombed house.

"Jan, wait for me. I think you're right. We may stand more chance by giving ourselves up than suffocating to death down there. I've heard they sometimes use gas to flush people out."

I was at once irritated and relieved. It *was* reassuring to have him there, familiar and friendly, but somehow his words crassly underlined my own cowardice. To my shame I wanted to cry, "Shut up, I've been through more than you. *I* know what the sewers are like. You should have braved it once, too." But I just nodded acceptance and avoided his gaze. Thus were laid the foundations of a strangely ambivalent friendship which has lasted to this day.

And that is how, early on the morning of September 26, 1944, I was finally captured by the Germans. Or rather, that is when I surrendered, for there's no point in lying about that now! We surrendered with our arms in the air, a sight I am glad that Eva and Franek and, above all, Vasily never saw. Vasily would have shot himself rather than surrender.

It happened near the little park where we had assembled on August 1. To our great good fortune, we fell into the hands of the Wehrmacht, the regular German Army, and not the SS, who never observed the Geneva Convention and would have either killed us on the spot or sent us to Auschwitz. We were searched, and Antek had his watch confiscated, but the two young soldiers who performed the routine were talking and laughing between themselves and took very little notice of us. We were then marched with others to an assembly point in a military airfield some miles away. I'd had no sleep for a long time, my arm wound was very sore again, and like all the others, I was desperately hungry. So once we got to the airfield, it was with enormous relief that I heard the loudspeaker announce, "Soup will be served!" A cheer went up from what was by now a large crowd of prisoners as caldrons of some steaming substance were brought out. Then there was a wave of consternation: no spoons! How were we to get at this precious lifesaving liquid without spoons? With our hands, one at a time? Surely impossible.

Then someone must have noticed a pile of discarded tins on which we all swooped. I have no idea where they came from, but the important thing was that they served as the crucial implements. Mine had contained sardines, and I was thankful for the tiny drip of strong-flavored oil in the bottom, remembering what Henryk had told me about its nutritional value. It was a bizarre sight—all those men drinking their rations of watery pea soup out of old tins, gingerly and carefully, to avoid cutting themselves on the jagged edges. Some, perhaps those less accustomed to hunger, did drink too greedily and I noticed blood trickling down several chins. To my irritation, Antek managed to cut his finger, and I had to bind it for him with cloth torn from his sleeve.

Later that day we were taken to a transit camp in an abandoned railway depot, where there was nowhere to sleep but on the bare cement floor. No blankets or covers of any kind either, and by the end of September the nights in Poland can be quite cold. Soon after our arrival there we had to stand in line to be inspected; they were looking for Jews, of course, and also—so it was said—for Poles who had mistreated German POWs. German soldiers—ex-POWs—marched up and down, staring into people's faces; Antek and I merited scarcely a glance, but every so often they lingered for a few moments by some poor unfortunate victim, and afterward several men were marched away. Within minutes we heard shots from behind one of the outbuildings.

The next day it was on again to another transit camp, stiff-limbed and still cold from our night on that unrelenting floor. Conditions at the second place were basic, but at least we were fed bread and soup and each given a blanket and a wooden bunk to sleep on, which seemed almost a luxury! We spent about a week there, maybe more, and many times during those days our numbers were swollen by new contingents of Polish prisoners. Each time I eagerly scanned every approaching silhouette, every face, for a sign of Henryk's slim, straight figure and dear, familiar features, but always in vain. And I wasn't the only one to be continually disappointed in this way. Szymon, who had fought in our platoon and who had likewise refused to evacuate through the sewers, although we didn't discover that until we met up at this second transit camp, was also searching very anxiously for someone. His younger brother. Like Henryk and me, they had become separated at the beginning of the Uprising. I can't remember the full story, but I know that Szymon felt very guilty about not having stayed by his brother's side. He claimed that one of the last things his mother had said to them was "Stay together as long as possible; there will be no one else you can trust." Poor Szymon! He was unusually tall, with huge hands and feet, and in our platoon he had been the butt of lots of cruel jokes because of his clumsiness and ungainly appearance. I don't think he'd ever been allowed to take command of a rifle.

Then came the day when we were taken to a nearby station and herded onto trains—or, more accurately, into the cars of a goods train. We were under no illusions. We had been told that we were prisoners of war and were being taken to a camp for POWs in Germany; certainly we had been more or less treated as such since our capture, but what were we to believe now? I, for one, who had seen too many trains leave the *Umschlagplatz* in Warsaw destined for Treblinka, knew that it was not possible to trust Nazis driving closed-in trains. But of course, I couldn't say as much to anyone: even with Antek I never made any allusion to my past, for fear of being overheard or of inviting an indiscretion on his part.

As we crowded into the train, I felt the old enemy claustrophobia rise like an electric current within me. The freight car was very full, though not packed to capacity, and I resisted the momentum which would have pushed me into the middle, making sure I was as near the door as possible. That way I could keep my eye firmly on the slits at the top of the doors. When the doors were shoved to the closed position from the outside and I realized that there was no handle or lever on the inside which could have opened them in an emergency, a wave of nausea threatened to engulf me. We were left there in the dark and without knowing when the journey would begin, probably for about an hour. I managed to keep the panic under control by concentrating hard on Szymon, who was talking to someone else about chess moves. Then, unexpectedly, the doors were torn open again, and someone barked orders at us to get out. We discovered from one of the prisoners who spoke German and had asked the guard what was going on, that some relief organization had made an inspection of a few of the cars and had lodged a complaint that there were no sanitary buckets on board. The matter was now being rectified! There was a general easing of tension; if we were being granted the luxury of buckets, then we were, surely, prisoners of war.

And we certainly needed the buckets. Conditions in those other cars, carrying their human cargo to the concentration camps, must have been almost beyond endurance. As we trundled very slowly through western Poland and on into Germany, we made frequent stops of different durations, and each time the sides of the car would be pulled back, allowing us to chuck our slops out onto the line. Even so, the smell was really foul by the time we reached Berlin. Every time the doors were opened, I took in greedy gulps of air, and when they were clanged shut again, I squeezed as close to them as possible so that I could peer out through the cracks in the boards and persuade myself that I could get out if necessary!

As we approached Berlin, Szymon hoisted me onto his shoulders so that I could see out through the slits under the roof. I remember Antek saying excitedly, "This is the first time I've been abroad!"

How he could feel the slightest quiver of excitement at being in Germany I couldn't begin to understand.

Altogether the journey took about three days and nights. We stopped for several hours in Berlin, where the German Red Cross provided us with soup. Having heard about the bomb devastation in the city, we were surprised, when the sides of the car were pulled back, that the houses which could be seen from the station were intact—in fact, spruce and tidy with little or no sign of rubble. After a while, however, someone noticed that what we were staring at were only facades, with no buildings behind them. We fervently hoped that they would prove symbolic of the state of the German Reich!

By the time we arrived at our camp near Bremen, I was really quite used to the train and no longer suffering from waves of claustrophobia, but it was a great relief to be allowed out into the fresh air. After three days of virtual immobility and almost nothing to eat, the three-mile march to the camp was physically exhausting, and several of the prisoners fainted on the way. My arm, still not completely healed again, ached badly.

The camp, or stalag, was in the shape of a huge square surrounded by barbed wire, but it wasn't overlooked by the sinister wooden turrets one associates with concentration camps, and there was only one armed guard to each side. The square was divided down the middle by a central avenue, and on either side were three or four compounds, reserved for different nationalities. The buildings were makeshift and of wood or metal, except for a separate barracks in brick for the guards.

For several days we were kept in a compound for arrivals, and on our second day a large consignment of new prisoners arrived. For a few moments hope flared again as I scanned the faces; then I realized that they spoke a different language—Slovak—and had not come from anywhere near Warsaw.

I was a prisoner of war for seven months, and my life for the whole of that time was dominated by two overwhelming preoccupations: hunger and fear of my Jewish identity's being discovered. The first I shared with every single one of my coprisoners. The second was secret and furtive, shared with only two people; without them I would, almost certainly, have been discovered.

But the great collective theme of camp life was hunger. Officially we had three meals a day. First, there was breakfast: coffee, and nothing else. Caldrons of foul-tasting coffee, which was far worse than the stuff we had brewed from chicory or roasted wheat grains in the forests. Then, at midday, came the *main* meal. Or rather, our only meal. That usually consisted of soup made from turnips and always with traces of fat floating on top which made it look revolting. Occasionally there would be cabbage in the soup, which was marginally better. With the soup we had boiled potatoes and a dark, dry, heavy sort of bread.

"This is made of sawdust," groaned Antek, as we chewed on it for the first time. And in all seriousness, I think he was probably right. We did get a tiny pat of margarine with the bread, and for "pudding" there was a spoonful of curds with jam. I think the jam was made of beetroot; I recognized it from the stuff Mrs. Stefa used to make at the orphanage, though hers tasted better! On Sundays came the highlight of the week: porridge, made from oats. We looked forward to that from the middle of the week onward. That may be why I can't bear to see you turn your nose up at your mother's porridge on cold winter mornings!

In the early evening we had tea. Literally. Tea made from herbs, and nothing else. If I have gone into more detail about my diet in the camp than at any other time during the war, it probably reflects the amount of time and energy we spent collectively thinking and talking about it. I coped with it better than most, simply because I was more familiar than the others with extremes of hunger. At least we knew we would get a meal every day, paltry though it was. Antek found the lack of food particularly difficult, and I would regularly give him one of my potatoes. I felt I owed him that at least, for reasons which I'll explain a little later.

The big monthly event in the camp was the arrival of the Red Cross parcels. They contained unimaginable luxuries like tins of sardines and corned beef, powdered milk, chocolate, and cigarettes. These parcels led to a lively commerce; one cigarette, for example, was considered to be worth one cup of soup or one slice of bread. There was one man, Stanislaw he was called, who was so addicted to cigarettes that he would try to sell his soup portion for a week—once even ten days—ahead! The poor man was so desperate for tobacco that his "business" partners seemed prepared to let the transaction go ahead until our hut leader intervened. He couldn't stand by and watch Stanislaw bargain away his life for a smoke! I didn't smoke, so I bartered my cigarettes for extra chocolate or powdered milk, which I would keep to share later on with Antek.

Because of the discipline I had acquired in the forests, and in eking out meager supplies with Henryk in Warsaw, I was not one of those who devoured the entire contents of their parcels immediately. Antek, however, could never resist doing so, and as a result, by the evening of the first day, he would become very morose, eyeing people who had supplies left with surly ill humor. I could never entirely free myself of the suspicion that if he were pushed too far, he might be reduced to blackmailing me in order to obtain double rations. Perhaps that was a very unworthy thought, but well intentioned and friendly though Antek was, he was also moody and unpredictable, and I had learned wariness and mistrust in Europe's most demanding school, so I regarded the extra luxuries I kept by to share with him as a sort of insurance policy.

Sometimes prisoners would succumb to the temptation of stealing food from other people's parcels. If they were caught, they were dealt with severely by a sort of kangaroo court. The hut leader would preside, two witnesses would be called, and if found guilty, the accused would be led up and down the central corridor in the hut, with people jeering and spitting at him and the belt with which he was to be beaten tied around his neck. Then the belt would do its work: thirty strokes on the bare bottom. Once Antek was caught stealing from Stanislaw's parcel. Stanislaw himself didn't really mind as he saw it as an opportunity to earn some extra tobacco. But I was alarmed at the possible effect of the punishment on my friend's morale, and though I usually took pains not to cross swords with anyone, this once I spoke out at the risk of angering the two prosecution witnesses.

"He told me he was going to give up smoking and would let Stanislaw have all his cigarettes from now on," I lied.

"He should have made the arrangement with Stanislaw beforehand," said the first witness, not without justification. He was a thuggish-looking man whom I'd always taken care to avoid. "That's no defense."

I stood my ground. "I agree. But he has been very faint and unwell recently, and that makes him vague. Perhaps he thought telling me was pledge enough."

Several others who were listening seemed swayed, including Szymon, whose chess-playing skills had given him a new status since the end of the Uprising. The hut leader reduced the sentence to twenty strokes of the belt. Antek's gratitude was, however, lukewarm. "Thanks, Jan. But now I'm condemned to a life without tobacco!"

Once or twice, as I listened to the endless complaints about our starvation rations, I was sorely tempted to cry out things like "In the ghetto there wasn't even the assurance of one meal a day. What did you do to help us then?" But of course, to do so would have been very dangerous. Not, to be fair, that any of my coprisoners, especially those who had also fought in the Uprising, would have been likely to turn me in to our German guards. But you could never be sure. I had learned that it was better to think of everyone as untrustworthy unless I had proof to the contrary. And there's no doubt that anti-Semitic views were still rife. Once or twice I overheard remarks that tempted me to commit murder; they are better left unrepeated. When that happened, I made an effort to remember Stefan and Fela and Father Klyza and Granny, and Igor in the shop in Warsaw overlooking the ruins of the ghetto, and to tell myself that they were but a few representatives of millions of other fair-minded Poles who abhorred what the

Nazis had done to the Jews almost as much as I myself did. But even so, I hung on to the secret of my identity as to life itself.

And in those close quarters there was, of course, one particularly likely way in which I could be found out: through the discovery that I was circumcised. This, at the very least, would cause suspicion and awkward questions among my fellow prisoners; it could not be risked!

Fortunately the lavatories were in cubicles, so I was safe from that point of view—until, during the coldest part of winter, some of the prisoners began to dismantle the wooden partitions for burning in the inefficient stoves which were supposed to warm the huts. We were left very much to our own devices by the Germans, and I was afraid that all the cubicles would have vanished before the damage was discovered! In fact, there was an inspection of the wash and lavatory hut before the last two had been demolished. That was the only time I saw our German captors really angry and punitive, for most of the time I have to admit that we were treated according to the standards of the Geneva Convention. We were always ravenously hungry, but one has to remember that food by that time of the war was generally very scarce in central Europe and our rations were well above those in the concentration camps. But on this occasion our lunch rations were halved, and we were made to stand outside in the cold for an entire day while the rest of our compound was subjected to a meticulous search.

Everyday washing was not a problem as we would just strip to the waist and douse ourselves as quickly as possible with the icy water. If I wanted to be more thorough, then I'd choose a moment when I knew the wash hut was deserted and Antek would keep watch at the door for me. The dangerous time was the monthly communal showers, when all our clothes were removed and taken away for disinfecting. Apart from the bliss of the warm water and the unusual feeling of being really clean, these occasions were for me an ordeal from beginning to end. It was then that I relied completely on Antek's help, and on that of another prisoner, Kasimierz, who discovered that I was a Jew in a way which I'll explain later. One of them would go very close in front, the other to the side of me, just before we got to the pile of discarded clothes, and like that we would swiftly undress and pass on into the showers, taking care to get as near to one of the walls as possible. Afterward, Antek would fetch three towels from the pile that was left near the door and bring two back for both Kasimierz and myself so as not to be too obviously singling me out. Often there weren't enough towels to go around, so Antek usually had to curtail his shower to make sure he reached them before they were all taken, and once, in fact, he only just managed to get the last one. That meant that he and Kasimierz had to run, naked and wet, to the hut where all the clothes were being steamed to disinfect them. In terms of discomfort, putting on the wet clothes was the worst moment, completely undoing any sense of well-being the warm shower might have induced; for me, though, the damp, clinging embrace of those gray overalls was a blessed relief. The shower was over for another month!

And now back to Kasimierz and how he came to know that I was a Jew. One day Antek and I, together with several others, had been out on a work detail beyond the perimeter fence, fetching potatoes and turnips from the trenches where they were stored and taking them to the communal kitchen outside the main gate. It was hard work, and on our rations, physical effort exhausted us very quickly. We got back ready to collapse on our bunks. When we reached the hut, we saw that we had been joined by several new arrivals. One of them was leaning over the bunk immediately below mine. I couldn't see his face, but his slight build and fair coloring were Henryk's. They say that one's heart leaps with joy; there is no better way of describing my sensation at that moment. I ran toward the stooping figure, his name on my lips.

He turned and stood up straight. I stopped in my tracks. He was nearly a head taller than Henryk; I had never seen the man before in my life. I just went on standing there before the stranger, my arms still held open in redundant welcome. It was the acutest, most intense moment of disappointment in my life. Sometimes, in waking from the cruel magic of dreams, which have convincingly raised Henryk himself and other loved ones from the dead, I have relived its hollow, crippling pain.

The stranger was gentle.

"I'm sorry," he said. "Really sorry. Who did you think I was?"

Immediately that wily caution, which had become a sort of sixth sense, reasserted itself.

"Oh, my uncle Henryk. We got separated in the Uprising." The newcomer, Andrei, asked me a few questions in case he could help. I told him I thought, but was not certain, that Henryk had been in the Old Town, working as a doctor. That was as much as I dared divulge; Andrei, who had not even been in Warsaw, couldn't help me. I noticed that another new arrival, a small dark man, was listening to us from the top bunk on the other side of the aisle, but thought little more of it at the time.

I climbed into my own bunk, the middle one, and turned my face to the wall. I didn't want to talk to anyone and had no wish to get up again, even for the midday meal. When it was time, Antek clambered down from the bunk above.

"Are you coming, Jan?"

"No." Antek had witnessed the little scene with Andrei but seemed not to have grasped its significance for me.

"Aren't you hungry?"

"What do *you* think?"

"What's the matter?"

"I thought that new man was Henryk. He looked like him from behind. I know now I'm never going to see him again."

"Don't be silly, Jan, you can't know that. He's probably in another camp. Come on, Jan, you must eat."

"I don't want anything."

"All right. Can I have yours then?"

"Yes."

"Cheer up, Jan"—patting my shoulder—"I expect he's a prisoner somewhere. And, after all, Henryk wasn't actually a relation, was he?"

I hated Antek at that moment. In fact, I don't think I've ever forgiven him for the remark, born as it was of a facile, insensitive assumption and hurting more than any deliberate insult could have done. How dared he dismiss my grief simply because Henryk didn't bear the right label; he may not have been *in fact* my uncle, but *in reality* he was so much more—father, uncle, friend, all in one. I couldn't bring myself to speak to Antek for a while; I wanted to forget all the things which bound us together. Our shared temporary burial under the collapsed house, his uncomplaining readiness to curtail the pleasure of a warm shower in order to protect me, the fact that he was Granny's grandson, and the only person I still knew, and was ever likely to know, who had actually met and spoken to Eva. I wanted, simply, to *hate* him.

I'm not sure whether it was the next day, or a few days later, when my intuitive knowledge of Henryk's death was confirmed. I found myself alone with the small dark man, whose name was Kasimierz and who had been listening to my conversation with Andrei. We were on the work shift that had to pump excrement out of the latrines and spread it on the ground outside the perimeter fence. A very unpleasant job, but at least it only lasted for about an hour and a half, and it wasn't nearly as exhausting as transferring supplies or humping wood.

"This smell is dreadful. It reminds me of the sewers in Warsaw," said my companion suddenly. I could feel his eyes on me, waiting for a reaction, so I kept shoveling and registered none. But how tempting it was to compare notes, to say, "When were *you* in the sewers?"

Eventually I said, as casually as I could, "You're from Warsaw then?"

"Yes. I was in the Uprising, too, in the Old Town, until we had to evacuate through the sewers with the wounded on stretchers. Carnage it was up there. And I knew a Henryk who looked like Andrei."

I straightened up then and looked him in the eye.

He went on, "He was a doctor. Your uncle was a doctor, you said, didn't you?"

"Yes."

He looked at me so intently that I think I knew, the moment before he asked, what his next question was going to be.

"And was he a Jew?"

It never even occurred to me to disclaim blood relationship with Henryk. I nodded.

"Don't worry," he said. "I'm not going to give you away. I was a member of the People's Guard, a Communist. I fought alongside several Jews during the Uprising, and it was a privilege."

I could have embraced the man, shit-laden shovel and all.

"Do you know what happened?"

"Yes. But keep working because this isn't going to be easy for you to hear. It's better to keep moving." That's when I learned the worst.

"Henryk worked very hard under impossible conditions. He performed operations in candlelight and under shell fire in a basement hospital in Miodowa Street. There wasn't much he could do, but he very possibly saved several lives, for a short while at least. One day I helped carry a man whose leg had been shot away into a dressing station in Bielanska Street. I recognized Dr. Henryk; apparently the two nurses there had been brought cases far too difficult for them to handle, so he'd been sent over to help them. He asked me to go and search for water, which was almost impossible to get hold of in the Old Town by then. Many of the wounded died of thirst and hunger before they died of their wounds. The poor devil I'd carried in was groaning, 'Water, water, please, water.' I was just leaving when Henryk called after me, 'Try the churches. Holy water. . . .'

"Just moments after I'd left the building, there was a particularly loud explosion. A several-ton shell had landed nearby, burying the dressing station under the rubble. One nurse survived, miraculously, but Henryk, the other nurse, and all the wounded were dead when they were eventually pulled out."

Not for one moment did I stop shoveling the feces. "How did you know he was Jewish?" I noticed that my voice, which seemed to come from a long way away, was very calm.

"The nurse told me. I don't know how she knew. But she said he had changed her view about Jews; he had worked so selflessly all through the Uprising. She said he was the best doctor she'd ever assisted, even though he was having to do things like amputate limbs more out of guesswork than training, for of course, he was not a surgeon."

My pride in Henryk and what he had done really did help me to bear the final news of his death. At the time I did not succumb to fever, as I had after witnessing the deportations, or sink into depression, as I had after the murder of Eva and Franek. I just went on much the same as before, treasuring in my heart and in silence, the memory of the man who had been my third father, my "uncle," and my friend. But I am not sure that I ever properly mourned Henryk, and perhaps that's why he haunts me more today than any of the others. Perhaps, Richard, because in so many ways he was a model stepfather. I suspect that in failing you, I am letting him down, too.

In any case, Henryk was the last person I was to love, or feel deep commitment to, for a very long time. For many, many years, in fact. There was, after all, very little of myself left to commit. And then there was for so long that insidious, almost superstitious belief that my love must be tantamount to the kiss of death. I only hope for your mother's sake and yours that the old spell has lost its power.

JULY 18, 11:00 P.M.

Dear Katie,

I've come to the point where I will have to write to Misha. I had my punishment from the Head—at last—today. A quarter share in the cost of cleaning the wall and loss of all privileges for the first half of next term, as it's so near the end of this. Too lenient. I feel

I've escaped scot-free. Doesn't the old fool realize how serious it was?

I've made several attempts at starting a letter to him, but they all sound so silly somehow. I wish you were here to help me; you're much better at that sort of thing than I am.

"I feel I must write to make a confession." No, too dramatic.

"After all you went through when you were my age and younger, I don't know how I can . . ." No. Sounds a bit false coming from me.

"You say you've been privileged to feel proud of the people you love. Well, I'm afraid that this time you're in for a monumental disappointment." No. That rather assumes he loves me, and I can't do that. Hell, this is a difficult thing to write. There's just too much to say all of a sudden. Perhaps it would be better face-to-face, after all. I'll sleep on it. Maybe the perfect wording will come to me in the middle of the night. Maybe. Wish you would—come to me in the middle of the night, I mean!

Love you. R.

Kasimierz was as good as his word and never, by hint or glance, put me in any additional danger. Once or twice when we were alone, he tried to help me talk about Henryk, but somehow I didn't want to. I wanted to keep what was left all for myself. But it did help to know that he had met and respected him; I think I would have liked him for that alone, even if I hadn't liked him for himself. But he was an educated man, a teacher by profession, and perhaps because of my age, perhaps because time hung heavy during the long, cold winter evenings, he offered to start teaching me English. "It looks as if it'll be a useful language to have, the way things are going," he said with a grin.

Antek wanted to join in and, as he knew some Russian and French, started off at an advantage. I was not particularly competitive, but I did quickly discover that I have a linguistic facility, and for some reason Antek found that difficult to accept. I think he rather liked the idea of being protector or guardian to a poor little uneducated Jewish waif; maybe, deep down, he had never really seen me as his equal. Whatever it was, he didn't like it when Kasimierz showed obvious pleasure and surprise at my rapid progress, and eventually he stopped coming to the sessions altogether. "You get on much better without me," he said sulkily. Despite my irritation, I had to make a point of sharing more than usual of my next Red Cross parcel with him. I couldn't risk alienating him. He *was* still the protector and guardian of a poor uneducated Jewish waif, despite my newfound skills. I enjoyed the lessons partly because I found the intellectual challenge stimulating, partly because I knew I was doing something that would have pleased all three of my fathers—and my mother, too, for my own parents had badly wanted their children to have a better education than they themselves had had.

After discovering what had happened to Henryk, I began to think more and more about Eli. I thought of the way she had shrieked when she realized that the little smuggler's pulley whisking her to freedom from Kozla Alley was taking her away from everything familiar. I wondered again, as I had so often, whether they had comforted her well and what she had been told about us, her family. Was she still alive? And if so, when would she read Rachel's little account of her early life—if she still had it? The thought of Rachel's unformed handwriting brought sudden and unexpected tears to my eyes. That's something I was learning. The river of sorrow may run much of its course underground, but it has a way of surfacing in unexpected places. Special sheltered little places. The other night, for instance, I was cooking supper while your mother was doing evening surgery, and the potatoes boiled dry because I was called away to the phone. I saved the pan before it got too burned, but not before I was overwhelmed by the memory of a certain night in Warsaw, when I ruined some other potatoes as I waited for Henryk to return home.

* * *

Liberation! I can't even tell you the exact date of our liberation, though it was in the last week of April 1945. For days the thuds and rumbles of artillery fire had heralded the approach of the front, and we could identify which direction the liberation would come from. Then, one morning, we woke to find that all our guards had disappeared during the night. There was no point in attempting to escape as columns of German troops were passing by almost continuously; one company even stopped and set up some heavy guns just outside our perimeter fence. Then, perhaps two days after our guards disappeared, *they* came.

For me the incongruous visual image conjured up by the word *liberation* is of men in goggles! Like creatures from some other galaxy they came, Americans, the men in goggles, driving their column of white-starred tanks and armored cars. We watched from the guardless gate in awed fascination as they proceeded steadily down the hill, on the unpaved road opposite the camp. The procession gathered a sort of relentless momentum, and running ahead of them into our different compounds, we looked back in breathless wonder as they spurned to stop at the gates but just kept on coming, flattening them in one long and gloriously symbolic gesture. I can hear again the crash and crack of crushed timber, my abiding aural image of liberation, and even now I see my arms prickle with gooseflesh as I recall the scene.

Suddenly there were tanks in our compound itself, and the men in goggles were calling to us in a strange, slurred language which, thanks to Kasimierz's lessons, I recognized as English. They jumped down from the great bulk of their vehicles, pushed back their goggles, and began moving among us, pumping our hands, and clapping us on our shoulders. I couldn't help wincing as one of them clasped me by the still-tender scar tissue of my upper arm.

"You're free, you're free!" they kept repeating. I understood the words. That is to say, I could translate the English into Polish and Yiddish. But no doubt for everyone in that camp the word had a different meaning. Many faces were streaming with tears, including that of the huge thug who had been Antek's prosecution witness. But mine was dry; for me the words really had no meaning.

Free! The freedom of my prewar childhood was now too remote, forever hidden in the shadows cast by a ten-foot-high wire-topped ghetto wall. I simply had no conception anymore of a life without the occupation, without hiding, without war, without fear. "A sort of freedom" was how I had once described partisan life to Franek. But I knew that the freedom of forest warfare was not the freedom the men in goggles thought they were bringing us with their wide, white-toothed smiles.

Free! In the midst of intense physical relief, I sensed the stirring of a great slow shudder of lonely grief. There were too many lost people with whom I should have been sharing that moment.

But the general jubilation was infectious. Everyone was hugging everyone else, stuffing into their mouths the candy which was liberally handed out by those amazing creatures from outer space, and there was a general lighting up of cigarettes. In the confusion I caught sight of Antek and Stanislaw sitting quietly side by side, enjoying their first companionable smoke since Antek's trial! Food was brought in from the trench stores outside the fence, and for the first time since my days with Stefan and Fela over seventeen months before, I could eat as much as my stomach would hold. Vegetable stew it was, to be sure, but richer than we had known it and in copious quantities, supplemented by tins of American meat and followed by sweet, sticky canned puddings. You can imagine that I was by no means the only one to mark the first night after liberation with an ignominious and severe dose of diarrhea!

The following day was something of an anticlimax. The large gates were reerected by the British, who came in after the Americans had left; they wanted to prevent us from leaving the camp, not unreasonably, because we were still in the midst of the operational war zone.

The British guarded us for about a week. But now we all knew that it was only a matter of a little time before we would be able to leave; the rigid camp routine disintegrated, and for several nights running many of the others got drunk on the bottles of wine which they found discarded by the Germans in the supply trenches. Remembering Henryk's words of caution, I was very careful not to drink much, unsure of how well I would keep my story to myself if my tongue were loosened by alcohol.

So, ironically, it was with German wine that we celebrated the German capitulation and then, when the British soldiers gave us the glad tidings, the final end of the war on May 8. Oddly, I remember very little about my reaction to that news; momentous though it was, it seemed just a logical next step after the great turning point of liberation. Overnight, liberation had freed me from a permanent sentence of death from which only a chance mixture of other people's goodwill and self-sacrifice, my own quick-wittedness, and a great deal of extraordinary good luck had granted me reprieve. I don't think I've ever completely lost my sense of gratitude to the British and the Americans for lifting that death sentence. But what liberation had not yet done was grant me the freedom to reclaim my identity—to be me, Misha Edelman, Polish Jew. "When will it be safe to tell?" was a question which had already begun, with an insistent little rhythm, to drum inside my head from the first sight of that column of white-starred tanks trundling down the hill. For the moment it was best to keep silent. There was no way of knowing how much danger still lurked among my fellow prisoners.

Once the British left us to our own devices, there began a wave of looting. People would leave the camp to roam around the devastated local villages and come back laden with goods of all descriptions after ransacking the deserted houses. Although I must admit to enjoying the extra supplies which these raids produced, not least the soft bedding, I was shocked when china and silver, cameras and bicycles began to appear in the camp. If that sounds rather puritanical under the circumstances, remember that I had been used to strict rules of behavior—not only in the teaching and example of Korczak but also in the partisan code which allowed us to steal food, clothing, and medical supplies but never luxuries. When Antek came back one day thrilled with a camera he'd found, I could only think of Eva's pang of conscience when she'd grabbed the tablet of soap off a market stall. I tried to share in Antek's delight—we had been through so much together, and it was still important not to alienate him—yet I was uneasy about the whole thing. I didn't join the looting parties, but I suspect that might have been more from reluctance to expose myself to temptations than from any true sense of honor.

When Antek suggested that together with Szymon and a few others, we should leave the camp and try and find General Maczek's division of the Polish Army, which we had heard was occupying an area near the Dutch border, I couldn't summon a great deal of enthusiasm. But there seemed little point in staying where we were, and it was hard to know what else to do at that stage. Kasimierz, the only other prisoner I felt remotely attached to, was going to try to make his way back to Poland. As a Communist he hoped that the Soviet invasion might signal the start of a bright new future. This had already given rise during the preceding months to many a heated debate among the prisoners in the compound, but Kasimierz was not to be dissuaded. Poor Kasimierz; I kept in touch with him, and in 1963, when I went back to Poland, I visited him. He was extremely welcoming and cordial and outwardly supportive of the Gomulka government, but somehow he let me know, perhaps in the wistful way he asked me questions about my life in England, that he was deeply disillusioned.

While Antek and I were still deciding when and with whom to leave, Stanislaw and another ex-prisoner were blown up by an unexploded mine on their way back from a local village. It was a salutary reminder of the many dangers still lying in wait just beyond the perimeter fence.

The former leader of our hut and someone else who spoke German went off in search of a pastor to bury our two comrades. As we had known Stanislaw quite well, we felt we ought to postpone our departure until after the ceremony. Perhaps if that accident hadn't occurred, the whole course of my life would have been entirely different.

PART 3

...AND IN BEGINNING AGAIN

But you, when the time comes at last
And man is a helper to man
Think of us
With forbearance.

BERTOLT BRECHT,
"TO THOSE BORN LATER"

The very day on which we committed Stanislaw's body to German soil, a Polish army truck arrived at the gates, looking for volunteers to join General Anders's Second Corps in Italy. As we'd have an armed escort and transport for the entire journey, that proposition sounded a good deal more appealing than attempting to make our own way through mine-strewn war-devastated territory to the Dutch border, on the off chance that we'd be accepted by one of the Polish units there.

The journey to Italy was long and uncomfortable; the Polish Army truck was crowded, hot, smelly, and noisy, yet it was the first journey I remember making without fear, and in a strange way I enjoyed it. I sat hunched up at the back of the truck, as close to the opening as possible, and, with my head resting against the tarpaulin side, I watched the ravaged world go by. Everywhere you looked there were refugees—homeless, lost, and often wounded. Sometimes they straggled in lines along the roads, all that was left of their belongings on their backs; sometimes we would see them huddled together on the verges in dismal little encampments around a wisp of smoke. We saw all manner of uniforms and clothes, though rags were the most common uniform of all, and we must have heard snatches of all the languages of Europe. The saddest sight was the children who were on their own, usually barefoot and painfully thin. Often they would run after our truck, desperate for anything to eat. We nearly always threw them something, and once I had to look away when three small children started fighting one another viciously for a crust of bread. I remember that a few of the onlookers laughed and cheered them on, reminding me of Igor's story of how the burning ghetto had proved an attraction for sight-seers. But the displaced children made me think of my sisters, particularly of Eli, because I was all too certain of Rachel's fate. It was not impossible that one of these little urchins—and it was often difficult to determine their sex—could be Eli herself.

But for all the chaos, for all the evidence of the devastation which the "civilized" peoples of our continent had suffered, there was an undeniable excitement in traveling across frontiers and seeing new scenery, new countries. The Alps, on that clear, warm May day as we approached the Brenner Pass, positively assaulted me with their beauty. I felt close to tears, though whether it was from wonder that the world could still contain such lovely sights or from grief that I would never now share them with those I loved, I cannot say.

It was in Ancona that I had my first ever glimpse of the sea. Antek, who had been to the Baltic as a child, was almost as thrilled as I was.

"It's so blue—just as blue as the picture books!" he kept saying. But as we stood looking toward the distant horizon, with nothing between us and the islands of Yugoslavia, I was entranced by the sense of space even more than by the color. For the boy who suffered so badly from claustrophobia it was like gazing at endless possibility, at the wide, wondrous face of freedom itself.

The regime at Ancona was by no means arduous. Our principal function was to guard army equipment and stores, as we did for a few hours each day, and to take part in physical training to keep, literally, fighting fit. But it was often easy to forget that, as we had plenty of time to relax and enjoy the Italian sunshine.

Our final destination was better still. It was a camp near Bari in Apulia, which had been set up specially to accommodate the flood of refugees which kept arriving to swell the corps from different parts of Europe. We were not hungry because, though the food was monotonous—usually thick soup in which floated a piece of tough meat—it was plentiful, and we were paid some money, which we could spend in local cafés and restaurants. We were free to do what we wanted in our spare time, and Italian classes were available, so Antek and I both dropped English in favor of this rich, mellifluous new language. Like so many other central and northern Europeans before me, I fell in love with Italy. The landscape of Apulia, the heel of Italy's boot, was not as spectacular as the mountains farther north, but the rolling hills dotted with quaint white bulbous buildings and brushed with the soft silvery green of olive trees had an appeal of its own. The olives held a particular fascination for me. There was one tree just outside the camp gate to which I became particularly attached; it must have been really ancient, for its trunk was massive, but also blackened and bent, a twisted mass of gnarled sinew, so that I thought of it fancifully as the tree of sorrow. And when, in the winter, it produced its crop of bittersweet fruit, I felt the achievement like a personal triumph.

It wasn't just the sunshine, the sea, the landscape, and the suddenly plentiful food that acted as balm on the weary and war-battered recruits to the Polish Second Corps. The attitude of the local people also played its part. Despite the fact that they had been on the other side in the war, I never once encountered hostility or resentment from an Italian. Antek took a fancy to one of the girls from the local laundry business which served the camp, and several times we were both invited to her home. We ate her mother's delicious fish pasta and savored the rare new luxuries of being welcome in a private home, well fed and gloriously unafraid. I had the feeling that if I had suddenly decided to tell them I was a Jew, they would have carried on cramming spaghetti into their mouths without raising their heads! Antek's relationship with Maria quickly soured when it became evident—much to my embarrassment—that she was more interested in me! That put a stop to our visits to the cool apartment with the flowered wrought-iron balcony and sent Antek into one of his sulky moods for several days. Later he transferred his affections to a girl who worked in a café in Bari, and after we'd been vetted by her brother, we were invited to a meal at her home, too. It really did seem as if Italy's reputation was well deserved: the land where foreigners are welcomed like brothers. If you've heard differently, I don't want to hear it.

Perhaps it is only in retrospect that our eighteen months in Italy seem like an extended holiday. But certainly for the first time in my adolescence I was healthy; sufficient food, warmth, air, exercise, and, above all, the absence of fear saw to that. I tried not to think of the immediate past; I suppose I must have known, at some level, that my mental survival depended on living in the present.

I did make a start at that time to search for Eli. I wrote to the Polish Red Cross, via some PO box in London, but I never received a reply.

At this time I was governed by a double taboo against talking of my past: Reluctance to disturb the fragile tissue of recovery was one; reluctance to reveal my Jewish identity—now acting almost like an ancestral prohibition—was the other. Since being in Italy, I had continued to be careful not to show myself naked, but it had been much easier because bath and shower arrangements were more flexible and relaxed.

Then the day came when I parted from my secret, when I publicly became a Jew again. I had expected the moment to be one of huge relief; in fact, the deception had been a part of my life, a part of *me* for so long that I felt quite bereft without it, exposed and vulnerable like a mollusk without a shell! We were off duty and on the beach at the time: Antek, myself, and three other men, all of whom had been in the Soviet Union. Two of them had been in the infamous gold mines on the river Kolyma. We were discussing the future and the choice we had been given, either to return to Poland or to go to England, where, we had just been informed, a resettlement corps was to be set up with the purpose of gradual demobilization.

One of the others said, "In many ways I'd love to go home. See my mum and sister—she had twin boys at the beginning of the war, and I've never even seen them—but I don't know that I can face life under the Communists, even at home."

At this Ludwik, who had been at Kolyma, spoke up. "You sound undecided. Let me tell you a thing or two. If you think life under the Nazis was harsh, you haven't seen anything yet. I love my family, but not as much as I hate the bloody Russians. There's no choice for me: I can't go back to a Poland in Russian hands. Even if I never see my own children again . . ."

There was a silence, while we tried to take in the bleak desolation of those words. I thought sadly of Ilya and Vasily, but dared not say anything. Then, to my utter amazement, Lek, the other veteran of Kolyma, volunteered, "I don't think there's anything to choose between them. But at least I don't have a dilemma about family. Mine all perished in the Bialystok Ghetto—not before they'd put up a bloody good fight, though." I had been shoveling sand over my outstretched legs as I listened to the discussion, but now I saw my hands drop their loads and fall, involuntarily, into the little trenches I had scooped out on either side of myself. No one else seemed taken aback. I looked at Antek, but he was lying on his stomach, his head facedown on his arms, giving nothing away.

Ludwik nodded. "Maybe you're right. Nothing much to choose between them. Barbarians, all."

I fixed my eyes on the creamy frill of foam at the water's edge: seaweed spread a dark untidy stain just below the surface, which lay still and smooth as glass. My heart had started to beat very fast; I couldn't stand the suspense any longer.

"Are you Jewish then?" I asked Lek directly.

"Yes, Jan, I am. If I'd stayed in Poland, the Nazis would have murdered me as a member of the racial enemy. As it was, in Siberia, I only just avoided being murdered as a member of the so-called class enemy." Lek had told us before about some of his experiences on Soviet soil; his five-thousand-mile journey across the Siberian wastes standing in unheated, windowless cattle cars made my journey from Warsaw to near Bremen feel like a trip on a luxury express.

I looked out to sea, where a battleship was passing like a prophecy across the edge of the world, and I knew this was the moment.

"I'm Jewish, too."

There was another silence, and then suddenly Lek had taken my arm in his two hands and was pumping it up and down. I watched in shame as my skin became rough with goose pimples and hoped he hadn't noticed. Five of Lek's fingers were missing, and the sight made me absurdly squeamish. He had lost three through frostbite; the other two he had cut off deliberately in order to buy time in the camp hospital, a respite from the murderous regime of that Arctic hell. He looked into my face, and in his near colorless eyes, dulled from seeing too much for too long, there was a new spark.

"So, a little brother! Jan—of all people! I'd never have guessed."

My heart turned over at the words *little brother*. But I answered him quickly, guilty at my reaction to his physical touch and anxious not to offend him.

"No, well, that's how I managed to survive. Yes, I'm from Warsaw. I was in the ghetto." Gradually I answered their questions, and a skeletal version of my story emerged from its temporary burial.

When they'd finished asking me questions, Ludwik suggested that the discovery should remain a secret with that little group on the beach.

"There are plenty of men in the unit who could still make life unpleasant for you. We've never talked openly about Lek being a Jew, and there's no reason for them to know about you either."

So it was only to be a partial disclosure after all. Nevertheless, it was a turning point for me, the first feeble fluttering of a phoenix wing.

Antek was very quiet in the days which followed, and I assumed he was somehow offended that he was no longer the guardian of my secret. But jealous and possessive though he could certainly be, on this occasion I did him an injustice. One day we borrowed bicycles and rode to one of the nearby villages to a café from where there was a lovely view of the sea. He told me then how troubled he was over the decision that had to be made, very soon, of whether or not to return to Poland. As the youngest of four sons he had been very much his parents' pet, and he told me that day he missed home more than he'd ever liked to admit—especially since he'd heard that a second brother had failed to return. I remember looking at him with a new compassion and with a pang of guilt for the intense irritation I had often felt toward him. But the many stories of our comrades' experiences in the Soviet Union were sobering in the extreme and had made Antek realize that a return to Poland in Communist hands was likely to be a return to a prison state. It was an agonizing dilemma for him, and there was very little I could do to help except listen sympathetically. I hoped that he would decide to go to England with me but dared not say anything that could be construed as pressure.

What decided him eventually was a letter from his mother sent via relations in France but, even so, dressed up in elaborate code to fool the censors. Dear Aunt Krysia, she wrote, was sick, very sick; her illness prevented her from doing the things she wanted to do or going where she wanted and even seeing some of the old friends she wanted to see. She could no longer get to church, and running the farm was becoming more and more difficult because of the constraints of her illness, and this in turn meant that she often went hungry. She knew the news would worry Antek, who had always been very fond of his aunt, but she felt it was only fair that he should know the position. Antek received the message loud and clear, for he had no Aunt Krysia!

And so it was that Antek and I found ourselves, one evening in November 1946, standing at a ship's railing and watching helplessly as Italy, in the form of the Bay of Naples, to where we'd been transferred the week before, slid out of our lives. It was to be eighteen years before I could afford to go back.

It took us six days and nights to reach Glasgow, my first sea voyage, and during the first two days I fervently hoped it would be the last. We had rough seas almost from the moment we sailed out of the Bay of Naples, and nearly everyone was violently sick. I recovered from the worst on the third day, when my appetite returned, and I made capital out of Antek's and other people's queasiness by using their meal tickets to obtain extra rations! Poor Antek was terribly sick, day after day.

"I should have gone back to Poland after all. At least I could have done that by train," he groaned. I knew he was very troubled by the decision he'd taken not to return, and one night, as we all slept crowded together on one of the covered decks, he cried out in his sleep for his mother. I didn't tell him as I knew he would have been ashamed— however unnecessarily—but in a wave of tenderness I huddled closer to him. He was now, after all, my only friend, and we needed each other badly.

As we turned around the corner of Europe at Cape St. Vincent and began to head northward, some of the sadness I had felt at leaving Italy began to fall away. To settle there had never been on offer, and so I had always regarded it as a transitory haven. And for me there was no dilemma like Antek's over returning to Poland, for there was no one there for me anymore. Except, possibly, Eli, and who knew where she was by now? It would be no more difficult to search for her from England than from Poland, easier perhaps.

I remember standing on the upper deck the night the worst of my nausea had subsided. A scatter of stars glimmered, caught like beads in a veil of cloud. I looked down at the dark swell below and realized that I knew scarcely more about the life awaiting me in the country called England than I did about life in the mysterious fathoms beneath us. New people, new places, new language, new customs, new rules. Nothing and no one familiar—except, of course, Antek and the few others who'd been with me at Bari. Szymon we had lost touch with back in Ancona. But I was young, and healthy again, and my apprehension was shot through with excitement. It would be a life in which I no longer had to hide and pretend; I could again be Misha Edelman, Polish Jew, protégé of Dr. Korczak, ex-partisan and resistance worker. I would learn to speak good English and then study medicine and be successful—to be worthy of my miraculous survival, to do credit to those who had loved me and given me so much that was good, even in the midst of squalor, carnage, and brutality. Under the pale starlight they all passed in slow procession before my eyes, their smiles fragmenting and dissolving in the rise and fall of the steep, dark ridges which hurled us on our way.

After a while I was joined by Lek. We stood in silence for a while, and I tried not to look at the way his poor mutilated hands gripped the railing like claws. Presently Lek, who was in his early thirties, said, "You're young, Jan. You have strength and, more important, hope. It will be up to you to bear witness and make the most of your survival—for all their sakes." I was startled by the way his words echoed so exactly my own thoughts, and looking at him more keenly, I noticed that his teeth were chattering.

"You're cold," I said, and putting a hand on his shoulder, I could feel how he trembled even beneath the thick material of his overcoat.

But he shook his head vehemently. "No, Jan. I'm not cold. At least not because of the weather; nowhere can be cold after Siberia. It's just that I'm afraid, that's all. I don't think I can face a new life—not now. Not after Kolyma."

He turned toward me, and I saw that his face was streaming with tears.

"I never shed a tear there. Not one, in twenty months. Not in front of those bastards. But now"—he shook his head as if in surprise at himself—"but now, beginning again, I just don't think I can do it."

His wasted body became convulsed by sobs. I held him in my arms and felt them coming from his very center with an elemental force. All I could do was pat his back like a baby's and whisper platitudes about how everything would be all right once we got to England. I think only at that moment did I finally understand that human endurance has its limits, while human ruthlessness and cruelty do not.

We reached Glasgow on a gray, dank morning toward the end of November. I'm sure that if we had come straight from Poland, I wouldn't have noticed the predominance of gray, but after the dazzle of the *mezzogiorno* the contrast was cruel. Almost immediately we were transferred south to a camp near Henley in Oxfordshire.

It was there that I first officially reclaimed my name. Stupidly, perhaps, I hadn't practiced the signature I'd been unable to use for over four years, and when I came to write it for registration, my fingers gripped the pen with paralyzing rigidity. Halfway through I had to stop and look up at the sergeant on the other side of the table.

"Don't worry, son. We'll take your fingerprints instead." The Polish soldier beside him translated for me. The English sergeant smiled, and I could see he meant no harm; he merely assumed I was illiterate. I bent over the book again and wrote "Michal Edelman" with slow and deliberate purpose. Then, after it in brackets, I wrote "(Jan Damski)" and, with a final, much quicker flourish, put a cross through the latter. Strange, but it wasn't at all with pure satisfaction that I did so; after all I had been Jan Damski for such a long and important period of my life. And that was how I was known to so many people, including Vasily, Franek, Eva, and Henryk.

"What was all that about?" asked Antek as we left the hut. He'd been slightly ahead of me in the queue. I shrugged and said, thinking of Lek's words, "Beginning again."

Antek looked at me thoughtfully and said, "I wonder if that's possible?" He took my arm in one of the fraternal gestures which made his difficult moods worth putting up with, and we went to the NAAFI hut where you could buy tea and sticky buns. But the business of the signature left me feeling troubled, confused, and oddly disloyal. Until then I had tended to think of my survival as a fact, something that, for better or worse, had already happened. From that moment I began to realize that survival was a complicated process which was only just beginning.

I'm not sure, Richard, how interested you will be in the things that happened to me after arriving in this country, as they can hardly be described as exciting, but I've pledged to explain how I came to be part of your family—if you can accept that that is what I am!—and so I need to give you a brief outline. And after all, those things, too, are very much part of my story and have a bearing on our relationship.

My earliest memories of life in England are conditioned by the vicious cold of that winter. By the time of the first snowfalls and blizzards we had been transferred to another Oxfordshire camp, at a village some ten miles from Oxford, and we frequently had to clear paths in snow which reached to our chests. The metal huts proved to be effective conductors of the cold, and the heating provided was woefully inadequate for such conditions.

Lek and Ludwik ended up in the same hut as Antek and myself; I think we must have arranged that somehow. I can't really remember.

"You should have married that nice little waitress in Bari," Lek used to say to Antek, as he stood over the wood-burning stove warming what were left of his fingers. "No one would have had me, but you had your chance to stay in Italy!" Someone would then make a crude joke, and we'd all laugh. Poor Ludwik's laughter invariably ended in a coughing fit which racked his emaciated frame and was painful just to watch. At the end of February he was taken to a hospital—I can't remember where. Antek, Lek, and I visited him a couple of times, but he died shortly afterward.

Lek was sitting on his bed drinking scotch whiskey out of a bottle when he heard the news.

"Kolyma means death. We all used to say so," he muttered. Neither of us had ever again referred to his outburst that night on the ship, but I knew he was wondering now how long it would be before Kolyma caught up with him, too.

The Polish Resettlement Corps was set up as a purely transitional arrangement to help those Polish troops who did not want to return to a Communist Poland to resettle in civilian life in Britain or to facilitate their eventual emigration elsewhere. I was never tempted to go to the United States or Canada as, illogically, I felt that by staying in Europe, I stood more of a chance of eventually finding Eli.

The corps aimed to give people like myself, who wished to stay in Britain, an opportunity for instruction in the English language, as well as some form of vocational training. Instruction in the English language! Well, I know the intention was honorable, but the English tuition in our camp turned out to be, frankly, a waste of time. We had two teachers from the British Army, each as ineffective as the other.

By that time I knew that I was an able linguist, not only from my Yiddish and Hebrew experience but also from those lessons in English with Kasimierz at the prisoner of war camp, and from the fact that I had picked up a fair amount of Italian with ease. I was also only too aware that to get anywhere in this cold new country, I had to master its language. It became an obsession. I regularly spent a high proportion of the little money I had on books, devoted hours to making long lists of vocabulary—with a rather pathetic emphasis on medical words, designed to further my ambition to train as a doctor—and, after about six months, reached the stage where I could read a serious newspaper with little difficulty. The trouble was, of course, that because I had such limited contact with English people I couldn't practice the spoken language, and I had little or no idea how good my accent was. Antek and I would test each other on vocabulary, but I suspect we would have sounded very comic to any native speaker who happened to overhear us.

There were grants available for higher education, and to further my dream of following in Korczak's and Henryk's footsteps, I applied for one, though I can't remember exactly at what point that was. In any case it was an utterly forlorn hope in view of the fierce competition there was for such grants. I was suddenly acutely aware of my half-finished education. The main preoccupation of my teenage years was not learning but survival. And now, what did I have to show for all that surviving? Certainly nothing that would impress the British authorities sufficiently to give me a place at one of their universities. I believe most of the available places went to Poles whose studies had been interrupted, but who had at least some grounding in their chosen subjects. I could hardly blame the British for that. I knew, logically, that it wasn't my fault either, yet for a long time I couldn't help feeling that I'd let them down, once again: the very people to whom I owed my continued existence. And I suppose that a vestige of those feelings has survived in my passionate desire for you, Richard, to make the most of your education.

Antek and I were in due course apprenticed to a builders' firm. We were collected and brought back in a van, and as the camp was isolated in the country with a very infrequent bus service, we had little or no chance to meet English people outside work, of our own—or of any—age. I was apprenticed in an informal way to a nice man called Jim, who was slow and thorough and took great trouble to show me what to do. He used to bring a packed lunch and a hot drink in a thermos every day, and I remember that his wife always put in something sweet, like a piece of homemade cake, which he'd insist on sharing with me. He must have told his wife about me because after a while two slices appeared regularly in his lunchbox. The only trouble with Jim, the first Briton I spent any length of time with, was his accent; he was originally from Glasgow, and I understood only about one in every twenty words he uttered! It was very frustrating.

We worked for the builders until the late summer of 1947, just after my nineteenth birthday, when we were given the chance to help with the harvest on a local farm. Antek was keen to do that and persuaded me to join him. It was pleasant to be out in the open air, and I enjoyed the physical exertions, but I missed my Glaswegian friend's kindness and natural courtesy, for the farmer and his family treated us with contempt. Several of us from the resettlement camp worked there, and none of us was ever allowed to set foot in the house, even to eat our sandwiches if it rained. One day Antek had an upset stomach and asked if he could use the farmhouse bathroom, but even that request was refused! When someone complained on Antek's behalf to the man who was a sort of foreman, he was asked in no uncertain terms, "What will you bloody foreigners want next? Just be glad you've got a job at all."

Bloody foreigners! I'm afraid it was an attitude with which we were to become very familiar in the months and years ahead, and never more so than when Antek and I were finally demobilized early in 1948 and, from a temporary base in a hostel in Oxford, started the search for permanent lodgings. That search was a desolate experience, and I was thankful that at least there were two of us. We would buy the local paper and visit every bed-sitter or lodgings which was advertised, whether or not it was for one or two people.

I suppose it's only fair to remember that for many English people a central European accent combined with a fair complexion means German, and in the late forties *German* still, very definitely, meant "enemy." It seemed that the very characteristics which had saved my life in wartime Poland now made me the object of suspicion and dislike.

"We don't take foreigners" was the ubiquitous message, delivered sometimes with embarrassment, sometimes politely, couched in different words, sometimes all too forthrightly. I remember one man, whose forearms were covered in tattoos, demanding to know where we were from. Stupidly, instead of saying "the Polish Army" or "the Polish Resettlement Corps," which he might have tolerated, we replied naïvely, "Poland."

"Communist bastards, eh? Not bloody likely," and he slammed the door in our faces. For all the laughable ignorance of his reaction— why should any Polish Communists have made their way to England, even if the Soviet regime had allowed them to do so in the first place?— it brought us close to giving up.

"Perhaps we should have gone back after all," said Antek. "There's nothing for us here; no one wants us." But as often happened when he was despondent, I seemed to find some extra strength from somewhere; on this occasion I remembered Jim's kindness, and that gave me hope.

"Let's keep going. Maybe we could put an advert in the paper ourselves. Then we'll know that anyone who replies is prepared to take foreigners."

And that's what we did. We were working for another building firm in Oxford by then, and we asked a sympathetic workmate to help us word it accurately. We received one reply, from a Mr. and Mrs. Johnson whose son had been killed at the Battle of Arnhem in 1944. They had been impressed by the stories, told by some of his comrades, of the bravery of the Polish paratroopers there and thought that in memory of their son they would like to offer us a home.

During all this time I had begun the serious search for my sister Eli. I wrote again to the Polish Red Cross and, absurdly, began to expect a reply after about two weeks. I remember playing silly superstitious games with myself, like delaying visits to my pigeonhole for two or three days in the hope that my self-control would be rewarded. After a couple of months I had almost given up hope and was wondering whether to write again. After six, when Antek's parents had written to say that the office of the Polish Red Cross had been burned to the ground in the Uprising like most of the rest of Warsaw, and with it almost its entire collection of records, I did give up hope, but I did write again. Then, a year and a week after my first letter, I finally received an acknowledgment! In retrospect, that was an efficient performance when you think that almost every member of the Polish population must have lost at least one person in the war. What they told me was just sufficient to keep my hope alive: They had transferred my request to the International Tracing Service, by then situated in Arolsen in West Germany, which had a special section devoted to tracing children who had been lost or separated from their families as a result of the war.

I also wrote to the Central Committee of Polish Jews, which, I was told, had a good Records and Statistics Department. But of course, it could only register Jews who cared to be registered as such; even after the war there were many who continued to conceal their true identities, and it was also possible that Eli's foster parents had never told her she was a Jew. Perhaps they'd never even told her that she wasn't their own daughter. Later, when the Central Committee moved its premises to 60 Sienna Street, I knew a fresh surge of hope, for the orphanage had been in Sienna Street, and I had some absurd superstitious notion that that might bring me luck. But nothing happened. They *were* able to confirm Henryk's death for me, however. It took place on August 26, 1944, the very day, according to Antek's memory, when the Stuka bombers had all but buried us alive. I also learned through them that Henryk's cousin Joseph, who had organized my escape through the sewers, had survived the war and had emigrated to Israel. It is a matter of lasting sadness that I never discovered what happened to other members of the partisan band.

Antek's parents were very helpful and wrote to, or contacted in person on my behalf, every family in Warsaw by the name of Sulek— that of Eli's foster parents, which Korczak had made me promise not to write down as long as the war lasted. But even that endeavor, which lasted for a couple of years, for it is quite a common name, drew a blank. One man did say that some young relatives of his had adopted a little girl during the war and had fled Warsaw because they were being blackmailed. The same story I had heard via the former neighbor and clearly the people I was after! But he had lost contact with them at the time—they were distant cousins, and he'd never known them well—and he was sorry he couldn't help. However, another branch of the family, who might be able to, had emigrated to Pittsburgh in the United States, and he passed on the American address. I remember writing to these people, my hand trembling so much that I had to start the letter three times. But eventually it was returned by the post office with a scribbled message saying, "Unable to deliver. No Sulek at this address."

Every time I moved I sent my new address both to the Central Committee of Polish Jews and to Arolsen, in the ever more forlorn but never quite extinguished hope that Eli herself might someday make an inquiry about her family. The likelihood was very faint indeed, because even if she was alive *and* had been told the full story, she would also, no doubt, have been told how Dr. Korczak went to his death along with all the children in his orphanage. She would suppose that she was the last surviving member of her family. But it was, nevertheless, a comfort of sorts to know that over there in Arolsen my details were somewhere in those four miles of reference cards—one, or maybe more as I don't know how many headings I was entered under, of the forty million entries relating to some twelve million people.

Antek and I spent most of that first year as civilians working in the building firm. The evenings were split between English classes and doing casual work as washers-up in a restaurant, in order to collect a few savings together. Although we were both anxious to continue our education, we knew that our first priority was to become proficient at English. In the restaurant it could be very frustrating because we were treated with a sort of genial contempt, our mispronunciations and grammatical errors being taken for signs of stupidity. In our free time we would often walk around Oxford, trying to resist the temptation to talk Polish between ourselves.

Not that we were unhappy. We bought secondhand bicycles and explored the countryside at weekends, and we took great pleasure in our growing competence in the English language. And during this period we were grateful for the quiet, unobtrusive friendliness of our landlord and landlady. It was they who introduced us to a club for refugees run by the wives of two Oxford academics. I was wary of identifying myself too much with other foreigners, sensing that the more contacts I had in the refugee community, the less likely I was to be accepted by English people, but it was extremely difficult for us to get to know any English people in the first place, and it was comforting to talk to other refugees facing the same sort of struggle.

For Antek the introduction to that club was to have far-reaching consequences. One evening a lady who helped there brought along her daughter, Lizzie. Antek fell instantly and madly in love with her. This is not Antek's story, so I won't go into great detail; suffice it to say that the family, who were well to do, liked Antek and took him under their wing. Having ascertained that he was making progress in English and had a good head for figures, Lizzie's uncle took him into his firm of accountants as an apprentice. Fifteen years later Antek opened his own firm and, as you know, "is doing well," as they say when people are making money. When their first daughter was born, I was asked to be her godfather. But I am jumping way ahead!

As you can imagine, Antek's involvement with Lizzie meant that I started to spend a lot of time on my own. I had met and had mild flirtations with one or two girls from the English class and the restaurant where we washed up, but there was no one I was interested in devoting much time to. In those days I was still very preoccupied with perfecting my English and earning some money as a form of security. And anyway, close relationships, as I had learned, were not safe.

I had by this time resigned myself to the fact that a medical career was out of the question, but I really had no idea what else might be both realistic and sufficiently challenging. Painting and decorating was a respectable trade and satisfying in a way, but it wasn't what my parents or Korczak or Henryk would have wanted for me. And it wasn't what I wanted for myself.

Then, one day, Mr. and Mrs. Johnson's two young grandchildren came to stay. They were energetic little boys, and I could see that the Johnsons, who were quite elderly grandparents, were quickly worn out. I volunteered to take leave from work for a couple of days to help look after them. I thoroughly enjoyed myself, and at the end of the second day Mrs. Johnson looked at me thoughtfully and said, "You know, Misha, I think you should consider getting a job with children—in a children's home, perhaps.''

Sometimes you can almost physically hear a suggestion or an idea click into place. Of course, that was exactly what I should do! Why hadn't I considered it before? It was obvious I could never be a doctor now, but I could perhaps do something to help children who for whatever reason were separated, as I had been, from their families. I didn't need particular academic qualifications for that, I would be doing something useful, I had relevant experience from my own childhood, and, above all, I would to some extent be following in Korczak's footsteps. That was definitely what I should do. And there may have been another reason for my sudden decision. I knew that the Johnsons would soon be moving from their semidetached house to a bungalow outside the city and that I would have to find other lodgings; a job in a children's home might provide me with somewhere to live, somewhere, perhaps, to belong.

I can see Mr. Johnson now, his bald head gleaming as he peered over advertisements with his magnifying glass until, one evening, he announced triumphantly that he had found "the answer." I remember his exact words because "answer" it most certainly did not turn out to be. Neither the home whose advertisement he spotted that night nor the other two where I was to work over the following few years. Despite some individual staff who did try hard, the regime of each place would, in different ways, have reduced Korczak to despair. Of course, the children were better nourished and clothed than any of Korczak's charges had been in the ghetto, but beyond that there was no comparison. Occasionally I would try and suggest an improvement—the introduction of some bright plants into a particularly drab building was one small one—but I met only hostility and unpopularity in the process. "Who does he think he is?" I overheard someone say on one occasion in a silly voice, which I suppose was meant to be an imitation of my accent. If I was looking for a place to belong, I had only succeeded in feeling more of an outsider; if I was trying to follow Korczak's example, I had succeeded only in dishonoring him—or that's how it felt.

Yet it was nostalgia for Korczak and his enlightened respect for children which led me one evening to a curious paradoxical discovery. I was thinking about the particular children I'd been with that day, and despite everything, despite *everything*, I saw that I had had enormous advantages in life. Not only had I benefited from Korczak's affection and kindness, but I had also had parents who loved and valued me, friends who had risked their lives for me. I thought of Jenny, aged six, found by police locked away in her bedroom, severely undernourished and filthy, rejected by her parents in favor of her brothers, and of Jimmy, who would always walk with a crooked gait because his stepfather had broken both his legs and they had not been properly attended to at the time. I thought of those things and was disgusted by my own tendency to self-pity. I realized then that thanks to my own mother and father, and thanks to my two surrogate fathers, Korczak and Henryk, there was an inner core of me that through all the misery had remained inviolate. Whether it would have withstood the systematized brutality of a concentration camp I have no way of knowing; as it was, I recognized for the first time that evening how privileged I had been.

Eventually I obtained a post in a Rudolf Steiner school, where the children were treated well, though even here there was a contrast with Korczak's homes in that there was a glaring lack of discipline. But at Pillsberry Hall there was emphasis on outdoor and craftwork, which were considered therapeutic, and I myself actually learned to milk a cow and beat copper! I felt reasonably comfortable there. I wasn't the only one with a foreign accent—it was, in fact, run by a nice Swiss couple—I enjoyed the outdoor ethos of the place, set as it was in many acres of parkland, and I had a reasonable amount of time to myself.

For the first time in my life I had access to a piano. There was an old one tucked away in a basement room of the big, rambling house, and I used to shut myself away in an attempt to teach myself how to play.

I was struggling one day with some very easy piece, wondering why it was so difficult for my left hand to be doing something different from the right and wishing there were some simpler way to be loyal to Vasily's memory, when one of the peripatetic music teachers surprised me in my labors. Graham took pity on me and offered to give me tuition at a reduced rate on the grounds that because of his other commitments, lessons might be erratic. To begin with, that seemed an excellent arrangement; I was quite excited and even mentioned it in one of my letters to Vasily's grandmother in Kiev. Graham was encouraging, and when I told him I was particularly interested in Russian and Eastern European music, he initially went to great pains to find me simple but attractive little pieces by composers like Kabalevsky or Khachaturian. After a while, when I suppose he realized that he was fighting a losing battle, the lessons did indeed become erratic and, what was more frustrating, unpredictably so. I'd spend a week trying to perfect a piece and be waiting at the appointed time all keyed up for his comments—only to sit and wait until I realized he'd forgotten all about me. He was always apologetic afterward, and it was hard to be cross for long as he was so nice, but the lessons eventually came to an end through drift rather than by formal agreement. It was actually a relief, as I had realized that "the echo of God's voice," to remember Vasily's words, would never be heard in my poor renderings! But at least I had tried.

Pillsberry Hall's main problem from my point of view was its isolation: There were only two buses a day to and from the nearest market town—and the nearest library. But that is how, over five years after arriving in England, I made my first English friendship of any significance. It was with Tony, the English teacher, a bachelor in his mid-forties, with whom, as you know, we are still in touch.

One day I heard him asking if anyone wanted a lift to town as he had to go to the library. In those days, the early fifties, it was something of a luxury to own a car, and I jumped at the opportunity. It was one of those black Fords with wide running boards along the sides. We'd scarcely spoken to each other before that day, but we quickly established a rapport. Tony was taking two Dickens novels back to the library. He was an enthusiastic Dickens fan, and he encouraged me to give him a try. I protested that his books would all be too long and too difficult for me, but Tony disagreed, advising me to start with *Oliver Twist* as I would find the subject matter immediately appealing! And that, in brief, is how I acquired a sort of tutor or mentor. My confidence and my spoken and written English improved in leaps and bounds as a result.

But not only that. I also conceived an absorbing interest in English literature more generally and began to devour the novels of many other writers, both nineteenth and twentieth century. Strange that the Polish Jew, who until war broke out at the age of eleven had scarcely ever heard of England and who didn't set foot in the country until he was eighteen, should fall so much in love with its literature.

I enjoyed looking after the children and didn't mind some of the menial tasks that had to be done—after all, no task had been too menial for the highly qualified Dr. Korczak, so who was I to complain?—but I would look forward to my next off-duty hours and a return to Dickens's London or Hardy's Wessex downland, where the characters helped to populate the empty spaces of my new life.

I looked forward to Antek's coming to stay for an occasional weekend and to speaking Polish for a change. It was good to see him—there is a level of mutual knowledge and understanding which comes from shared exposure to prolonged danger and hardship and which goes well beyond like and dislike, even beyond love and hate—but all the same we had moved apart. He was absorbed with Lizzie and her family and the forthcoming marriage as well as with his accountancy exams. And he made fun of my new love, eyeing the pretty blond school nurse and suggesting that I might do better to devote my time and energy to her rather than to books.

The children at Pillsberry were what was known as "maladjusted" though the truth was, of course, that they were often rather well adjusted to very bad situations. They were by and large from broken homes in very poor areas of London. Many of them could barely read and write when they came to us. One of the aims of the place was to teach them basic literacy skills, and surprisingly, many of them *were* more literate by the time they left despite the lack of discipline in the classrooms.

It was thanks to my work at Pillsberry that the seeds of my new ambition were sown: to be a teacher. I talked about it to Tony, who was encouraging but realistic; becoming qualified would be a long and demanding process. The best way for me to do it would be to read for a degree by correspondence, and in order to be accepted anywhere, I needed at least five O levels and two A levels, so the whole process would take about eight years if I continued in full-time employment at the same time. But it could be done.

It was. I was just twenty-three; I had a steady job which provided me not with riches but with enough money for the fees, with accommodation and adequate spare time. The children could be exhausting, but on the whole the staff were friendly enough, and of course, I had no closely competing emotional ties. In any case I knew I had to do it. The job I was doing was useful, but it didn't stretch me any longer in the way I wanted to be stretched. In fact, I enjoyed it much more once I started studying; perhaps being more fulfilled in one area of my life gave me fresh enthusiasm for the others.

I shall gloss over those years because I don't imagine they are of particular interest to you, and I'm sure you're waiting to hear how your mother's path and mine came to cross. But just before I come to that, I should mention that Antek married Lizzie in 1954, with me as best man. It was a pleasant rather than a joyful affair, overshadowed by the recent news of the death in Warsaw of Granny and the fact that the rest of the family, locked as they were inside Communist Poland, could not attend. But two years later, just after the birth of their first daughter, the situation in Poland eased sufficiently for Antek's parents and one surviving brother to be able to come across. Although I had never met them before, we had heard so much about each other and they had gone to such strenuous efforts to help me find my sister that when we finally came face-to-face, we embraced as if we ourselves were long-lost relatives.

It was a rapturous reunion for Antek, and I did share wholeheartedly in his joy. Yet when I watched his mother fussing over her little granddaughter, I was also pierced by sadness. My mother would never see her grandchild. Even worse, maybe there never would be a grandchild. All of a sudden it became very important that there should be. By then I was reasonably used to the idea that Eli might be dead and that I could well be the last surviving member of our family; I wasn't yet used to the idea that when *I* died, the family would die with me. But to become a father, I first needed to fall in love, and it was beginning to seem as if I had been drained of the capacity. I went out with a few women over the years, of course, and with one—the social worker for one of the boys at Pillsberry—I had a relationship which lasted for nearly two years but which broke up because of my preoccupation with the correspondence degree. Until I met your mother in 1965, no woman claimed my total commitment, perhaps because only by then did Eva lie in peace in her forest glade.

For eventually, in 1963, after Antek and I had both acquired British citizenship and could travel to Poland with reduced fear of being detained, we went back. Needless to say, I went in person to the Polish Red Cross and to the Committee for Polish Jews, and I went to have a look at Eli's last-known address in the suburb of Ochota. By then the house had become part of a school. It was all in vain, as I had been virtually certain it would be. Eli and her foster parents had simply vanished without trace.

One day while Antek was with his parents, I took a bus journey to Parczew. It was strange, but even at a distance of over twenty years, I couldn't bring myself to use the Warsaw–Lublin railway line. That had been "our" journey, Eva's and mine, one hot and terrifying day in August 1942, my first day of freedom. I wanted it to remain like that in my memory, forever.

I suppose I had some absurd notion in my head that I would find that fatal forest clearing and pay my respects, finally, to my twin friends. But even with my previous knowledge of the area and what I thought was a fairly clear recall of Henryk's description of the place all those years before, I soon lost my way. It was inevitable. The forests seemed denser than ever, and I was almost immediately besieged by clouds of blackflies, which were even more persistent than I'd remembered. I'm ashamed to admit that I gave up after only a couple of hours. I didn't belong there anymore; the boy in the torn shirt and ragged trousers, who stripped the clothes off corpses without a tear and stole to stay alive, that boy had gone. Vanished, like Eli, without a trace. Searching eagerly for familiar landmarks and finding none, it was as if I were visiting the forest for the first time. Perhaps I had expected the wind in the trees to carry echoes of fireside songs, but it *was* only the wind in the trees. Perhaps I had expected to glimpse in the shallow, stagnant pools reflections of dear though only half-remembered faces, but I saw just reeds and lilies and a few wild duck. I discovered then that the most cherished images of life as a partisan survived in my memory and not, as I had expected, among the dark acres of pine and birch which had been their first home. It was the same when I paid a pilgrimage to the house which Henryk and I had lived in on Miodowa Street. Partly rebuilt and smartly painted, it was no longer ours; I had no business there, and neither did Henryk's ghost.

But first I had had a mission to accomplish back there in the forest. Finding a clearing which was approximately the right distance southwest of Parczew, I knelt in the soft, peaty earth and, with a trowel I'd brought from England, dug a small hole at the foot of a pine tree. There I planted a pot of scarlet geraniums which I'd carried through what by that time felt like a hundred hostile thickets and half a million flies. I knew they wouldn't last, for shady woodland is not their habitat, but I wanted their message of hope to flare in the gloom, however briefly: an offering for Eva and Franek because of all they had continued to mean over the years—love and loyalty, youth and generosity, energy and a certain reckless courage. The geraniums provided a symbolic little link with Rachel and my mother, too—if perhaps a rather sentimental one. But why not? After all, not one of those who died is in a grave or permanent resting place that I can visit. I have no way of paying my respects except in symbol, prayer (despite not being a believer), and memory. And in what I have done with my survival, of course, which still belongs to them: at once my greatest burden and my greatest blessing.

Dearest Katie,

This is a copy of the letter I eventually wrote to Misha. Not very good, I know, but I just felt I had to write something.

I'm longing to see you—I'll show you some of this amazing stuff then. I don't think he would mind.

Rich

JULY 19

Dear Misha,

I'm writing to you because there is something you should know before you come back from Australia. I don't really know what to say about your letter or story or peace offering or whatever it is. "Thank you" doesn't seem quite enough, somehow. Yes, as you hoped, it has explained a lot, and it has also changed the way I think about you in many ways. But whether it will make a difference to the way we get on—well, I suppose we won't know that until you get home.

This is what I have to tell you. Those boys you've never liked, Micky and Sam Fox and that lot, wanted to pay the Head back for

*expelling Rob Davis. And I must say I agreed that that business was
really unfair, and the Head deserved some repercussions. Anyway,
they decided that one way of annoying him would be to paint some
graffiti on the playground walls—and I mean big ones—so as to hit
everyone, but particularly the Head, in the eye every time they go
anywhere near the playground. I went along with it, though I
honestly didn't know what they were going to write or paint. My job
was to be one of the lookouts. It wasn't until they'd almost finished
that I realized what they were doing.*

*They were painting two huge black swastikas and daubing the
words* Jews belong in Israel. *The Head, as you know, is Jewish.*

*But there's worse to come. When I saw it, I laughed. I LAUGHED.
I DIDN'T SAY ANYTHING. Okay, I didn't realize until I read your
story just exactly what a swastika stood for, but I had a pretty good
idea, and I should have objected and tried to stop them, then and
there. That's what the Head has failed to punish me for. Not for
being part of the exercise in the first place—we're all being fined
for that—but for not having the courage to make a fuss when I
realized what they were doing.*

*I don't think there's any more I can say. Except that I didn't
want you to hear about this from anyone else. And I'm sorry, really
very sorry.*

*I hope it's going well in Australia. Many happy returns of the
17th, by the way.*

> *Love,*
> *Richard*

It was not all that long after I returned from Poland that I first met
Jack, your father, who by then was working freelance as a foreign
correspondent. I liked him instinctively; there was something immediately
appealing about his tall, hunched-shouldered figure and shy,
warm smile as he got up to greet me.

We had been introduced by Jack's cousin, your uncle Henry, who was a colleague of mine in the school where I was teaching at the time. Jack was writing a series of articles about Eastern Europe, and he'd got hold of some Polish samizdat material which he wanted translated, so Henry put us in touch. Samizdat is literature which, forbidden by the authorities, circulates secretly between dissidents, usually in home-typed or even handwritten form. Jack's idea was to try to trace the patterns of repression behind the Iron Curtain in the twenty years after the end of the war. He showed me a poignant picture of a line of young women in head scarves, stooping to clear a vast area of rubble with nothing but their bare hands. A small child stood apart from them, a hand clapped to his mouth. The reason was not difficult to discern, for just in front of him lay a corpse, obviously just uncovered. I gave a start wondering, absurdly, if the corpse could have been Henryk's, for the caption below the photograph read "Warsaw 1945. What was it all for?"

I was impressed by the amount of research Jack had done and by his knowledge not only of the war years but also of subsequent developments, and assumed that he had particular interest in Eastern Europe. Later, when he went off to Indonesia to gather information about the horrendous massacres there in 1965 and 1966, and later still, when he went to Greece to report on the use of torture under the colonels, I understood that his interest was not so much in any particular region as in the mechanics of repression itself. In a sense, your father and I are traveling in different directions: I have spent all my adult life trying to escape or at least to come to terms with the effects of savage persecution and terror, whereas Jack, who by virtue of his background and education could have had a life of comfort and security, seems actively to seek out what is oppressive, dangerous, and threatening. Whereas I ran away from such forces, he turns around and confronts them, seizing every opportunity he can to challenge them. Perhaps if there had been more Jacks in Germany in the 1930s, the history of Europe might now look significantly different.

My liking for him was reciprocated, and we went on meeting regu-

larly even after I'd done the Polish translation. One day Jack said—
I remember it very well, we were having a drink in the Cock and Bull
at lunchtime—"I'm going to see my ex-wife and son tonight. Why
don't you come along?" I wasn't at all sure that I'd be a welcome
addition, but he persuaded me.

"No, do come. Things are particularly sticky at the moment, and
it'll ease the atmosphere." In fact, I was only too happy to be persuaded: Life in the school holidays could be lonely, and the date was
August 1, the twentieth anniversary of the outbreak of the Warsaw
Uprising and of the last time I ever saw Henryk. August has always
been a difficult month, full of anniversaries I would like to forget, but
occasionally, when I have done so, the remorse has been unsparing.
Anyway, I was intrigued to meet my new friend's family.

I wonder if you remember the first time we met. You were ten, and
I remember it very well indeed. You were halfway up the lamppost
outside the house when we arrived and to my horror were obviously
intent on getting to the top. While we stood and watched, you shinned
up with apparently no effort, clung to the top with one hand, and
waved delightedly down at us with the other. Jack then called sternly,
"Come down now, Richard, that's dangerous." But not before he had
applauded the performance with unmistakable pride!

That was the first shock, and your mother was the second! The front
door was ajar, presumably for you, so we walked in at the same time
as Jack rang the bell to announce our arrival. She was sitting at the
kitchen table and looked up, slightly startled, from her task of shelling
peas. Her dark hair was swept sleekly up in a knot behind her head,
and she was wearing a simple deep blue dress. I fell instantly and
irrevocably in love with her!

And the rest you know. How Penny and I married just over a year
later and how I moved into the house in Christchurch Road with you
both. You and I got on well together for quite a long time; I think the
trouble started around your fourteenth birthday, when you began to
go out in the evenings and come in whenever you felt like it. Perhaps

I have intruded too much on decisions which should, more properly, have been your mother's and Jack's, but after all, I am the one who lives in the same house with you whereas Jack spends a good deal of his time abroad. All the same, after the examples I had had you'd think I might have learned to do it properly, wouldn't you? Ironic really. I always thought of Korczak, who cared for two hundred children at a time, as my model, and I couldn't even cope with one! And what's more, all this started about the time when I'd begun to suspect that I couldn't have children of my own.

It was a beautiful April day last year when those suspicions were confirmed. As your mother and I walked back from the clinic after receiving the results of the tests and the dreaded yet not unexpected news of my infertility, it seemed that everything in the world was fruitful and fertile—except me! The gardens were bursting with the brightness of daffodils and polyanthus, and everywhere there seemed to be cherry trees obscenely laden with blossom. For months I felt a profound malevolence against everyone who had, as I saw it, succeeded in an area of life in which I had so signally failed: who had managed to produce a child. I conveniently forgot that Korczak, fulfilled, rounded, and father figure extraordinary, had never had a child of his own. I was deaf and impervious to any words of comfort or reason. I purposely avoided all my colleagues at school who had young children as they never seemed to talk about anything else. I couldn't even bear to visit Antek and Lizzie anymore; by then they had a growing family of four, and I hated them for it.

It didn't help that at thirty-eight with a well-established career as an eye doctor, Penny was somewhat ambivalent about starting all over again. "The worst thing of all," I said to her one day, "is that after I die, there'll be no one in the world with any connection at all with my family." I thought of Jack's photo of the women of postwar Warsaw and its caption, "What was it all for?" I asked that question now, with anguish. "Why all that surviving? It feels as if I'm letting them die all over again."

I think it was when we went for a walk in the country one weekend, and I expressed resentment of a mare with a foal, that Penny realized things had gone too far and began to be seriously worried about me. By that time you and I were clashing almost every day, and tension at home was very high. Penny had to be worried to consult Jack, because as you know, she takes a pride in her ability to make independent decisions. And I know she consulted Jack, because I caught them talking about me when I came home from school earlier than expected one afternoon. Jack then proposed a walk.

It was perhaps no coincidence that he suggested we go across the suspension bridge toward the woods. We stood with our hands on the railing, the chasm yawning deep and menacing below.

"You know what I think might really help?" said Jack. Before I could reply, he went on. "I think you should get on with writing that account of what happened to you in Poland and afterward. I've often said that to you before, and I think I do understand why you've always resisted it. But maybe now, Misha, it's become a sort of obligation. For the sake of your relationship with Richard and—and as a way of coming to terms with . . ."

"Sterility," I finished for him. How clever Jack was being: "obligation," "for the sake of"—playing into my already overactive conscience. I was angry and ashamed, and I knew in some deep part of me that he was right. He issued the proposal as a challenge that I had to rise to, not so much because of what had happened in the past as because of what was happening in the present. In other words, for the sake of our little family and the tensions which could, potentially, rip it apart. And most particularly, for you, my stepson, the nearest I will ever have to a child of my own. What your dad was saying that evening, high above the river, was that the time had come to pull myself together. Not in so many words, because that is not his style, but I received the message loud and clear.

And it struck me, thinking about it afterward, what an extraordinarily generous message it was. There is nothing possessive or jealous about your father. I love him for his concern that you and I should get on better together, his willingness to share you for *your* sake, as I do for so much else: his easy charm, his recklessness, his extravagant generosity, his questioning approach to what most people take for granted in this world, and, above all, his readiness to put himself at risk for the sake of an ideal or a principle he believes in—or, as has happened, for a colleague. He, I know, would disclaim that as a quality; he says he just gets high on danger and calls his risk taking a form of self-indulgence. Perhaps he's right, perhaps not. Who is to judge?

And so, thanks to Jack, I began to write about six months ago. It was a laborious business, for I kept having to check that the sentences were properly English in every nuance; that was extremely important to me, a matter of both personal and professional pride. I may teach English literature, yet it wasn't until I began this task that I fully understood what an immensely delicate and complex piece of machinery a language is. In fact, I think my preoccupation with the English helped in an odd way to keep under control the emotional effects of so much concentrated recall. First Jack and then, after he went off to South America, your mother patiently answered all my queries. I started writing it in the winter, and progress was reasonably steady until April, when I had reached the part relating to the Uprising.

And it was then that the miracle happened. I ached to record it there and then, but its place is here, at the end, so I hope you will bear with me if I now repeat what I know you've heard discussed a hundred times over the past couple of months.

It was a Saturday morning, when Penny was at her emergency clinic and you were in France on the school trip, so I was alone in the house. The post arrived late, as usual on Saturdays. There was just one thing that morning, a typed envelope with a German stamp. I couldn't think who it might be from as none of us has friends in Germany. Then I looked more closely at the postmark: Arolsen! I sat down on the bottom stair and began to read.

Dear Mr. Edelman,

With reference to your inquiries initiated in 1946 and the subsequent correspondence, I am writing to inform you that we have received from South Australia an inquiry from a Mrs. Elena Jackson, née Edelman, daughter of Mr. and Mrs. Moshe and Lili Edelman, who is looking for her brother and sister, Michal, known as Misha (d.o.b. 17.7.28), and Rachel (d.o.b. 18.5.32).

As she also mentions that they were once resident at the orphanage run by Dr. Janusz Korczak, with whom she has always assumed they died in August 1942, it would seem from our records that you are the brother concerned.

We are delighted at this successful outcome and have pleasure in forwarding her address.

It was as if all the bells of Bristol pealed out in that moment. I put my head on my knee and wept—and wept and wept. With a clarity that stung my eyes I saw again the scene in our mother's room in the ghetto, where Rachel and I had taken Eli, a toddler of eighteen months, to say good-bye. If only Mother could have heard this news!

Then the need to tell someone took over! I was so excited that I had to keep moving around as I dialed Penny's number at the clinic and waited endless seconds for someone to answer.

"I'm afraid she's with a patient. Is it urgent, Mr. Edelman?"

"Urgent? Well—no, no, please don't mention I rang." On second thoughts, I wanted to see her face when she heard. But I couldn't wait three hours for her return. So I dialed Antek's number in London. He and his family had moved there a year or so before, from Oxford, and we'd been invited to visit several times, but so far I'd made a number of excuses for I now found it impossible to cope with Antek as a paterfamilias. To me four children was almost a dynasty, and it seemed so terribly unfair. But now it was different! As I spoke to Lizzie, I heard a child crying in the background; perhaps I would mind again in the future, but then, at that moment, I didn't mind at all. Eventually Antek came to the phone.

"Misha, this is a rare pleasure," he said in Polish, perhaps to underline the note of reproach in his voice, but I ignored it.

"Antek, you are the first to know." Even in the midst of my euphoria, I knew how much that would please him. "A miracle has happened. *Eli* is *alive!*" Communicating the news seemed to give it validity and truth. I kept repeating the three words to myself, over and over again, so that I didn't take in what Antek said or answer his excited questions, for several moments.

I wanted to telephone Australia that day, but Penny restrained me. "It'd be too much of a shock for the poor girl," she said wisely. "She obviously thinks you've been dead since 1942; at least you've always known that she might be alive somewhere." And so, instead, we sent a telegram. A letter would have been too casual, too slow. But it was not an easy message to word.

"Joyful news received from Arolsen today. You are alive. I searched for years and virtually gave up hope. Writing. Your brother, Misha."

Penny had to dictate it to the operator for me as I didn't trust my voice. And when she put the receiver down, she turned to hug me, her own eyes full of tears.

Very soon letters and photos began crossing each other on their way around the world. Probably the main reason why my searches had been in vain was that Eli's foster parents had continued to receive blackmail messages even after moving away from Warsaw, so they had been forced to part with her to friends of theirs who after the war emigrated to the United States, where Eli grew up. Sadly her original foster parents were killed in the Uprising in Warsaw, where they had returned after reluctantly letting her go. She is now living in Australia because when she was at college, she met, and later married, an Australian student who was on a year's scholarship to the States. And, most wonderful of all, she has a little girl, Rachel, who is three years old.

She finally wrote to Arolsen after seeing a TV program about the International Tracing Service, which described other reunions between relatives who had believed one another long dead. I can't wait to hear more about her past, as you can imagine. I have broken into our savings and booked a flight to Adelaide for the first day of the school holidays—my school holidays, for yours, as you always point out, don't begin until after mine! I plan to be there, as you'll know by the time you read this, for most of the summer. You were probably pleased to hear that I won't be joining you and your mother and grandparents at the place they've taken in Devon. I'm glad Katie is able to come with you for a while, though.

Once I had booked my flight, the point of writing my story began to reassert itself with new urgency, because I knew I had to finish it before I left for Australia. Not only would you then be able to read it in my absence, but it would also help to prepare me for the reunion, as if I were somehow putting my house in order.

So that, while perhaps not the end, is the point where I want to stop. I hope, Richard, that when I get back from Adelaide, you and I might begin again. If, to echo Antek, beginning again is ever possible. But in the meantime, take great care of yourself and your mother while I'm away.

Affectionately,
Misha

AFTERWORD

That is probably where this collection of papers would have ended had it not been for a sudden and tragic development. In Uruguay, where he had gone to report on the activities of the National Liberation Movement, the Tupamaros (who had sprung to worldwide notoriety when they kidnapped the British ambassador, Mr. Geoffrey Jackson, earlier that year), Jack Buchanan was killed. He was shot accidentally by police during a raid on a Tupamaros safe house. The Uruguayan authorities, already embarrassed by Geoffrey Jackson's prolonged detention as a hostage, made strenuous efforts to minimize bureaucracy and have his body flown back to England within days. What follows is an unfinished letter from Richard to his girlfriend, Katie, the day after the funeral.

JULY 27

Dearest Katie,

I still can't believe what has happened. Of course Dad was often away for months at a time, so I suppose it'll be awhile before I finally realize that he's never coming back. NEVER. When he was here, he was always so—well, alive, if that doesn't sound too stupid.

It was good of your mum to bring you down for the funeral yesterday. I couldn't take it all in, so I don't suppose I thanked you for coming. But I wanted to write now and tell you the

*extraordinary thing that happened in the evening, after everyone
had gone home.*

I went back to the churchyard because I wanted to be alone at
the graveside. I was just standing there and thinking about Dad
when I happened to look up. There, walking toward me, with a
bulky package under his arm, was MISHA. Katie, I swear to God I
thought I was hallucinating. I thought Dad's death had pushed me
over the top; it was actually quite scary.

As he drew closer, he said softly, "Don't be alarmed, Richard. It
is me." He came to a stop on the other side of the grave.
"Richard, I'm so terribly sorry."

I just stared at him, dumbfounded, but eventually managed to
stammer stupidly, "But—but you're in Australia."

"I couldn't stay there after this had happened. In case—well, in
case I could help in any way."

"But Eli. What about Eli?"

"It's all right, Richard, Eli and I have found each other. That's
what matters. We have the rest of our lives to keep in touch. She
and her husband are planning a trip to Europe in a couple of years,
anyway."

I just couldn't believe it. After all the excitement, all the
planning, all that money. After all those years.

"But you were only there just over a week—all those plans you
made."

"They were full and wonderful days. And my little niece is a
delight—a replica of Rachel whom she's named after. But I don't
want to talk about it now. This is where I belong at the moment—
with you and your mother."

Then he frowned and said, less firmly, "But if it feels as if I'm
intruding . . . ?"

I couldn't have that, could I? "No, of course, you're not
intruding. Does Mum know you're back?"

"Yes, she told me where she thought you'd be. I also rang her *earlier from the airport. I really wanted to be here for the funeral, but the wretched plane was delayed in Singapore.''*

We both looked down at the grave between us. I knew that yet again, Misha was saying good-bye to his best friend, and I couldn't help wondering how many other faces besides Dad's were looking up at him at that moment.

Eventually he said, ''I've brought something for him.'' He went to the end of the grave and removed the wrapping from his parcel. Inside were two bloodred geraniums and a little trowel. He handed me the trowel, and then, kneeling down, we took it in turns—first me, then Misha—to plant a geranium at Dad's head. When we'd finished, Misha put a hand briefly on my shoulder. I was a bit embarrassed, but it made it easier for me to mumble,

''Misha, there's a letter in the post. You won't have got it. I . . .''

''Your mother's told me. About the swastikas?''

I hated hearing him say the word. I felt evil, Katie, evil.

''I'm sorry, Misha.'' Isn't it silly, the same word for stepping on someone's toe and for expressing regret when someone dies? And for when you've done something you're really ashamed of?

He didn't say anything for a moment, and again we both looked down. I was thinking, almost angrily, Surely you didn't have to die to bring us together?

Then Misha said, ''I know you're sorry, Richard, and that's what's important to me. But we both have a lot of work to do now, you and I. We have to find the answer to that question of Henryk's, if you remember it. We have to make sure that our phoenix can sing. Otherwise, what was it all for?''

ACKNOWLEDGMENTS

During my research for this book I have been grateful to receive the generous help of a wide variety of people and in many different ways. I hope they will understand that they are too numerous to mention by name.

There are, however, three people to whom I would like to express particular appreciation: to Dr. Keith Sword of the School of Slavonic and East European Studies at London University, without whom Misha would have had great difficulty in finding his way to England; and to Mr. Kasimierz Kozlowski and Dr. Zbigniew Pelczynski, here in Oxford, who patiently and uncomplainingly delved into their pasts to "lend" me some of their own experiences for my story. They alone will recognize a few scenes in the book, which I only hope I am returning in acceptable condition. To them I owe a special debt of gratitude.

—C. L.